MW00883341

Raluca might have said something more, except at that moment she broke out into a fit of terrible coughing. The gravity chair lurched and swayed.

Disgusted, I looked on as she convulsed just off the ground in front of me. Sure, I'd coughed before. Who hasn't? But never like that. There was spittle spraying from her mouth. Her eyes were blood red. "George Walker!" She gasped for breath.

What did diseases look like, anyway? I had heard of them before, but I thought they were just the fancy of vengeful learnbots.

I glanced fitfully to the left and to the right. Not far away at one end of the runway was a set of squat, square buildings, but I didn't see any diseases.

Were they furry? How many legs did they have? Did they get you in your sleep?

I took a step back and bumped up against Van Johnson.

"What will happen to us?" the former host of Ten Things I Hate About Treason stammered nervously, clearly horrified by the turn of events.

Raluca managed to get her coughing under control. "Eventually, you'll be terminated, of course," she wheezed, wiping her lips with her sleeve. "But first we'll have your trial."

The author was born in Cranston, RI, in 1973. He attended the Johns Hopkins University where he graduated with a degree in Computer Science. Currently, he resides in Amsterdam, the Netherlands, and spends his summers in Narragansett.

For Darice –
It was a
pleasure
meeting you!

[signature]

Thank You
For Your
Cooperation

Adam Wasserman

For Apollo

the Light
and
the Word

First Edition, November 2011
Copyright 2011 by Adam Wasserman
All rights reserved

ISBN 978-1-105-25812-1

lulu.com

Chapter 1

Every once in a while you see something strange. Sure, life in the Bunker is remarkable in itself. It is, even if you believe all that crap they pawn off as history. Everyone knows human beings aren't meant to live their whole lives underground. No one needs to tell you that. You feel it in your bones. But you get used to it. It's the only thing you know. There's nothing strange about sleeping stacked up on top of one another like briny strips of Algatine in a can, eating slop, and blindly following the orders Control hands down. At least not to me there isn't. But like I said, about a yearstretch ago I saw something strange. Something real and strange at the same time. And I don't care what those smack addicts in the Underground say. They're all traitors anyway.

It was after breakfast and I was out with the crew cracking open stones looking for uranium ore. It's what I did every morning. It's what I did all afternoon, too. Working in a uranium mine is the fate Control assigned to me the moment it approved my birth and entered me into the Communal Registry. Like the Bunker, it was all I'd ever known.

My crew is decent enough. We all get along. Sure, there's the occasional scuffle, a broken bone maybe, but the medibots patch you up and you're as good as new. Why hold a grudge?

So like I was saying, I had just put my drill through the rock and was about to sift through the pile of rubble at my feet when someone called out.

"Hey, Terry!" It was Clyde. Nice enough fellow once you get past the smell.

"What?"

"Is that you?"

"Is what me?"

"There! On the tube!"

Annoyed, I looked up. I didn't need any distractions. We were behind on our quota, and there was precious little time to make it up. I was about to snap at the boys to get cracking, but I never did manage the words.

Normally at that time of my daystretch they're blasting the Anthem of The Patriot or dispensing hygienic advice or going through the most recently updated Thousand Most Wanted list. But that morning when I looked up at the tube, I didn't hear or see any of that.

What I did see was a man who looked very much like myself, trying desperately to diffuse an alarm.

A lot of people look like each other from far away. But this guy was a spitting image, right down to the crooked nose and oversized knuckles and uneven teeth.

In the background, the shrieking of the alarm was mixed up in the louder groaning of what sounded like huge cogs and gears turning. They were badly in need of an oil bath.

Underneath the video feed was a moving banner. TRAITOR CAUGHT IN THE ACT!

I gulped.

"... how he ever managed to land on the asteroid in the first place. Your friends at Homeland Security have initiated an investigation and several terminations have already taken place. It isn't yet clear who this traitor was, and – those of you who've already seen this feed know what I'm talking about – it's unlikely he'll be identified from the primary evidence alone."

"Is that because all the primary evidence is floating around in space?"

"That's right, Bob. It's just a chunky red spray. Not much you can do with that."

The invisible cameramen chuckled.

"If any citizen has information which leads directly to the identification of this criminal and the subsequent arrest and termination of his co-conspirators – "

"Sorry to interrupt, Felix. But here it comes."

"Is it boom-time, Bob?"

The man in the feed was sweating profusely. He must have known what was coming.

"It's boom-time, Felix."

The tube went black. A moment later, it lit up again. Bob and Felix were sitting behind their desks, smiling and cracking jokes.

"Hey, Terry," said one of the guys. "That bloke looked just like you."

"You got a twin brother or something?" asked another.

"No one has twins anymore, you cancerhead!"

"Who are you calling a cancerhead?"

"Control's got a strict One Child Only policy."

"Yeah, but it's only been in effect for the last ten or fifteen yearstretches! Ain't I right?"

I stood by while the boys argued. The whole experience was surreal. I knew I should try and put it out of my mind, but I couldn't. It was almost as if I knew I might be implicated in that sap's treason just for looking like him.

My PA lit up. The boys stopped arguing and stared. I pulled it out of its protective casing and opened it up. The head supervisor was looking at me from the little screen.

"Renfield?" he barked. "Did you see that feed?"

"Yes, sir. I did."

"The whole Bunker saw it." He paused as if carrying on a debate with himself. "Put Hal in charge," he finally decided. "And get your ass to my office! We've got to have a little chat."

George sat on the other side of his desk, eyeing me intently. In one hand he was playing absently with a rivet of some kind. He was in a pensive mood, so I decided not to interrupt. After all, he had a security clearance.

Once upon a time, George was one of the crew. But a few yearstretches back he turned one of the boys in to Control. Luca was his name. George accused him of belonging to the Underground, and whatever evidence he had was solid enough that Homeland Security was called in. They pump you up full of drugs that make you very agreeable, or else they use the enhanced techniques, but either way you end up confessing. Everyone confesses to Homeland Security. They dragged Luca away screaming.

When we thought the security cameras weren't looking, me and the boys debated whether or not Luca was actually guilty. But it was impossible to tell. That's the way it is with traitors. Anybody could be one.

After that they put Luca on meds and transferred him to a psychotic ward until he got better.

George got a promotion. I don't know what security clearance he has, but he must have access to better food. In the yearstretches since he's been our head supervisor, he's grown chunky. No one gets chunky eating slop.

"That guy looked just like you, Renfield. Wouldn't you say?"

I nodded even as a sinking feeling took hold of my stomach. "Yes, sir. He did."

"It was uncanny." George chewed on his bottom lip and played with the rivet some more. "You called in sick last weekstretch, didn't you?"

7

"Yes, sir. I did."

"Didn't show up at all the day after."

"I was sick."

"You could have called in."

"I wasn't required to! Regulations –"

George stuck out a hand. He swung his legs off the desk and leaned forward. He was trying to seem earnest. "You've been with us a long time. Never a problem." He gestured at the little, glowing screen on his desk. "Clean record. I mean, a few little altercations, a night or two in the slammer for drinking and brawling, but nothing serious. No treason." He smiled at me. "Terry, I've only got your best interests at heart."

Here it comes, I thought.

"Maybe it's best if you take some time off the job."

I was caught by surprise. "Time off?" I started to protest. "But, sir –"

George held out his hand again. I bit my tongue. "It's for the best, Terry."

Stunned, I stood up. All I could think about was how long I had until Homeland Security would come for me.

"Oh yeah, before you go..."

When I looked again I saw he was holding out a neat, little package.

"Do you mind taking this over to Central Management? I mean, now that you have some time on your hands."

So that's what this is about. I was relieved. He needs an errand boy, and I'm a convenient, no-clearance citizen obliged to serve my betters. Still, I hoped I could get back to the job after the package was safely delivered. You have to be useful in the Bunker. Otherwise, they get rid of you. You'd be accused of some treason and it wouldn't matter to Control whether or not you were actually guilty. There aren't enough resources for slackers.

My eyes narrowed suspiciously. "What's inside?" I asked as I reached over and took possession of it.

"Sorry, Terry," George replied smugly. He leaned back in his chair and put his legs back on the desk. "I'm not authorized to tell you."

The sinking feeling was back.

"So what's in the box?"

We were sitting at one of the many flimsy, fold-up tables laid out in a haphazard fashion across the floor of the Endurance Community

Dining Hall in Q-16 sector. I don't know if you've ever been there, but I'm pretty sure it's the largest commissary in the entire sector. It's got to feed thousands – maybe even tens of thousands – of hungry workers like myself. You name it and you'll find them swarming there. Builders, welders, food pit and reactor core attendants – the lowest of the low. Any time of your daystretch, Endurance is packed. The Bunker never sleeps.

Sitting across from me, unenthusiastically stirring her slop with a stained plastic spoon, Sally was peering at the package. I had set it on the table next to my tray.

"Beats me," I said and eyed the bowl in front of me warily.

"It's called Goulash," she assured me wryly. "Whatever that is." She still hadn't put any in her mouth. "The drink today is Yellow Flavor."

"It tastes the same no matter what Flavor it is," I grumbled.

"Watch your tongue, citizen," Sally hissed and jammed a spoonful of gunk into her mouth. She winced but somehow managed a smile.

"Calm down. No one's paying attention." I wasn't ready yet to try mine.

"They've upgraded the security. The cameras are equipped with lip reading software."

"I'll bet. They can't even keep the reactor core online."

"It's triggered by certain words," she went on and stuck more of the gunk in her mouth. "Facial expressions."

I still couldn't bring myself to try the slop. My stomach, not quite on the same page as my brain, grumbled loudly.

"Better eat it while it's warm," Sally advised me. She was right. As bad as it was, it tasted even worse after it hardened.

The first few spoonfuls were always the worst. Once I got past them, I was usually able to stop grimacing.

Sally's curiosity about the box resurfaced. "Who's it addressed to?"

If she weren't my girlfriend, I'd have thought she was being nosy. In the Bunker, people who are nosy tend to end up floating face down in a food pit or volunteering as shielding for the reactor core.

"Jeremy Whiles." I read the name off the box. "Building 6, Ronald Reagan Plaza, Q-7 Sector. Green Pastures Recycling, Recycling and Reclamation, Production and Logistics."

The man next to me suddenly looked up and peered over at us. Sally hadn't noticed, but I caught it out of the corner of my eye. I could have stared him down – hell, maybe I should have stared him down – but I gambled I'd gain some advantage if I pretended I hadn't noticed. I didn't. A stretch later, he was chatting softly away with the others at his rickety table. Chatting softly, just like I should have been.

"Ronald Reagan Plaza?" Sally muttered. "That's not far from Deeper Delvers, Inc. George probably takes the metro through it to get to work. He could have taken it himself!" She leaned closer. "Does it have a security clearance?"

It did. "Delta." The funny-looking letter was embossed in the upper right corner.

"Delta!" Unlike me, she managed to keep her voice down. "I hope you got a waiver to carry it!"

I had forgot to ask.

"I'll bet you can't even get in the building."

I hadn't though of that, either.

A smile broke out on her face. "Let's go find out."

"Don't you have to get back to the grid?" Sally worked as a first responder for Repair On Demand, a firm in the Housing and Construction conglomerate.

She shrugged and gestured at what was left of the slop clinging to the sides of her plastic bowl. Hardened bits were already flaking off. "I'll call in sick."

In the Bunker, you've got to survive. I don't know if God said it or some bloke named Derwin or whoever, but it's a fact of life here. You know it. I know it. None of us is a traitor, but everyone else could be. It's why those goons from Homeland Security are standing by the exit. Even the local commissaries could be targets. Biological, nuclear, electromagnetic – the attack could come from anywhere, anyone, it could be anytime. I'm glad those typhoids in latex and kevlar are there. Even if they scare me. They make me feel safe. Sort of.

We left the Endurance Community Dining Hall. They didn't scan our I-chips, and the security cameras didn't budge. Everything seemed okay.

Control isn't really concerned about us grunts. We're the vast majority of people here – but also the most powerless. Those with a security clearance are considered more trustworthy. They've been rewarded with greater access and luxury, but they are also saddled with responsibility.

Ironic, isn't it? The more privileged they get, the more Control tightens its grip. After all, where am I going to get my hands on a thermonuclear detonator?

The corridor outside the commissary was packed.

"Hey, keep close," I said. I don't know why, but I was more tense than usual. In the Bunker, you don't question such feelings.

But Sally knew what she was doing. She can handle herself. Even in the mean corridors of the Bunker. "Get dysentery," she said and pulled her arm away.

I love that woman. There's not another one like her.

Stretched out before us was a narrow, stunted tunnel lined with corrugated steel. The lighting came from unshielded bulbs that stabbed at the eyes. All around were fellow citizens, dressed in their own personal flavor of brown, grey, or Color of the Patriot – pewter, if I remember the announcement last week. Very metallic, in any case.

This was it, the Utopia that was the Bunker. The Anthem to the Patriot was blasting. The posters on the wall told us to be vigilant. Everyone was happy.

The crowd surged forward. We went with the flow.

Someone elbowed me in the kidney as he passed.

There is no way to identify citizens with a security clearance just by looking at them. According to Control – not to mention my old learnbot, Ms. Bits; after all these yearstretches I'd still love to have a go at her with my drill – ours is an egalitarian dreamland. Who am I to argue? But some of us are more equal than others. We have our ways of showing it, too. Chewing gum, for example. A little, handheld mirror. Hair gel.

Someone bumped roughly into me. I was set to give her a piece of my mind – a very swift, blood-letting piece – but some survival instinct insisted I look first.

The woman I had almost knocked over was standing on a flat, motorized bot floating a few centimeters off the ground. It was no larger than a dog.

Oh yeah, did I mention that stepbots and similar ambulatory aids are a perk reserved for Delta clearance and above?

I swallowed thickly. "Please excuse my behavior, citizen."

Fortunately, the woman was on meds. She was having trouble focusing. I darted to the side just as a column of guardians was passing by.

Sally was waiting just up ahead, trying to stifle a laugh.

"It's not funny!" I hissed even as I scanned for a security camera. Sure enough, there was one pointed a bit further up the corridor, right where I had been. The little red light underneath glowed sternly. It swerved even as I stood there gawking at it. It was trying to pick me out of the crowd.

"You should be more careful," she told me as we hurried along.

"I know, I know. I was thinking."

"That's a change for the better."

We were already coming upon the entrance to the metro station. The line was so long we were standing in it before we even got inside.

"This is going to take forever." But there was nothing we could do except wait.

I started to wonder whether or not George would have to wait. After all, higher clearance also meant access to doors and corridors off limits to the rest of us. Like that turnstile there. Could George have got past it? Because if so, there was no point to me carrying around this damned package for him.

But then again, why ask me at all?

It's only when you're idle that you start thinking about such things. And I know from experience that thinking things through can be a life-saving exercise. It's just that in the Bunker, you're usually too damned busy.

George was my supervisor. I didn't know him outside Deeper Delvers, Inc, and I certainly didn't know what clearance he had or what he had access to.

His clearance was at least Delta. The clearance on the package was Delta. I checked it again just to make sure.

A bearded man in a white, laboratory coat clutching a clipboard strode imperiously past us and up to the turnstile. As he approached, one of the Homeland Security goons scanned his I-chip. I guess he had been tagged, because a moment later the two of them drew their blasters.

"Easy now," one of them growled.

"There's nowhere to run," confided the other.

The bearded man stopped.

"It says here you're carrying anthrax," said the first goon.

The line of people waiting to get into the metro stepped as a single body away from the turnstile.

"No, I left the anthrax back at the lab," remarked the bearded man softly. There was something odd about his voice. "I'm on official business. Does it say that there, too?"

The goon peered at his scanner. "No. It says we got to arrest you. And be careful, too."

The second goon swallowed thickly. "Should I just blast him?"

"We got our orders!"

"I thought maybe he was acting – you know, threatening."

The first goon addressed the bearded technician. "Is there anything we should be aware of, citizen? Remember, you are responsible for any harm that comes to us. You could be charged with further crimes."

The technician laughed. The voice was decidedly tinny. Unreal, even. "Is there something you should know? Why, yes! I am a test run. A pretty convincing one, wouldn't you agree?"

At that point, the orderly line suddenly degraded into a mass of agitated individuals, all trying to get away. Given how crowded the corridor already was, we made limited progress. The hair-pulling and kidney punches didn't seem to help, but we doled them out anyway.

"Should I blast him now?" the second goon asked hopefully.

"A test run?" repeated the first goon uncertainly. "What does that mean?"

"I'm a hologram, but imbued with certain material qualities that, for instance, are able to return a reading to your scanner. Pretty neat, eh?"

The first goon, not sure what else to do, nodded.

"I could explain to you how it works, but you wouldn't understand."

There was a brief pause rife with uncertainty. "So what now?" the first goon asked hesitantly.

"Did I mention the bomb? I'm a test run, but I'm also a diversion. Efficiency, that's our motto."

"If we can't blast him now, Tom, then I'm working for the wrong side."

But the bomb blasted them first.

In the chaos and confusion that followed, I nearly got separated from Sally. Through the smoke, we could see the charred bodies of what had been goons just moments before. Behind them, a large hole had been opened in the station's wall. The hologram was nowhere to be seen.

An alarm was sounding, although it was hard to hear over the ringing in my ears. Several watchbots zipped into the area, their tentacle-like sensory perceptors extended and waving awkwardly about. It was then that I noticed – we all noticed – the security camera monitoring the entrance had been vaporized, too.

All citizens in the Bunker are loyal. This is especially true when we know we are being observed. However, in those rare moments when we know we are not, a strange thing happens. Our loyalty takes on new, previously unthinkable shades of meaning.

Afterwards, if confronted with evidence of this troubling, anti-social behavior, a citizen will readily agree that indeed everyone else was acting in a most criminal fashion. However, he himself was not, and he will brazenly explain why.

For example, no one wants to stand for hourstretches in a line, even if it is the loyal thing to do. So when an illegal but unobstructed entrance to the metro station suddenly appears and the security camera has gone offline, a number of citizens might decide to shorten their wait. And this is exactly what happened. I was among them. The others were traitors, you see, but I had an important package to deliver.

Sally, though, held me back. At first I didn't understand why, but then she discretely motioned towards a citizen standing near the watchbots barely visible in the swirling smoke. She had her PA out and was aiming it at the crowd of people streaming into the station. She was recording them.

As I was saying, all citizens are loyal. And one of the most important duties of the loyal citizen is to report – accompanied by detailed evidence – the crimes of her fellow citizens. After all, it is not only criminal negligence to witness treason and ignore it, but it also happens to be the most reliable way to get a security clearance.

I had never been to Ronald Reagan Plaza before, and – standing there now – my initial suspicions were immediately confirmed: there was no way they'd let us into any of the buildings. In fact, I was surprised we had even got this close.

Ronald Reagan Plaza is located in Q-7, the center of the vast nexus of the Production and Logistics conglomerate in the sector. But no work is actually done there. All around we could see the office buildings, high glass towers stuffed with managers filling out forms, and that means people with security clearances.

The ceiling was high – higher than I'd ever seen before. I didn't know the Bunker was capable of supporting domes that stretched so high. The top must have scraped the surface of Mars. Ventilation ducts weaved their way like metallic arteries across its surface. Their constant droning filled the air. I had never seen so many people before, either, except maybe jammed into a sweaty commissary. But here there was plenty of space to accommodate them. The plaza must have stretched two hundred meters from one end to the other.

The high buildings on all four sides of the plaza were branded with the names of the firms whose headquarters operated the conglomerate. They issued the directives which flowed ceaselessly to the supervisors in the field and they processed the statistics sent back into reports which Control subsequently reviewed. It was a process which should have led to the highest efficiency and most optimal allocation of resources. But like everything else in the Bunker, it worked out better in theory than practice.

Take the dome here above Ronald Reagan Plaza. At first glance, it looks like a technological marvel. But there are no technological marvels in the Bunker. All the technological marvels were built long ago, and we're just trying to keep them patched together. Take a closer look, and you can see the rust under the peeling paint. You can hear the buzzing of shorted wires. You can feel the dreadful throbbing of malfunctioning equipment. I'll bet my pinky finger the choicest offices in these buildings are located near the ground floor. In the Bunker, no one trusts the lifts.

Officially, we're a shining example of utopian progress. You can't improve a utopia because it's already perfect. Anything that isn't perfect is, well, the work of terrorists, traitors, and social deviants. That's why Control wants us to be vigilant. But everyone here knows the truth, even if it's treason to say it. We're slowly decaying. One daystretch the domes will crack and that will be the end of us. Some people actually believe we can turn the tide. Some of us actually believe this system can work.

I'm not one of them.

"C'mon," Sally said and pulled my arm.

We made our way across the Plaza, threading our way inconspicuously among our superiors. They didn't have to identify themselves. The cocky spring to their unyielding step was enough.

The entrance to Building 6 was unobstructed, but just inside the wide, double, glass-paned doors there was a checkpoint. Above it hung a large letter, glowing ominously in yellow neon. It was an Epsilon. It was the lowest of the security clearances, but even so, it was treason for us to be anywhere near it.

I stiffened, but Sally pulled us onward. I wanted to warn her this wasn't a good idea, but now that we were under surveillance, I decided it was safer to play it cool. I started to drum up all the innocent excuses I thought might help us avoid a reassignment to hard labor.

I wanted to go in front, but she was either ignorant (unlikely considering she was still alive) or on some kind of pep pill, because she kept snaking through my grip.

They scanned us. We got through the checkpoint.

I was shocked but had enough of a grip to continue as if I knew what I was doing.

What was I doing?

Sally had found the floor map. She pointed towards the listing for Green Pastures Recycling. It was on the sixth floor.

Next to the floor map was a bank of elevators. One stood invitingly open. When she made for it, my instinct for survival suddenly reasserted itself.

"Let's take the stairs," I suggested.

"How did we get through?" I squeezed the words out of the corner of my mouth. Stairwells aren't usually well monitored, but they're still outfitted with cameras. There was one at every switchback. The red light, though, wasn't always shining.

This stairwell had smooth, unpainted, cement walls and dim lighting. The stairs were flimsy structures made of hard plastex strung up like ribbons and held together with rivets that squealed as soon as your feet put pressure on them. Still, it didn't feel like it was about to give way. Whatever that means.

"I don't know," Sally whispered back. "Must have been a mistake."

I hate mistakes. They happen all the time. They usually end up badly, even if they don't start out that way. I started searching for quick escape routes.

George, you son-of-a-bitch. Why didn't you bring the damned package yourself? "It's a trap," I said. There were some other people in the stairwell, but no one was close enough to overhear.

"You always think it's a trap."

"Sometimes I'm right!"

Sally shrugged. She's being way too callous, I thought to myself. What's gotten into her?

She pulled open the doorway that led to the sixth floor. The hall was well lit by glow panels running along the top of the wall. A twisted stone structure – was it supposed to be some kind of art form? – about waist high stood on either side of us. A corridor stretched off to the left, lined on either side by opaque, plastex doors. To our right was the bank of elevators after which the corridor took a sharp turn.

"I think it's down this way." I followed Sally. We passed door after door. She was peering at the little plates mounted next to them.

"There." She pointed. Up ahead one of the doors was cracked slightly.

Maybe it was because it was the only door that was open. Maybe it was the heavy silence that hung in the air. Maybe it was just luck. Whatever it was, I sensed something wasn't quite right.

I pulled Sally back and rudely gestured for her to shut up. Then I slunk forward, and – holding my breath – peered carefully inside.

A man was sitting in a chair next to the door, cradling a laser pistol in his lap. He wore sunglasses. His hair was meticulously parted. His clothes were pressed. Homeland Security.

"Oh, shit!" I hissed and started to back away.

The goon heard me. "Someone's here," he announced and sprang up.

Fortunately, I had my own laser pistol. In a single, fluid motion, one hand reached into my boot and the other pulled the door closed. There was a bright flash of light and some smoke. When it cleared, the locking mechanism had melted.

"Where under the dome did you get that?" Sally asked, amazed, staring at the warm barrel of the gun in my hand.

But there was no time for that now. We ran down the corridor back the way we had come. The stairs loomed ahead. But they had become a deathtrap. I threw the door open and kicked over one of the stone sculptures. It started to tumble loudly down the stairwell. I hoped it would make the switchback. Even if it bought us mere secondstretches, they would be enough.

"What are you doing?"

The frazzled door to Green Pastures Recycling wasn't going to hold out much longer.

There was only one thing we could do. Something unexpected, and the risk of death was only marginal. "We'll take the lift!"

We made it to the ground floor long before they ever could. Even so, it felt like a long time. Once the heaving lift slowed to a crawl and we heard grinding. There was a camera in there, too, and if we had stood holding each other, cowering like we wanted, and somebody on the other side of that lens had had a hard time getting the morning's slop down, we'd still have had a problem even if we managed to get out of there. But, like I said, we made it. When the doors opened, we faced a panel of incredulous faces.

We might have taken bows.

It's only when you're thinking back that you know what you should

Adam Wasserman

have done. But at the time our thoughts were elsewhere.

We pushed roughly past our audience and headed for the checkpoint. My muscles relaxed somewhat when I saw they were only scanning the people coming in. The exit seemed to glow warmly, framed as it was by the artificial light from outside.

We stepped through the glass doors. The stale, recycled air of the Bunker washed over us. It was the same recycled air as inside, but somehow it felt refreshing. We pressed forward through the crowd until we neared the middle of the Plaza. I was sure we weren't being followed. They would have got us by now.

I grabbed for Sally. I was going to kiss her. Then I was going to chew her out, but I was going to kiss her first. But somebody shoved a laser pistol in my side, and I froze instead.

"Homeland Security," the voice barked clearly in my ear. I could smell the sour breath. A badge flashed briefly in front of my face. "Drop your weapon or I'll lay you down right here."

A vision passed through my mind. It was fat George. He was saying, *Do you mind taking this over to Central Management? I mean, now that you have some time on your hands.*

Central Management. The package was addressed to Production and Logistics. I didn't know what it meant, but now I was sure of it: George was setting me up.

I didn't know how or why, either, but I sure as hell was going to find out.

Chapter 2

It was a Search and Extraction team. They blindfolded us and tied our hands behind our backs with thin, flextex wire. It bit deeply into my wrists. Then they marched us off somewhere. I couldn't see, but I could certainly sense all the citizens who had stopped to watch the treason parade. If we were really unlucky, someone would be filming us and we'd make Ten Things I Hate About Treason hosted by Van Johnson. What loyal citizen hadn't spent much of his lunchtime distracting himself from the awful taste of the slop with Ten Things I Hate About Treason? The only footage they show is submitted by loyal citizens themselves.

Where there is a metro, there is almost always a transtube reserved for privately owned autopods, movebots, and the like. Of course, you need a security clearance to operate any of the vehicles in the Bunker. I'd seen some of the flashier models on plenty of vidshows. You know, the ones where the sinister and scarred Evil Traitor is out to blow up the Bunker, but the vigilant and daring Loyal Citizen manages to thwart him at the last moment? And now that I was being pushed into one, I wasn't even afforded the pleasure of seeing what it looked like. Still, they couldn't hide the push and pull of the centrifugal forces. I guestimated we were going pretty damned fast.

The ride didn't last long. Our friends in Homeland Security yanked us roughly out. I heard a dull thud and Sally grunted. A flash of anger coursed through me. But I knew better. I'd be a pile of hot, simmering ash before I got a single punch in, and she'd still be in the same bind, if not worse.

It was quiet here. There was only the heavy thumping of the booted feet of the Search and Extraction team and the hum of the air recycling system.

We slowed down. The high-pitched, pleasant bleep of a scanner approved our presence. It was followed by the slow hiss of the hydraulics as a security door gave way. The light brightened, and we quickened our pace.

In here, the sounds were more ominous. I wanted to slow down again. Now that I had heard them, I wasn't in a rush to get to our final destination. But someone smacked me in the nape of the neck with a truncheon and I thought better of it.

The screaming wasn't the worst part. Nor the sounds of what was causing the screaming: drills and saws and other industrial equipment. It was the sound that was made just before the scream, when the raw screeching of the drills and the saws and the other industrial equipment suddenly softened. Other times there was no scream at all, but what followed was a liquid sound, like a filled bucket tipping over. Or a handful of slop hitting the wall. More than once I heard someone throw up. I guess our tormentors were human beings after all.

I was pushed into a room. The others continued, presumably leading Sally to an interrogation chamber of her own.

"Already?"

There was a gruff grunt from the goon still standing in the doorway.

"But I just finished up with the last one." There came a belabored sigh. "Don't I get a break? I need a break."

I don't know how the goon responded. All I heard was the door slide shut after him.

There was a short, terse silence followed by another sigh. "Alright," the man muttered to himself, resigned. Footsteps approached. "You're not gonna like this. I don't care what the tag says."

He struck me with what I presume to be the heel of his boot square in my throat. I fell and struck the wall with the back of my head.

While I struggled to breathe, he tore the tag off my clothes and read it. "Trespassing. Destruction of Bunker property. Assault. Conspiracy to trespass. Conspiracy to destroy... Yadah, yadah, yadah." There was a brief pause followed by a low whistle. "Unauthorized possession of a firearm."

The heavy boot found its way back to my neck and clamped firmly down.

This is the end, I thought.

Actually, I'll be lucky if it ends like this.

It's hard to convince yourself you're lucky as the first waves of the dreadful panic that accompanies asphyxiation and waterboarding kicks in.

He tore the blindfold off.

For a few moments we stared at each other, blinking stupidly.

Danzel slowly removed the boot from my throat and set it on the floor where it belonged. "Terry Renfield?"

I coughed a few times, face red and burning. "George Walker."

In the center of the room, there was a mean-looking gurney with restraints and some equipment I cared not to look at. Off to the side was a desk with a comfortable looking, furry chair. In the corner was a banged up cleanbot. It was stained an ugly color of rust and idled softly. I imagined it got a lot of use in here.

Danzel retreated to his desk, still clutching the tag in his hands. "You're in a lot of trouble, Terry."

"Do you think you could do something about these cuffs?" I asked hopefully. For some reason, the back of my head was sore.

He didn't answer. He was obviously put out. "Where'd you get a firearm?"

But he knew as well as I that a citizen has his ways. They'll want me to give names, of course. "One of the guys on my crew."

Danzel glanced at his desk. A handycam lay there. He didn't pick it up. "Listen, Terry." He refused to look me in the eye. "We can do this the easy way or the hard way."

"I just told you, Danzel! One of the guys on my crew. He doesn't work there any more. Just give me a moment. The name will come." Who could I turn in and still sound credible?

"You think names will save you?" Danzel emitted an outraged humph.

"But, Danzel," I responded, my voice soft and inoffensive. I was trying to carefully shove the words one by one into his ear. "I'll tell you whatever you want. You can put it in that report of yours and maybe you'll get a promotion."

"I'm sick of the reports!" He threw the tag into the air. Collapsing on top of his desk, Danzel put his face in his hands. "George Walker, I've been doing this a long time."

My head was aflutter with uncertainty. It's one thing to know you're going to die a nasty death, but it's even worse to imagine a ray of hope. You don't want to allow yourself to believe in it, because it undermines the mental discipline you know you'll need. And yet – how can anyone resist hope, especially when the prospect seems real enough?

Danzel looked up at me again. His eyes were red. He looked very tired. It certainly did not look like the face of a man about torture me to death. "I've been doing this since we got out of the creche, Terry. Remember?"

"How could I forget?" My voice was as neutral and unassuming as possible. Who knew what triggers he had acquired. "You were real happy the day we graduated."

"A commission at Homeland Security!" Now it was his hands he threw into the air. "Who wouldn't be? They're the choicest assignments in the Bunker."

That wasn't exactly true, but I wasn't going to argue with him now.

His spirit flagged. His arms returned to his sides and his shoulders sagged. "Do you know what I do?"

"Yes."

But he didn't seem to think I really did. "I've been trained to cause and sustain an unbearable amount of pain. If you go at it long enough, whatever mental defense you're up against will break down and the only thing my assignment will want – the only thing that exists for him anymore – is the coup de grace. The escape of death. Because it's the only escape left. He's got to realize it himself, of course. He's got to say it. You can't prompt him. He's got to realize that life – whatever it was before – has come down to a few, very long hourstretches. It takes some longer than others, but they always get there. That's the art of the job, I suppose. I always carry on for a bit, even if they're begging. Just so the point really sinks in, you know? It's the things they say then that I usually put in the reports."

He snickered. "You know, they penalize you if you chalk up too many premature deaths. But I almost never let one go by accident. The lucky bastards."

Danzel wiped his nose with his sleeve. Suddenly he perked up. "We go way back. Don't we, Terry?" He smiled reassuringly. He was older, but now he looked somewhat like the Danzel I knew way back when. "I sure as hell ain't gonna do that to you."

I didn't know if he was telling the truth, but I felt relieved anyway. Looking around, I didn't see any cameras, but that didn't mean there weren't any. "Don't you think you should be – you know – careful? About what you're saying?"

But some measure of relief seemed to have washed over my old creche-mate. He waved my concerns away and jumped down from the desk. "Nah," he said dismissively. "They never bother us in here. I think it disturbs them to watch."

He strutted across the room and stopped where I lay on the floor, hands on his hips. A man looks very powerful when you're lying at his feet. A playful expression took hold of his face. "I still can't believe it! What are the chances?"

But there was something else on my mind. "What's going to happen to me, Danzel?"

He thew his head back and laughed. It was the large, throaty laugh of a madman.

Pretty soon he was helping me up and guiding me over to the gurney. He didn't strap me in. He just sat me down on it, and when I looked stable enough, he backed off.

"You ever think of Ms. Bits?" Danzel flopped into the comfortable looking chair behind his desk, folded his hands behind his head, and grinned. Some of his teeth were missing.

I held onto my cool, unperturbed facade for a stretch, the one I'd need to cling to if he went to work on me. But I really didn't see it happening.

"Hell, yeah," I finally responded and smiled a little one of my own. After all, I knew Danzel. We went way back. "Think she's still in operation?"

"I know she's in operation, Terry! My little girl's got her."

"No shit! You got a little girl?"

"Yep." Danzel thumped his chest proudly. "Two, actually."

"I don't have any kids."

Danzel cocked his head to one side. "Really? Why? You afraid Control won't approve them?"

I shrugged.

The look on his face turned a shade graver. It was frightening the way he was meandering from one emotion to the next. "After they become Wards, you don't get to see your kids much anyway," he breathed. "Maybe you're right."

I swallowed uncomfortably and attempted another smile, but I could feel how much my face didn't want it.

"Girlfriend?"

"Yeah." Now it was my turn to feel somber. "They dragged her in with me."

"Really?" He tugged roughly at his bottom lip. "I'm sorry, Terry. There's nothing I can do. Did you love her?"

My heart skipped a beat. "Yeah."

A look of fury forced its way onto Danzel's face. "Dammit!" Suddenly, he was on his feet again. "Utopia? This ain't no utopia. This is a goddamn prison! No, it's worse! It's hell. It's like being put in a pot of cold water over a slow flame. When does it get too hot, Terry?"

"Hey, Danzel. Relax." I quickly checked the ceiling once again for cameras. "Don't get yourself in trouble." Or me, I thought, but I didn't say it.

"Aw, you think I care?"

That attitude was exactly what I was worried about.

He scraped as far back in his throat as he could and spat out a ball of mucous. It landed with an audible thud next to his chair. "I hate this place, Terry. Look at me."

I did. I saw the eyes of a man who was speaking plainly and honestly. I felt bad for him. People who speak plainly and honestly in the Bunker end up as Voluntary Organ Donors. But I wasn't going to let him take me down with him.

"I feel like I'm choking to death. Too long now I've put one foot in front of the other, doing what they tell me, smiling when I'm cued. I can't stand it any more. At first I thought, just make it to your pension. Live the rest of your life in a meds-induced ecstasy. Doing nothing except grabbing the nurses' ass. Except I know now. Too many people who been through here been telling me too much of the same stories. Some of them got to be true." He swallowed thickly.

"Why don't you call in sick?" I suggested. "Take some time off. Get your head together."

But Danzel wasn't listening. The muscles on his face looked like someone was pulling on them. Suddenly, he had an moment of clarity, or he reached some kind of decision. He relaxed again, and the smile came back. "Remember that time we set off the fire alarms in that cement factory next to the creche?"

I chuckled at the memory. "They didn't get it up and running again for two daystretches. The manager spent a whole afternoon at the creche screaming and yelling. He knew it was one of us. But what could he do?"

"Or that time we found that capsule of nuclear waste hidden in the ceiling of corridor Q-15/TY-809?"

A low whistle escaped my mouth. "It's amazing, when you're young you think you're invincible. Nowadays if I found nuclear waste where it wasn't supposed to be, I'd have a core dump and get the hell out of there."

But Danzel was on a roll. The eyes were bugging out of his head. "Whose idea was it anyway to sneak into Good Living and drop it in a food pit?" Before I could answer, he was guffawing with laughter. "Fifteen victims, and ten fatalities!" He shook his head. "Man, we should have never grown up."

It's true. Even though they weren't my prouder moments, these are the unwritten rules of the Bunker.

Upon reaching five yearstretches of age, everyone becomes a Ward of the State and is removed from his parents' care. They will rarely, if ever, see him again. For the next eleven years, his new parent is a learnbot. His new brothers and sisters are his creche-mates. They live together, eat together, and sleep together. During that time, they are imbued with all the skills necessary to carry out whatever function Control assigned them on approval.

Wards of the State are untouchable. They can do whatever they want, and they can do it with impunity. Control is very strict about how its Wards are treated. If anyone so much as lays a finger on one, no questions are asked, but a swift termination usually follows. No exceptions are made.

At sixteen years of age, a Ward graduates and becomes a citizen. Forever after, he will look back on his years as a Ward and regard them as the best of his life.

My eyes grew misty. "Remember that time we tried alcohol?"

We chuckled together. He knew exactly what I was talking about. It was also the first time both of us tried sex.

"What was her name again?" I asked, scrubbing my brain.

Danzel shrugged. "Does it matter?"

We sat for a little while, reminiscing silently. I don't know how much time passed, but eventually one of us coughed or shifted and the reverie was suddenly over.

We looked at one another. We remembered the reason why we both were there.

"I have to tick the box that says, 'terminate'," Danzel told me solemnly. His eyes found the tag where it lay on the floor.

"I understand." I shrugged. "Thanks for not torturing me."

"I could do you a favor, you know." He reached into his desk and pulled out a laser pistol. "I could make sure you go painlessly. After all, I got such a high rating, an 'accidental' won't matter much." He smiled at me encouragingly.

I thought about his offer. It sounded good enough. "Can you go over and help Sally out, too?" I asked him softly.

He nodded his head and took aim. "Bye, ol' buddy."

"Hasta la vista, Danzel." I closed my eyes.

The door burst open. Shots were fired.

I opened my eyes. Danzel's lifeless body was slumping to the ground.

The first of Scorpio I ever set eyes on were his boots. They were shiny and made out of a strange but fascinating material I later found out was leather. That afternoon, sitting on a gurney in a Homeland Security interrogation chamber, I didn't know some people had the luxury of wearing animal skin. I didn't even know there were animals.

The man attached to the boots was standing just outside the doorway. Two heavily armed officers were blocking my view of the rest of him. Scorpio is rather short, you see. But I wouldn't remind him if you want to live very long. Scorpio is very sensitive about his height.

"You have done us a great favor, Terry," came a nasal, sing-song voice from outside the room.

I didn't know what else to say, so I said, "Great."

Scorpio laughed and took a loud bite out of something crunchy.

While I sat watching, two people darted into the room. One grabbed the lifeless body of my old friend under the armpits and dragged him away. The other sprayed something out of a plastic bottle where it had lain. A bit of the misty substance wafted over to me. It smelly slightly bitter and sweet at the same time.

Once they had gone, the two uniformed officers stepped in and moved to either side of the doorway. They stared at me stonily.

Scorpio and his boots followed.

I had never seen an Alpha clearance citizen before, but it was quite obvious that this was one. From what I had heard, these were the people who staffed Control, who ran the Bunker. Never mind that strange ball of white foodstuff with the green skin he held carelessly in one hand. Never mind the black-rimmed glasses with narrow, squarish lenses or the brown vest with buttons or the puffy pants that were tucked neatly into his boots.

He looked healthy. That was it. He had perfect skin and all of his teeth.

He never told me how old he was, but I'd venture to guess forty, maybe forty-five. He had a trim, little mustache and short, curly hair. His hands were manicured.

Very deliberately, he took a little, meandering tour of the chamber. He had a long, thin stick that he used to prod at things he was interested in. He casually observed the cleanbot and the tag. I think he even caught sight of the snotball glistening on the floor because he avoided stepping in it. He ignored the gurney and the tools of the trade nearby. He was especially interested in the desk. He took his time. At one point he seemed ready to sit in Danzel's chair, but then he prodded it a few times with his stick and decided against it.

Turning around, he tucked it under an arm and took a moment to look me over. "There are traitors even here in Homeland Security," he finally said to me. "Yes, I know, it's hard to believe." He took another bite out of the white foodstuff. It was getting smaller.

"What is that?" I asked.

"What? This?" Scorpio held the fruit out to me. "It's an apple. Would you like to try?"

Disgusted, I shook my head no.

He shrugged and continued chewing. "Danzel Croffton was an especially troubling case. I'm glad you could take care of him for us."

"Excuse me?"

Was I missing something? In the Bunker, you're constantly afraid that you're missing something.

Scorpio swallowed and cocked his head to one side. He stepped with one boot on the toe of the other and peered at me intently. "Please don't be shy, Terry. Your performance was absolutely brilliant. It's almost as if you knew we were watching. Leading him on like you did. Tripping him out. Getting him to confess. We knew he'd only do it for an old friend. If he thought the circumstances were intimate enough." He held the apple out again. "Are you sure you don't want to try? You have no idea what you're missing."

I blinked rapidly a few times. "Sure, I'm a loyal citizen like any other. Glad I could help."

Scorpio nodded his head approvingly. "Very good, Terry. I'm proud of you. I think we're going to get along just fine. Don't you?"

I didn't know what else to do, so I agreed with him.

"I don't think I've introduced myself. My name is Felix Tubman. I'm head of Homeland Security."

"Sector Q?"

He stood with two feet on the ground and started to pace slowly around the desk. "I don't think you understand. I'm the head of Homeland Security. All of it." He observed my reaction and seemed somewhat pleased. "This business with the gun and the trespassing. We are quite willing to look past it, you know."

Suddenly, he stopped. He was standing behind Danzel's chair. He folded his arms and leaned against it, peering at me intently. "Tell me about the package."

"It's not mine."

"So you say. Yet it was in your possession."

"My supervisor gave it to me. He asked me to deliver it."

Scorpio's eyes narrowed. "Yes, I know. What's his name?"

You damned well know his name. "George Varukas. Deeper Delvers, Inc, Q-8."

Scorpio took another bite of the apple. It had almost disappeared.

27

He started pacing again. "Do you know what's inside?"

"No. It has a security clearance."

"We didn't find a waiver on you. It's not very smart to carry things around a Bunker you're not cleared for." He had circled around to the front of the desk. He stopped there and faced me. "This George person. Did he tell you anything else?"

"No." I paused and frowned. "Actually, he told me to go to Central Management. But it's not what's on the box."

Scorpio perked up. "Central Management. I see." He finished the apple and flung what remained at one of the officers, who snatched it deftly out of the air and put it in a plastic bag. At the same time, he gestured impatiently for the other to approach. "And that didn't strike you as odd?"

"My mind was on other things." He was right. It was a very amateurish mistake. "I had just seen something disturbing on the tube."

Scorpio's eyes stabbed at me through the rectangular, black lenses. He didn't say anything, though. A moment later, he took the PA held out to him by the other officer and tapped intently at the screen. While he did so, the officer removed my cuffs. I rubbed my wrists gratefully.

A few stretches passed. I didn't know why, but I started to sweat. After all, I had just looked death squarely in the face and hadn't flinched. But this man – I couldn't put my finger on it.

Scorpio handed the PA back to his officer. "You have been very helpful, Terry. Thank you."

"You're welcome."

"Hand me your Card."

In the Bunker there was only one. Tucked into the casing next to my PA was the thin, plastic rectangle. I had recently loaded it up with a lot of credits. I retrieved it and reluctantly handed it to the officer, who passed it on to Scorpio.

He looked it over once and then returned it to the officer, nodding meaningfully.

The officer walked over to the wall where there was a small terminal. He inserted my Card into a slot underneath.

"I'm going to let you go now, Terry."

"Okay."

He smiled at me. "No, really. Your girlfriend, Sally Xinhua, too."

"Is she alright?"

Scorpio's smile grew slightly mocking. "What harm might come to a loyal citizen in here? She *is* loyal, isn't she?"

I nodded my head vigorously.

Scorpio stopped smiling.

The officer returned with my Card and held it out to me.

"You're now Epsilon-clearance, Terry. Congratulations."

My eyes widened. I stared at the Card. It looked exactly the same. "Why?"

"Take the Card, Terry."

I did as I was told.

"Thank you for your cooperation. From here we can only update the plastic. You'll have to make it official by popping into Central Management and filling out the necessary forms. Now, Colonel Alvarez here is going to place a collar on you. I hope you don't mind."

Before I could say anything, the officer pushed my head to the side and placed some kind of device against the nape of my neck. It was where my I-chip had been implanted at birth. After a moment, the device – it looked like a small, thick cylinder – was removed. I hadn't felt a thing.

Scorpio crossed the room to the entrance, the officer following closely in his wake.

"Is that it?" I asked, uncertain if I should get up from the gurney.

"That's it!" Scorpio replied encouragingly. "Oh, yes." He gestured at the officer who had disposed of the apple. "I almost forgot."

That one produced a very familiar looking box.

"You mustn't forget your package."

I looked up at him dumbly even as I accepted it.

"Despite what you've told me, the package is yours."

The officer pressed an official piece of paper in my hands.

"That's a waiver, Terry." Scorpio twirled the thin, long stick in the air in front of him. "The package is, as you know, Delta-clearance. The waiver will help you avoid any unpleasant misunderstandings. Don't you think it will be helpful?"

I nodded my head dully. This was all happening too quickly.

"Don't loose it!"

"How do I get out of here?" It was, really, the only question of importance.

"Someone will carry you."

"Carry me?"

"Yes. After all, you may now have an Epsilon clearance, but it's not enough, is it? We can't just let you casually note the route from the front entrance to the nearest Metro stop, can we? We have to run a very tight ship here at Homeland Security. The well-being of this Bunker depends upon it. I'm sure you understand. Goodbye, Terry."

I was about to protest, but the world went black before I could manage it.

Chapter 3

The package sat in my lap. It quivered every now and then as the metro car hurtled carelessly through the rough, unlit tunnels of the Bunker. Even though I despised it, I cradled it protectively in my hands.

"George is a liar! He's a thief and a traitor and I'm going to live to see the day they carry him off and erase his ass!" Needless to say, I was rather upset.

Sally, though, wasn't convinced. "What does George have to do with it? We got picked up because we were trespassing." She pointed at my lap. "Because you weren't cleared to carry that package!"

"I know he's involved."

"And that gun. How long have you had it?"

"I wouldn't be in this mess if it weren't for him."

"What mess?" She reached over and tousled my hair. "You've got a security clearance!"

The car lurched and we were thrown forward. The lights dimmed and blinked out. For a moment there was an impenetrable darkness. I clutched the package fearfully.

When the lights returned, it was still there.

"Why would an Alpha care about a case of simple trespassing? Answer me that."

Sally sighed and rolled her eyes. "He's an Alpha. Who knows what he was up to! Who cares, Terry? We made it out alive. All the body parts are in their proper place. Stop being so paranoid!"

"You'd be paranoid if they'd put a collar on you." My eyes narrowed. "Did they?"

"Did they what?"

"Put a collar on you?"

"No!"

When we had awoken, we were sitting on a bench in a public square in Q-3 sector. Like most public squares in the Bunker, it was really just the hollowed-out intersection of two major corridors. Unlike most public squares in the Bunker, taking up most of this one was a mass of agitated citizens. They wore shiny pins and orange hats. They blew horns and banged on drums. Sometimes they stomped their feet. It was a Caring Demonstration.

Like all Caring Demonstrations, the participants were holding colored cards, red or green. Those citizens carrying green cards had committed some minor infraction of the rules, such as jaywalking or swearing. Those citizens carrying red cards had been brought there by agents from Human Resources. They acted partly as cheerleaders and partly as thugs. After all, the holders of the green cards were on some kind of probation. Chances are, most of them would end up in a labor camp or terminated. Still, in the spirit of optimism and hope that characterizes every utopia, we are expected to do our best to find and help that single, lonely citizen desperately seeking to cure himself of his social deviancy.

Many of the participants holding red cards had been kidnapped or otherwise coerced. Not that they'd admit it. If asked, they'd respond with a forced smile that they were volunteers. What else would they be?

Who knew how long they had been there. They looked tired and ragged in their silly costumes, shouting out the slogans and singing the songs and otherwise following the cues of the Loyalty Leaders. Most of those worked for Human Resources, too, but no doubt a few moles from Homeland Security were mixed in for good measure.

When confronted with a Caring Demonstration, the safest and healthiest thing to do is to approach the nearest Loyalty Leader and enthusiastically request permission to join. This is exactly what we did.

We got our red cards. We were pushed into the crowd.

"Hold on tight to your card," Sally whispered to me under cover of the shouting.

It was sound advice. The holders of the green cards were forever trying to find a way to loose them, and the best way to loose a green card is to get your hands on a red one.

Immediately in front of us was a citizen holding a green card. I was about to ask him what he had done, but three other citizens wielding red cards muscled their way past before I could get a word in.

"Greetings, citizen!" said one.

"Hey, buddy," snarled another. She gave the first bloke a healthy shove. "This one is mine. Go find your own flaphead to care for."

"I was here first!" He grabbed firmly ahold of their unfortunate victim.

Meanwhile, the third one started pulling on the poor sob's neck. "Get scarlet fever, the both of you! He's mine."

"Not so fast!" screeched the woman and grabbed a fistful of hair.

Within moments, the citizen carrying the green card was lying unconscious at their feet in a pool of his own blood.

The citizens carrying red cards argued a few stretches longer about whose fault it was before splitting up and disappearing into the crowd.

Caring Demonstrations tend to develop into aggravated, disorderly affairs. This one had grown so large it was blocking the traffic along the corridors leading into the square. Those who complained were sucked in, which just complicated the situation further.

Needless to say, after a few hourstretches of screeching and jumping and banging a Special Ops squadron arrived and shot a few concussion grenades into the crowd.

In the ensuing confusion, we slipped into the metro and made our escape.

Oh yeah, and did I forget to mention? They gave me back my laser pistol. My very illegal laser pistol.

I asked Sally what she thought of that.

"I think you're overreacting." She put her head in the cup formed by my arm and chest. I knew that our conversation had – for the time being, at least – been terminated.

Still, my mind raced. I wasn't being paranoid. I was sure of that. I just didn't know what was really going on.

When we got back to Q-16 sector, Sally seemed concerned. "Can I leave you alone?"

"George Walker, Sally, I'm not a Ward of the State! Go on off to work. Text me when you're off."

"I don't know when it'll be, Terry. I skipped this morning, remember?"

How could I forget?

I promised I'd be good and off she went. As soon as she was out of sight, I made for the nearest terminal.

It was time to try out my security clearance.

A PA (or Personal Assistant) is a useful device. Everybody in the Bunker has one. It's about the size of your palm, lightweight, and it fits in a handy, radiation-proof case that's strapped to your waist. You can make a vidcall to anyone you want, wherever they are. You can take pictures and record video. You can download your personalized, pre-approved, mass-produced background and ringtone of your choice. It's linked up all the time. In fact, it's treason to switch it off.

You can do a lot with a PA, but there is one thing it's not very good for. There's no keyboard. There is voice recognition software, but it's treason prone. That's right. It's some citizen's idea of a joke. You speak one thing and it records another. A few hourstretches later, they're hauling your ass off to a reeducation center. Control denies there's a problem, and it's treason to argue with Control.

The Bunker is amply supplied with little cybercafes where you can order a cup of steaming sludge for a credit and hunker down behind a large, glowing terminal. It's certainly unproven that the high rate of ear, nose, and throat cancer has anything to do with the steady bombardment of alpha and other particles that comes from these terminals. Still, I always bring my combat helmet with me when I use one. You see, I'm very sensitive to noise.

The cybercafes in the Bunker are run by firms in the Developmental Engineering conglomerate. These firms compete with each other to provide the best service for the lowest price. It is strictly forbidden for any of the firms in the Bunker to form cartels by fixing the prices for their services.

No matter where you go in the Bunker, it costs two credits an hourstretch to use a terminal in a cybercafe, an exorbitant price.

The cybercafes are open to everyone in the Bunker, even those without a security clearance. Of course, they don't have much use for them. After all, there's not much they are allowed to be interested in. They can look up the metro timetable, for example. But they never do that. The metro timetable is only good for knowing when the metro will *not* arrive at the stop you'll be waiting at. They can also look up what consistency the day's slop will be at the local commissary and the color of the drink.

As I said, those without a security clearance are rarely to be found in a cybercafe. But I had a security clearance. As I sat in front of the terminal, combat helmet strapped on, and waited for an available connection, I was grinding my teeth in anticipation. What would the screen look like?

The first thing I saw was an advertisement.

In a strange way, I felt comforted. I was still on familiar territory. Whatever that means.

A bright, white background appeared. The Bunker's proud logo – a squat, two-story house with square windows and a rectangular door – was embedded in a circle in the center. A pointer of some kind revolved within the circle, leaving a little trail of dots after it. After some time, the pointer disappeared and dark letters and other symbols began to assemble on the screen. I instantly recognized the pattern.

Mixed in with the flashy, gaudy advertisements there were a few random pictures from the Thousand Most Wanted List. The faces had been manipulated to look incredibly monstrous and evil. Human beings – even in the Bunker – simply don't look like that. The background music was the same, too. The Anthem of the Patriot, done over in some horrible collision between trance and disco music. Familiar icons lined the bottom: a knife and fork, crossed, and a little subway car.

There was, however, a search bar at the top of the screen. I smiled. It had never been there before. It was exactly what I had been hoping to find.

I reached for the keyboard and typed in two words: JEREMY WHILES.

No results.

I added some additional criteria for good measure: GREEN PASTURES RECYCLING Q-7 SECTOR.

Even though I had been expecting the result, I sat for a few, tense stretches staring at the screen, not quite sure what to do or what to make of it.

There was no Jeremy Whiles. There wasn't even any Green Pastures Recycling. They had probably tacked the plate to the wall just before we arrived. It was probably already gone.

What could it mean?

The most obvious conclusion was that – whoever Jeremy Whiles was – even an Epsilon clearance wasn't good enough to pinpoint him.

Possible, yes. But I knew it wasn't the case.

So what was in the package? What under the dome would be addressed to a man who didn't exist?

I had no answers. Not yet.

The search bar held my eye. Now that I was sitting here and the two credits had been spent, it seemed like a waste to just get up and walk away. I thought I'd just look up a thing or two, some random curiosities that had been bothering me now for yearstretches.

You know, where did the slop come from? What was the surface of Mars like?

What was there before there was the Bunker?

Everybody knows that human beings came from Earth. It's the third planet in the solar system. But everybody also knows that human beings can't live there any more. We destroyed it. We pumped too many poisonous gasses into the air and we dumped too much industrial waste into the oceans. The temperature began to rise and the plants and insects and fish began to die off. The thick, stinking sludge that had become the sea rose up and inundated most of the places where people were living. Sickness and disease killed off anyone who managed to survive the elements and starvation. I wasn't sure what the Earth looks like now, and I didn't think anybody did.

Everybody knows the earthlings had colonies on Mars. It's the fourth planet in the solar system. So when the last people died on Earth, it didn't mean the end of the human race. There was the Bunker. I suppose we ought to be proud.

Everybody also knows that to prevent such a calamity from ever happening again, the early colonists created Control.

Control's primary function is to protect the environment. The very first inhabitants of the Bunker divined that to control the environment, one must control the economy. After all, it was the greed of a very few people that had resulted in the destruction of the delicate ecosystem that had been Earth's.

Unlike Earth, the Bunker's economy is not based on greed. It is based on egalitarian equality and fairness.

To accomplish its goals, Control has to have complete control over how many people there are and what jobs they have. Using very thorough and complex calculations, it knows at any given time exactly what the price of everything should be.

The security clearance system ensures that only the very brightest – only the hardest working and the most morally sound – citizens ever make it to the top. There are very few Alpha clearance citizens, but they are all exceptional.

I suppose that part of the reason most of us accept our place in the Bunker is that in theory the path to the top is open to everyone. Ours is a meritocracy. Any citizen of a higher security clearance can promote you as far as his own as a reward for exceptional service. It is treason not to. All the advertisements and vidshows and the endless incantations of the Anthem of the Patriot have driven the message home that if you are at the bottom of the heap, it's because that's exactly where you belong.

Stuff the meritocracy. Shove it up a dark, damp place where the neon lights don't shine until the eyes are bugging out of your head. I didn't create these rules. If I don't qualify as exceptional, there's something wrong with the criteria. Because I am exceptional.

I'm just very careful about showing it.

So, this is what I found out in that marvelous hourstretch. I want to share it with you.

The destruction of the Earth unfolded centurystretches ago. I don't know what a centurystretch is, and I'm not cleared to know, either, but apparently it's a long time.

What started out in a few underground tunnels has since expanded into a vast, convulsing city. The Bunker is huge. I never realized how large it was. There are eighteen sectors, each identified by its own letter. At that very secondstretch, three hundred and sixty-eight thousand, four hundred and one persons lived in them. The primordial sector – A sector – is the oldest. The last sector – Y sector – is not the newest. Rumors of the existence of a shadowy Z sector are the result of terrorist sleeper cells and should be disregarded. Each sector has been subdivided into a number of departments. Some sectors have more departments than others. My home sector – Q sector – has sixteen.

Every citizen has been assigned to one of the Bunker's conglomerates, each of which is wholly in charge of one aspect of its economy. There are eight of them: Human Resources, Homeland Security, Developmental Engineering, Housing and Construction, Production and Logistics, Central Management, Defense, and Procurement.

Human Resources has an exclusive monopoly on information. It is also responsible for the Wards of the State, health services, the prison population, and workforce (re)assignment. It produces and broadcasts all the entertainment on the tube, including the commercials, infomercials, and scammercials. The people over at Human Resources must be convinced that we are all idiots, because that's the only kind of person who would appreciate their sense of humor.

Homeland Security acts as a police force and judicial system all wrapped up into a single, unfeeling but omnipresent institution. They are nothing more than thugs armed with lots of weaponry and Control's complete trust. Avoid them as best as you can.

Developmental Engineering is responsible for the design and maintenance of all electronic, mechanical, and digital equipment in the Bunker. They do their best to provide us with a steady supply of power, design our PA's, and ensure the air stays inside. They are the closest thing we have to science, and they can't even get the lifts to work properly. Still, they preserve whatever knowledge is left over from the earthlings. It is their responsibility to ensure that it does not erode further.

Housing and Construction does pretty much what the name

suggests. They build and maintain things. When the things they build subsequently collapse and those responsible have been terminated, they return to the scene of the disaster and try again. Life expectancy within H&C is not a very encouraging datum once you find out you've been assigned to it.

Production and Logistics produces all the slop and runs all the factories. It also makes sure that all the things it produces are then distributed to those who need them. There are certainly never any shortages in the Bunker. If you need something (like air) in a particular place and it's not available, then either you're not cleared to have it or you didn't fill in the proper form. The boys at P&L are also responsible for collecting garbage and other waste products – such as dead bodies – and making good use of them.

No one is quite sure what Central Management is responsible for except writing documents and designing forms. However, they do this very well.

The last two are the oldest and the easiest of all the conglomerates to define. Defense blows things up, and Procurement obtains the raw materials from outside the Bunker required to replace what has been lost, blown, or used up.

The conglomerates are large, sprawling networks of office buildings and bureaucracy. Some, such as Homeland Security and Central Management, are largely self-contained. Others, however, farm out a good deal of work to privately-owned firms. These firms are operated by loyal citizens who have obtained a special waver from Human Resources. Such entrepreneurs (as they are called) apply for an available market niche and are assigned a preliminary budget for advertising. After that, they go to work cajoling, bribing, and (if all else fails) bullying other citizens into buying their products and services. In many cases, they don't even produce anything. They just obtain the regular, mass-produced junk from P&L, attach their own, flashy label to it, and double the price.

Deeper Delvers, Inc, where I used to work and that fat bastard George is the head supervisor, is a firm within the Procurement conglomerate.

The conglomerates operate under Control's watchful eye, consuming the resources Control makes available and producing the junk it has deemed necessary to facilitate a healthy environment. This junk is then distributed according to the free-market theory of prices and demand. The prices are set by Control and the citizens are happy to demand what is available.

It's a good thing for all of us Control hasn't yet figured out that the healthiest environment is the one without any people in it.

Citizens receive a monthly stipend based partly on their job assignment, partly on their security clearance, and mostly on the weather. By using complex formulae, Control ensures that the amount of junk being produced and the availability and distribution of the money supply is always the most optimal for the environment.

And if for some reason it isn't, you'd better have the right friends in the right places or risk falling on the wrong side of that equation.

As befits an egalitarian society, a great deal of the economy is geared towards fighting the ever-growing terrorist threat.

I scanned the data. Maybe it was because I just assumed it was doctored that I subsequently filtered it out. Later on, though, I would remember. You see, there is far too much being produced here for a population of several hundred thousand. We couldn't possibly use all those lightbulbs. Or that much reinforced concrete. Or surface-to-air missiles.

And little land rovers. Everyone knows the Bunker is a closed environment. But we also know it has exit points onto the forbidding surface of Mars. The land rovers are used to get around up there. The people who operate the land rovers wear ecopacks. These are loose-fitting, airtight environments that fit snugly around the persons inside. Ecopacks make it possible to move about freely on the surface of Mars, or an astroid, or any other environment lacking sufficient oxygen, air pressure, and surveillance.

Attached to the perimeter of the Bunker is a spaceport. It is used to get specially trained miners to the asteroids. Sometimes they come back. Other times they enter into permanent orbit around the sun. There are lots of asteroids in the vicinity of Mars. The asteroids are very convenient sources of water. The main problem seems to be the expense of getting it back here.

It's a very dangerous job, mining an asteroid. According to Control, the reason the miners all have Delta security clearance and are spoiled beyond belief is not because of the many disasters that can (and do) befall them. No. It's a small recompense for the fact that they have to spend much of their lives outside the confines of our happy, egalitarian utopia.

Of course, they eat the same, egalitarian food we do. The original settlers ate algae; in the Bunker, we eat Vitamim. Human Resources is armed with lots of stamps bearing the name. Calling Vitamin something treasonous like "slop" is strictly forbidden. Vitamim's basic ingredient is algae and fungus cultivated in Production and Logistics' laboratories. It is processed and given flavor in the pits. It's all good for us.

And there's an Underground. I already knew there was an Underground. Everybody does. But now I was cleared to know about it. Of course, just saying the word could easily land me in an interrogation chamber. My new security clearance certainly didn't protect me from that.

According to the terminal, the people that make up the Underground are a mix of various pathologs and psychotics. Most are deranged and easily identified by all the twitching and stammering. This calculation is most unfortunate for those citizens who happen to stammer because they have no other way of speaking. In any case, the Underground is very small and does not pose a threat to the continuing happiness and serenity of life in the Bunker.

The Underground is evil. Fortunately, it has been completely infiltrated by Homeland Security. Apparently, Control allows the Underground to exist so that terrorists and other social deviants have a convenient way to identify themselves. There is nothing to worry about. Its most dangerous elements are eliminated safely and immediately. No innocent people are ever terminated by mistake, and it all happens in places your average, loyal citizen shouldn't be and need not know about.

Let's see, what else? Oh yeah. Mars is a red, rocky planet swept by frequent sand storms. The atmosphere is thin and wispy. There are few clouds. All the water is frozen several meters below the surface, just above the tops of the domes. There isn't much, but P&L's recycling programs help us make do with what we have. Radiation from the sun and space is constantly bombarding the surface. It is a world populated by large, carnivorous creatures called dinosaurs. They kill just for the sheer joy of it. Even worse, there is no ceiling. If you aren't attached to anything (such as a land rover) you will fall upward and be forever lost in the vast emptiness of space.

The surface is, in fact, a forbidding, dangerous place and none of us who isn't cleared for it should ever want to go there.

I sat back in my chair and looked up.

They made it sound so goddamn interesting!

Back at the barracks, there was a surprise waiting for me.

I live – along with thousands of other citizens – at the very bottom of Q-16 sector. It is a dark, dreary place called the Lower Quarters.

Many of the lightbulbs have burned out and are waiting replacement from H&C. Some of the others blink and flash erratically. There is a constant, infernal buzzing noise.

The corridors are long, wide, and straight. They are always crammed. The Bunker is manned at every hourstretch, it is true, but not by everyone at the same time.

Just like every other barracks, Barracks One where I have my bunk is a large, cavernous hall. The beds are stacked eight high and are equipped with ladders for those fortunate enough to be assigned a top bunk. Although you must climb to get there, the higher you are, the harder it is to sneak up on you. Every daystretch in the Bunker, they find a few more sleeping, dead bodies.

The beds stretch out in perfect rows from wall to wall. They are heavyset and hard to damage. There is barely enough room for two people to pass between them. Although it never shows up in the reports, this fact is often the cause of the fights and brawls that break out from time to time in the Lower Quarters. Although I was still a Ward of the State at the time, I can still recall the carnage at Barracks Nine L-11 Sector. It was all over the tube. As far as I know, no one survived the havoc or the waves of interrogation that came after it.

Barracks One is no different than any of the other barracks in Q-16 sector. Well, almost no different. It has one distinct advantage: mine is the closest to the Endurance Community Dining Hall.

You might ask yourself how this is an advantage. It is a very reasonable question to ask.

With so many citizens living in such close proximity to each other, hygiene is an important concern. It is so important, in fact, that H&C periodically conducts surprise hygiene inspections. They make everyone stand outside in the corridor where one crew examines hands and scalps and another enters the barracks and checks the condition of the beds and the cleanliness of the chemical toilets.

The citizens over at Housing and Construction take their hygiene duties quite seriously. One might even go so far as to say that they are zealous. It is especially the younger recruits – the fresh blood as it were – that you have to watch out for. They will always find something. Whether it is a spec of dirt under the fingernail or a stain on your shirt or a wrinkle in your sheets, they are sure to find it. And if they can't find it, you can trust them to invent it on the spot.

It would be far too inefficient to identify all the beds and the citizens who belonged to them before inspecting them. Central Management has decided that these drills consume resources proportional to their usefulness only when those citizens who have failed are required to present themselves for punishment. Control (or – more likely – an Alpha highly placed over at Defense) has calculated that posting armed units with bed patrols would be silly.

As a result, hygiene inspectors are usually outnumbered one hundred-to-one on any given inspection.

When you have been tagged by a hygiene inspector and he demands that you accompany him, the safest thing to do is knee him in the balls and make a run for it.

At the Endurance Community Dining Hall, I have a friend who sometimes works handing out napkins. He usually lets me hide in one of the storerooms until the hygiene inspector gets bored or frustrated and goes away.

"You're a strange cat, Terry Renfield."

Hanging from the ladder by an arm, I froze.

A woman sat up in my bunk. The protective, plastic sheet she had placed over it crinkled loudly.

She was pretty.

Normally, when a pretty woman sits up unexpectedly in your bed and you happen to like women, you would be pleased. A lot of other ideas would flood your mind and you'd expect (quite reasonably so) that some of them had a good chance of coming true in the near future.

But I did not feel this way about this particular woman, and I happen to like women.

This woman wore a dark, grey suit with the Homeland Security logo embroidered boldly on the front. She was pointing a laser pistol at me.

"What do you want?"

"It's not very often," she went on, "that someone is taken into an interrogation chamber and walks out again a few hourstretches later. With the same illegal laser pistol he had when he went in. I checked. You're not an informant, and you didn't become one, either."

I shrugged. "So?"

"So?" Her eyes widened. "What's in the box?"

"I'm not authorized to tell you."

"We'll see about that." She lay the hand with the pistol in her lap. "I recognized you instantly. You look just like that traitor on the tube last night."

That sinking feeling told hold of my stomach again. I had been making good progress putting the whole incident behind me.

"The resemblance is amazing. I checked up on you, you know. You called in sick to work last weekstretch." She shrugged. "Of course, all the records show you were here in your bunk, reading and blowing snot out of your nose. The only places you went were to eat and shit. I even dug up some of the archive footage. And sure as nation building, there you were. You looked so cuddly."

I swallowed. "Why are you here?"

"Because there's something unhygienic going on. I can smell it."

"Looking for a promotion?"

She scowled at me. "Give me your Card."

"I'm Epsilon clearance."

Her eyes narrowed dangerously and the pistol lifted from her lap. "Don't play games with me, citizen. I checked before I came. You don't have a security clearance."

I waved my Card at her. "Sure I do. Just got one."

She hesitated. "But you're not registered."

"I just got it. I haven't had a chance to get over to Central Management."

Her shoulders sagged. "Who gave it to you?"

"Felix Tubman."

Her eyebrows shot up and her shoulders lifted. "Who?"

"You heard me."

"The Chief of Homeland Security?"

"All of it." I smiled.

She shook her head as if I'd just told a very bad joke. "I'm sure Mr. Tubman has better things to do than associate with common trash like you." She pointed her pistol meaningfully between my eyes. "Now hand over that Card!"

Needless to say, I was reluctant to do so. There's a hundred things she could have done with it, and all of them meant trouble. She might have confiscated it, for example, or she might have planted some kind of evidence of treason. Even worse, she might have used it to try and blackmail me into revealing whatever treason I was already involved in. Which admittedly would have been difficult because no one had yet had the decency to let me in on what it was.

There was only one thing I could do.

I lunged and tried to snatch her laser pistol from her grasp, but she was almost as fast as I was. Still, I managed to wrap my hands around the barrel. We struggled for a very short time before I felt it go off.

We stared at each other, wide-eyed. One of us was suddenly very dead, and the other was very much trying to figure out which one it was.

Chapter 4

"What was she doing in your bed, Terry?"

"George Walker, she tried to kill me!"

The lines on Sally's face hardened. "You didn't answer my question."

There I stood in corridor Q-16/UIT-12, not far from the entrance to Barracks One. Streaming by us on both sides was a crowd of dazed citizens, returning properly medicated from a long, hard shift at the iron-ore furnaces. Their daystretch had just ended. The citizens designated to replace them, just as dazed, were headed in the opposite direction. Their daystretch was about to begin.

The heavy, plastic-wrapped bundle I held with difficulty in both arms kept getting jarred. The package was gripped as delicately as possible under one arm.

"Well, what did she want?"

"I don't know," I replied between clenched teeth. After all, the middle of corridor Q-16/UIT-12 was not the ideal place to be having this particular conversation. "Do you think you could help me now?"

"I don't know," she replied casually and bit a fingernail.

The ex-Homeland Security agent's feet caught someone in passing on the shoulder. I received a rough shove in return. "Watch where you're going, buddy!"

I leaned over and whispered in her ear. "There's a dead body inside this thing. I'm not kidding."

A small knot of living Homeland Security agents marching in lock-step down the corridor caught our attention. They looked like they were on a mission. In fact, they *were* on a mission. It was a Search and Extraction team, and I had a pretty good idea who they were looking for.

Sally's attitude suddenly improved. "Looks like they want to find out why she didn't report back."

We stood still as hardened Vitamim until it was clear they were making for the entrance to Barracks One.

"Okay," she said, reaching over and taking the package. "Let's make a move before they put the department on lock-down. We have to be quick."

It's times like this I know Sally is my girl and no one else. After all, it was my mess. If she walked away now and left me to go down in a hailstorm of laser light, she'd get off scott-free. But now she was using words like "we" and "let's". Now it would be her ass out there swinging in the breeze along with my own. I'd do the same for her, and she knows it.

We turned and sprinted forward. But I only got a meter before I slammed into something fleshy, smelly, and unyielding.

It was a thick, bearded citizen wearing soiled overalls. He was leering at me. A few of his crooked teeth were missing and his lips were terribly chapped.

This man was clearly in violation of a number of sections of the General Guidelines on Sanitation and Hygiene.

A wonderful thought flashed through my mind. If I turned him in, Control might be inclined to forget about the accidental killing of a simple Homeland Security goon. After all, there were so many of them. Who was going to miss just one?

"Hello, Terry," the smelly man grumbled. The voice was low and gritty as if he were carrying around a gravel depot in the back of his throat.

I had never seen this citizen before in my life.

"What you got in the bag?"

"Some breath mints. Want one?"

I didn't have to look to know the Search and Extraction team had already entered the barracks.

"Terry!" It was Sally. She was anxious. "Now's not the time for socializing."

"Didn't think I'd be able to track you down, eh? Well, Lance Trevor is just full of surprises. Anyway, you weren't hard to find."

"Uh, I'm kind of busy, Lance."

"I'll bet you are." He reached into the carrying case at his waist and whipped out his PA. "I recorded the whole damned thing. Saved me a lot of trouble, too."

I swallowed thickly. "Recorded what?"

The deceitful grin grew wider. "You thought you could just crawl back into your old life and pretend nothing happened? Well, it's payback time, chump."

There are simple truths in the world – even in the Bunker – and one of them is this: before I pay anyone back, I like to know what for. And frankly, I wasn't interested. Another time, another place, I might have been mildly curious, suspicious even. But I had other things on my mind. This flaphead would have to wait.

Of course, a citizen's options are limited when he's burdened with a fresh corpse. The only thing I could do was take a crack at one of his kneecaps.

Lance – whoever he was – let out a grunt of pain and collapsed to the floor.

We kept on running.

Behind us arose a dreadful hollering. It was Lance, of course, calling to the Search and Extraction team or the security camera or whoever else was watching and listening.

"Oh, shit!" Sally said.

We were running through the corridors of the Bunker with a very big, very unsanitary problem. I couldn't just explain it away, and there were cameras everywhere. Even worse, I had no where to run to.

Things were looking pretty bad.

Sally, however, did have somewhere to run to.

I had been with Sally for almost four yearstretches, and I thought I knew her pretty well. Turns out, I was wrong.

As we ran up the corridor, pushing our way through the crowd and suffering the occasional glancing blow in return, there was only one question on my mind. "Who was that guy?"

"Shut up and get your pistol out!"

Someone up ahead had noticed our approach and was steeling himself for a confrontation, but Sally body checked him first. She's small but wiry.

"I can't!" I panted. I'm a tough, fit guy, but carrying around an extra fifty kilograms of weight was wearing me down. "I've got my hands full!"

Sally frowned at me. "Are you still holding that?"

"What else do you want me to do with it?"

"Dump it!"

"Where?"

By now, the commotion had attracted the attention of the cancerheads milling around at the head of the corridor. They stood there, taking up the entire T-intersection. They were waiting for us. I didn't know what they intended to do, but I was sure we wouldn't like it.

As we closed on them, I gathered every last ounce of my strength and heaved the body. Three were bowled over and toppled loudly to the floor.

We passed right on through the gap in their line. No one tried to stop us.

"Now get your gun!" Sally shouted at me.

I knew what she had in mind.

I got my gun. The security camera above us was swiveling eagerly in our direction. Just before we came into focus, I took it out with a nicely aimed shot at the lens. A gentle mist of fine, partially vaporized plastex shards rained down on us. We held our breaths, covered our mouths, and stepped aside.

I made to turn left, but Sally wasn't having it.

"C'mon!" I cried to her, taking a few steps forward.

But she held back, shaking her head adamantly. "Trust me, Terry."

A bolt of laser light struck the wall not far from my face. It was the Search and Extraction team. Peering back the way we had come, I could see we had a good start on them. Our passage through the corridor had stirred the traffic up into confused, little knots that were difficult to dodge or barge through.

There was no sense in arguing. Hell, I didn't know where I was going anyway. I leapt after Sally.

The traffic here was a bit thinner. It made running easier, but spotting us would be easier, too.

I kept hitting the cameras, at least the ones I knew of. Not all of them are obvious. But I'm a good shot – always have been – and didn't miss a single one.

"Where are we going, Sally?"

"Just trust me," she repeated, almost pleading. It seemed to me like she was looking for something.

Whatever it was, I'm glad she found it. Because the laser fire had started up again. One of the bolts passed between us and struck a very surprised young woman. Alas, she had just been added to the swelling ranks of collateral damage in the war against terrorists and social deviancy. I was sure she'd make the Loyalty Stretch on the tube.

Considering the most probable futures I could think of, the Loyalty Stretch didn't sound so bad. After all, the Loyalty Stretch isn't necessarily a deadly affair. It's just an uninspired, fear mongering collage of current events. Ten Things I Hate About Treason hosted by Van Johnson, however, always is.

We turned into a little access corridor on the left. I had hardly noticed it. It was poorly lit and seemed deserted.

"Is anyone home?" Sally shouted into the dimness.

"What?" But she wasn't talking to me.

Up ahead there was an alcove blocked by a vending machine. It was, of course, an odd place to be selling tins of Algatine, but maybe it was the only refreshment available to the poor souls unfortunate enough to be on assignment down here. Much to my surprise, though, the vending machine slid aside, revealing a gnarled, stunted woman with knotted hands and a nose far too big for her face.

I saw Sally do something strange. She pushed the palm of her right hand against her forehead and wiggled the fingers.

The dwarf woman quickly repeated the gesture and waved impatiently at someone standing behind her. At once, three people stepped out into the corridor and started looking busy. Two of them were carrying repair tools, probably for the vending machine. The third positioned himself just down the corridor and – head cocked and listening – waited.

Oh, I get it. When they burst into view he'd be just another random citizen, minding his own business.

"No, ma'am. No one's passed this way for at least five minutestretches. You must be looking for another deserted access corridor."

Sally ducked into the alcove. I followed. The gnarled, ugly woman glanced at me with scarcely concealed hostility.

"Here are the keys," she said to Sally and pressed a plastic button into her hands.

"Where?" Sally demanded, looking around expectantly.

They slid the vending machine into place behind us. And just in time! We could already hear the heavy, booted feet of the Search and Extraction team coming down the access corridor.

The dwarfish woman did not respond. She simply walked to the back of the alcove and pressed against it. A small panel popped off.

"Thanks!" Sally put a leg through the opening, turned, and raised an eyebrow at me. "Well, what are you waiting for? Come on!"

We were speeding down the transtube in a sleek, silver autopod. Sally was driving.

"Why didn't you tell me you were in the Underground?" Alright, I'm man enough to admit it. I was pouting. I'll bet you would, too, if the woman you'd been sleeping next to for four yearstretches suddenly turned out to be somebody else.

"Try and understand, baby. There are rules to this kind of thing. One of them is you're not supposed to tell anybody." She was gripping the joystick so tightly her knuckles were white. Artfully, she dodged the slower vehicles in front, all the while maintaining a careful eye on the situation behind.

It sounded reasonable enough. However, at the time I wasn't in the mood to be reasonable. "George Walker, I didn't even know you could drive." I leaned back in the seat and pouted some more. After all, if anyone should have been driving it was me. *I* was the one who always wanted to sit behind the joystick.

A sudden thought occurred to me. "Are they going to try and make me join? I won't, you know."

"First we've got to get someplace safe. Then I'll get in touch with Brutalizer. She'll know what to do."

"Brutalizer?" I scoffed. "What kind of name is that?"

"We have our own names in the Underground. So we can't trace each other back to the real world."

"You got a name like that?"

"Sure."

"What is it?"

She hesitated. Maybe I was asking her to break another one of their rules of secrecy or whatever. But I didn't see that it made any difference now that I knew the only secret that mattered. She must have come to the same conclusion, because she said, "They call me Complicity."

I laughed. "Did you make that up yourself?"

She put a hand out and pinched me on the thigh. When she spoke next, her voice was no longer pleading. It was quite serious. "Listen, baby. You got to remember to call me that. Complicity. It's important. My life could depend on it."

"Okay, baby."

"Another thing. When you meet these people..."

"What?"

"Try and control yourself."

"What do you mean, control myself?" I was offended.

"Try and be nice. That's all."

"Aren't I always nice?"

"Just try. These people are dangerous."

"I'm dangerous!"

"Yeah, but so are they."

Our conversation was cut off when she noticed a large, heavily armored flybot coming up on us from behind.

"We've been tagged!" she hissed and pointed.

On the dashboard between us was a series of monitors, one of which showed the situation out back. Sure enough, inching its way carefully through the gap between the tops of the vehicles and the curved ceiling of the transtube was some kind of military bot. A multitude of perceptors like oversized ears and strands of hair was crowded onto its thick, grey-green skin. I could spot at least two banks of heat-seeking missiles under the stubby wings and a laser canon mounted on the top. It was pointing vaguely in our direction, trying to get a lock, ignorant of or ignoring the innocent citizens all around.

"Hold on!" Sally cried.

I held on.

Sally pulled hard to the right where there was a narrow gap between a large, slowly moving truckpod and a busbot. I was jerked so hard to the left I almost fell out of my seat.

The asphalt where our autopod had just been melted under a heavy rain of cannon bolts. Bits and pieces of the road pounded the vehicle, some of them large enough to burn little craters into the hard plastex.

The unfortunate movebot driving behind us never had time to avoid the firestorm. It slid headfirst into the hole that had suddenly opened in the ground. A stretch later it was struck from behind and both movebots exploded violently.

Our autopod shuddered as the shock waves thundered past.

Some of the wreckage flew out of the fireball straight up into the air and almost clipped the flybot. It veered dangerously.

"Good," Sally grunted, straining to control the various forces pushing and shoving the autopod. There was only a small amount of space between the busbot in front and the truckpod behind. "That ought to buy us a few stretches."

"George Walker," I muttered as I collected myself from the floor. "How did you stay in your seat?"

"Push the button!" It was the only thing she would say to me.

There were a lot of buttons, and none of them was labeled.

Sally had one hand on the joystick. The other was tapping urgently on the monitor closest to her. She had pulled up a schematic of the transtube. Somehow, she managed to pinpoint our location. The map looked like a mesh of multi-colored lines, some of which crisscrossed. The whole thing had a vaguely three-dimensional feel. I wondered how she could read it.

There was a red button on the passenger side door about level with the seat. It was a bit larger than the others.

The busbot in front was filled with Wards of the State on some kind of field trip. The unhygienic typhoids were crowded around the windows, ooh-ing and ah-ing at the destruction. We couldn't hear the jokes they were making, but they laughed grandly at them. A few in the back were making faces and rude gestures at Sally and me. One kept drawing a finger across her throat and sneering.

Maybe this was the button Sally was talking about.

"No, not that button!"

A small, mining drill extended from the nose of the car. It was a long, sturdy rod with a three-headed, riveted torso that churned violently, ready to plunge itself into stone as hard as granite. I was impressed. At Deeper Delver's, Inc, we'd have had a much easier time making our quotas if we had only a single machine like that one.

It was an interesting device to have on an autopod. What else had they equipped this thing with?

As I said, there wasn't much space between our autopod and the busbot. The mining drill cut easily through the back of the bus. The girl who had been threatening us with imminent death dissolved into a fine, red spray which coated the rear windows.

The Wards of the State who had crowded around the side windows stopped telling jokes.

"Good going!" Sally said, glancing nervously at the rearview monitor. The military flybot had made it past the gathering fireball we had left behind. More and more movebots were crashing into it, but it was of no interest now. "We're stuck to the busbot!"

The transtube curved slightly and we were momentarily cut off from our pursuers.

Behind us, the truckpod lurched dangerously. A trail of smoke plumed out the back. It was then that I noticed the markings.

This truckpod – I could hear the slow, rumbling of its strained motor even inside our autopod – was painted with a symbol well known in the Bunker to be synonymous with sickness and death. It was a barrel circumscribed by a circle. It meant that the truckpod was carrying some kind of incredibly safe but also incredibly toxic payload. It meant that it would be incredibly stupid and dangerous (not to mention treasonous) to disturb it in any way.

I had an idea.

I got out my laser pistol. "How do you open this window?" I asked, banging on it with the tip of the barrel.

"What?" She glanced at me sideways. I could tell she was wrapped up in the calculations required to plot a safe course.

"The window!" I shouted. "Open it!"

"The switch under the handle!"

There were two switches, one closer and one farther away.

"Don't hit the eject switch!"

"Which one is the eject switch?"

"The silver one!"

They were both black.

Sally was preoccupied, making sure we didn't crash into a wall, and I had to decide, so I flipped the one farther away. It didn't do anything. I flipped it the other direction. The window cracked. "Ah-ha!" I cried and kept it pressed. The transparent pane steadily lowered.

The world outside was a cacophony of screeching, bellowing, and roaring. Even worse were the gasses and the smells. We both broke out into fits of coughing.

I turned around and kneeled. With one arm I pulled the back of the passenger seat to my chest, trying to brace myself as best I could against any sudden moves Sally would make. The other arm had the gun. I put it out the window, aimed it at one of the truckpod's tires, and fired.

I saw the driver's face as I pulled the trigger. He looked unpleasantly surprised.

For an unexpected, heartfelt stretch, I felt sorry for him.

Then I reminded myself that there are no innocent saps in the Bunker. More likely than not, he was some kind of criminal, probably dealing anonymously in black market goods on the net or hacking into people's Cards and stealing their credits. I was doing the Bunker (and myself) a favor.

The truckpod lurched to the side and skid on one of its axels. A shower of sparks sprayed the transtube wall. The driver started to frantically pound at the dashboard.

The truckpod started to fall back, giving us some room. This is exactly the effect I had wanted.

The effect I had not wanted was the sudden degeneration of the locking mechanism at the back of the flatbed. The gate flew open, and whatever crap he had been carrying started to unload onto the transtube floor.

"Oh, shit!" I exclaimed.

I couldn't see what it was, but I was very glad every moment put a little more distance between the truckpod and ourselves.

I got my arm back in before the flybot rounded the curve and bore down on us.

"Shut the window!" Sally mouthed to me. She didn't have to tell me a second time.

The window seemed to close far more slowly than it had opened.

The truckpod was falling farther and farther behind. The military flybot was almost directly over it.

That's when whatever the truckpod had been spewing exploded.

It was a violent blast, even more powerful than the first. The window sealed a few moments later, but not before a plume of nasty fumes snuck inside.

My eyes were burning. Pain shot through my throat and into my lungs.

"Slam on the brakes!" I tried to shout. But my voice had been reduced to a hoarse whisper.

"What?" Sally, trying desperately to maintain control of the autopod, frantically rubbed her eyes.

"The brakes!"

She didn't seem to understand.

I didn't know how this damned thing worked or I would have stopped it myself.

But she did understand. I don't know if she actually heard me or just figured it out for herself.

We now had a wide berth behind us.

Sally pulled back suddenly and hard on the joystick. I was thrown suddenly and hard against the windshield.

The force was enough to rip the drill – still spinning menacingly – out of the back of the busbot. It started to pull away from us, too.

I guess Sally had already plotted our course because without her intervention the autopod veered suddenly to the left and crossed all three lanes of traffic. I screamed because I thought it was taking us into another movebot or the transtube wall.

Fortunately, the bot's CPU was still functioning well enough that it didn't crash into anything solid, which – as everybody knows – happens from time to time.

Sally pulled the autopod over in front of Good Seasons Nuclear Power Facility and threw her door open. It lifted wearily into the air, jerking and whining, as if it were an old person. I thought it might fall off.

"C'mon!" she cried, one foot already on the ground outside. "What are you waiting for?"

My head hurt and my eyes were blurry. "What about the autopod?" As beaten up as she was, I was loath to give her up.

"Leave the autopod!" She got out, took two steps towards the facility, and looked impatiently back.

I most certainly did not want to leave the autopod.

It remained idling at the curbside. The mining drill was still extended and spinning. A few interested citizens had gathered around.

Another distraction, I thought. Our friends from Homeland Security would spend some time here – only a little, but time was precious enough! – collecting evidence before continuing the pursuit.

Of course, it wouldn't be very difficult to figure out where we had gone next.

A massive, plastex imitation of Nutty the Happy Neutron waved at us above the main entrance.

Everybody in the Bunker knows Nutty the Happy Neutron. Nutty is a pudgy little figure with tiny little balls like ioun stones floating around his head. He is always smiling and waving. He makes frequent cameo appearances in commercials, infomercials, and scammercials to remind us all how friendly and safe nuclear power is. There's nothing to get worked up about!

I never feel good when Nutty the Happy Neutron is in the vicinity.

"George Walker, Sally!" I whispered to her hoarsely as we ran inside. "We'll be trapped in here!"

But she ignored me. Running up to the front desk, she slammed a fist down on the counter and blurted out, "Bonzo, we have an appointment!"

The young man behind the counter stared at her, dazed. Apparently, he wasn't called Bonzo, and he didn't know anyone who was.

There were a few other people standing in the lobby. A good number of them had radiation suits on.

"Shouldn't we have a radiation suit?" I asked. I was a bit worried.

Looking around wildly, Sally cried out, "Bonzo! Are you here? Is anyone here? George Walker, we have an appointment!"

Fortunately, there was someone around who seemed to know something about this mysterious appointment.

Approaching from among the stragglers in the lobby came a middle-aged woman. "This way," she instructed quietly, taking Sally by the elbow. "You're late. We almost started without you."

Disappointed that nothing treasonous was underway, the other citizens in the lobby lost interest. The security camera, though, with its ominous red light glowering just underneath, was fixated on us.

"They're right behind us!" Sally whispered anxiously as we passed through a heavy, reinforced door.

Our escort, though, maintained her slow, bureaucratic pace.

We were passing through a cavernous maze of cramped tunnels seemingly propped up by thick piping. The light was dim and had a reddish tint. The doors were all heavyset and made of something stronger than plastex – very solid looking – and had to be operated manually. Occasionally, we passed someone, but these corridors were mostly deserted.

There were more cameras than I was used to. Each one swiveled to follow us as we passed.

There were signs plastered on the walls. Most of them were scrawled with letters in a font too small to read in passing. But Nutty the Happy Neutron was everywhere. Apparently, he had a lot to say.

For example, I was able to read this while pausing for our guide to open one of the doors: "In the unlikely event of a core meltdown, remain calm. Sit on the floor and put your head between your knees. Oxygen masks may drop from the ceiling. Place a mask on yourself before assisting others. An attendant will come fetch you as soon as it is safe to evacuate."

Eventually, we left the tunnels and came out into a wide-open space. It reminded me of some of the shots of the surface fleet I'd seen on the Loyalty Stretch. The vehicles were lined up in a vast, unobstructed area called a hangar. Like the hangar I had seen on the tube, there was a lot of activity going on here. Unlike the hangar, this place wasn't being used to store and retrieve massive objects, and it wasn't unobstructed, either.

As far as I could see, there were tall, cylindrical structures separated by clearly marked paths. Each one was topped by Nutty the Happy Neutron. Nutty was smiling invitingly.

An alarm of some sort was going off.

At first, the sound of the alarm made me uncomfortable. But when I saw that the workers carrying fuel rods were as puzzled as I was, I knew it was only us. We were the cause of the alarm.

Our guide quickened her pace.

The workers stared at us as we hurried past. There were four of them. Each one was holding onto one end of the zirconium encasing of a long, narrow, fuel rod. I observed how nonchalantly they wore their radiation suits. The headgear was thrown back, exposing the long, braided hair. Their gloves dangled from a belt. They were chewing gum.

Chewing gum! The lucky typhoids. But I reminded myself that the work of a reactor core attendant was almost as dangerous as that of a miner on an asteroid. Who knew how much longer those guys would live? And their deaths were not likely to be sudden or pleasant.

One of them dropped his end of the fuel rod. It struck the floor with a loud bang.

"Shit!" the one at the other end said.

"Get bronchitis," muttered another.

"Did the casing crack?" demanded a third.

The bloke who had dropped it picked his end up and peered at the underside, all the while chomping loudly. "Naw, looks okay."

"Are you sure?" pressed the third one. "The cracks could be too small to see."

The attendant shrugged. "We'll find out once we load it in the reactor, won't we?"

His companions guffawed and carried on.

The door behind us burst open. "There they are!"

Sally caught my arm and tugged me along. Still, I managed to catch a glimpse of the Search and Extraction team. Someone had already drawn her pistol and was aiming it at us. Just in time, one of her companions caught the barrel in a gloved hand and pushed it roughly to the ground. "Not in here, you flaphead!"

Before I knew it, we were passing swiftly through another door. The sign above it read: "REACTOR CORE #8".

If I thought the first tunnels were cramped, this one was even worse. I had to stoop to pass along without smacking my noggin on the pipes. And they were hot! The whole area was steamy and damp.

We were in the tiny containment dome that capped the core itself. The left wall and whatever shielding it had been plied with was the only thing separating my fragile bodily functions from the nuclear hell on the other side.

What a waste of water, was my first thought. Then I wondered where the water was coming from.

There was an intermittent hissing noise from somewhere above.

I started to sweat.

The door behind us banged open. The Search and Extraction team piled in. Our view of them was blocked by the curvature of the dome, but they couldn't be far behind.

Moments later, our guide opened another door in the outer wall and darted out, gesturing excitedly at us to follow. Now she wanted us to hurry up!

Sally and I clambered out. She threw the door closed. That's when I noticed we weren't alone. Two other people were waiting outside.

One was looking at us grimly. He looked vaguely familiar. The other was standing in front of a control panel mounted on the outside of the containment dome.

Painted in broad strokes on the back of the door was a large depiction of Nutty the Happy Neutron, waving as always. A balloon hung near his mouth. The text in the middle read, "Nuclear Energy is Safe and Efficient!"

As soon as the door clicked shut, the woman in front of the control panel touched the screen. A red light flashed over Nutty's head.

A valve opened somewhere. There was a great deal of hissing. From inside I thought I could hear the sounds of screaming, but it didn't last very long.

The valve closed.

Over the top of the door there was an LCD display. "OUT OF ORDER", it read.

"Here." Sally pushed something small and rectangular into my hands.

I didn't have to look to know what it was.

Chapter 5

Sally, our guide, and the two others deposited me outside a janitor's closet where they disappeared to confer privately. I stood staring at the back of the door for about thirty secondstretches before I came to my senses. Quietly, I snuck up and pressed my ear against it.

"Does Renfield suspect anything?" asked one. That was our guide.

"Nope. Not a thing." The voice was unmistakably Sally's.

Did I suspect what? And why hadn't she told me?

They kept on talking, so I kept on listening. There'd be time enough for thinking later.

"Everything is going rather smoothly," said another. It was the man. "No glitches. Kind of weird, huh?"

"Renfield's right outside this door and knows all about us," our guide retorted dryly. "I'd call it a significant glitch."

"Why did you have to fly?" asked the man.

"Terry killed someone," said Sally. "Homeland Security."

There was a low whistle.

"Homeland Security?" repeated our guide. "You think they –"

"Of course not, Alibaba! He's dead. He never talked to anybody. You saw the feed."

"You don't know who he talked to before he got to the asteroid," the man pointed out.

"He's trustworthy," Sally insisted. "If he said he'd keep quiet, he kept quiet."

A twinge of jealousy arced through my chest. Who was this smack addict she was talking about anyway?

"I'm sure he was sincere, Complicity," our guide sneered, "but we have no idea what happened to him after we sent him off. People will do the strangest things in order to survive."

"Scorpio could be double crossing us," suggested the man.

There was a moment of silence.

"Cut the crap," snapped a third female voice. Hers was unfamiliar. I imagined it was the woman who cooked up the Search and Extraction team. "Homeland Security is like every other conglomerate. It's manned by back-stabbing, ambitious citizens all looking for a leg up on their comrades. Who knows what this agent wanted, but it certainly didn't have anything to do with us."

"Can you be so sure?"

"I can sure as hell find out. But until I do, we assume it was a coincidence."

The others agreed.

"I was afraid Terry would recognize you back at the reactor, Starbuoy," said Sally.

"It was a weekstretch ago when he showed up for the brain scan, Complicity!" retorted the man. "It's almost impossible he'd remember."

"Yeah, well, we chose him specifically *because* he isn't like most other people."

"Yeah, but not in that way."

"You two had a conversation."

"I gave him some pills!"

"You operated the scanner."

"Right! The *brain* scanner! He couldn't see me with his head inside. After that he got up and went home."

The unfamiliar, female voice broke in. "Complicity! Starbuoy! Let's not argue. Scorpio's instructions are that we proceed according to plan if nothing's amiss."

"What about Terry?" asked Sally.

"Let's worry about Renfield later. It was a bitch getting him to work with us the first time."

"Okay," they all agreed.

"And the surveillance?" Sally wanted to know. "Something's got to be done about the surveillance, Brutalizer."

"You left quite a trail, Complicity," replied the unfamiliar female voice. "I've got contacts in Developmental Engineering with a direct link into the central database for Homeland Security, Q sector. Even as we speak, your faces and any other data that could be used to identify you are being replaced by some random convicts' terminated yesterday."

"So who has the envelope?" asked Starbuoy.

I heard something tear open. There was a short silence.

Sally spoke up first. "How are we going to get a message through to Lakshmi Bunker?"

"Does anyone even know where it is?" asked our guide, or Alibaba, or whatever you want to call her.

"I don't think it's on Mars," said Starbuoy.

"There are six Bunkers on Mars," Sally said. "Hebes, Ganges, Aeolis, Apollinaris, Elysium, and Hecatus."

"Lakshmi's not one of them," observed Starbuoy.

"If it's not on Mars, then it's got to be Venus," said Brutalizer.

That's when I stopped listening. I had heard enough.

I knew I had to run, and I needed as much of a head start as I could get.

My head was spinning. I was suffering from information overload. What was so special about me?

I looked at the package in my hands. Scorpio and George and whoever else was involved can get bronchitis, I thought, and threw it to the floor. It landed with a little thud.

My heart was racing. I think I was on some kind of autopilot.

Was Sally my girlfriend or my enemy?

They seemed to know so much about me.

I had never seen any of them before. Except the man. He had looked familiar. What had they called him again?

There's more than one Bunker?

When I started paying attention, I saw that I was well on my way back to the lobby. But I went back and picked up the package anyway.

Sally was concerned enough to want to know what they were going to do with me. But I can't trust her.

Who was this guy she was talking about so fondly?

She helped me escape from the Search and Extraction team. True. But she brought me to these guys. And they *chose* me.

For what?

I certainly wasn't going to *do* whatever they *chose* me for until I found out a lot more about it.

At least now I knew why I was running. I couldn't trust Sally.

Once I found out what they expected from me, I might be able to understand. Only then would I be able to forgive her.

I hoped I wouldn't have to kill her. Or worse, what if she had to kill me? George Walker, that would suck.

I threaded my way through the corridors of Q sector, knowing I was safe. At least I knew that!

Now I remembered where I had seen that cancerhead! He was working at the clinic when I was sick.

It was nothing more than a coincidence, of course. How could my being sick have fit into whatever sinister scheme they'd hatched? I went to them! They couldn't have known how I'd be feeling that day!

Unless, of course, they planted a virus in my overalls.

In my mind, I played back the conversation I had listened in on. I couldn't make sense of it all. For one, I had never worked with anyone in the Underground before. Certainly not any of them. And certainly not that typhoid at the clinic!

Maybe they meant Sally. I thought back. Had I inadvertently helped in her secret missions just because she's my baby? Aside from blowing up the transtube and a military flybot, I couldn't think of anything that would qualify.

And I never got any pills from that smack addict. He ought to count himself lucky if he doesn't ever run into me in some dark access corridor.

I didn't go home from the clinic right away, either. In fact, I don't remember much after the scan. When I woke up, I was still in the hospital. They told me the flu I had was pretty bad.

But the medibot gave me some meds and sent me back to the barracks to rest up. I was out of commission for two daystretches.

That's probably what he meant, really. I was thinking too much. You can get lost in your own logic, especially once you start mincing the details.

People make mistakes. They remember things the wrong way. They choose a word to explain something that means something else to you. It's easy to distort the facts without even meaning to.

So, there's more than one Bunker. That was a revelation.

That's when I knew. I was going to try my luck in one of the other Bunkers. It didn't matter which one.

After all, I couldn't stay here.

Turns out, having an Epsilon clearance is good for more than a search bar in a cybercafe.

As time went on, my wandering became more determined. My thoughts stopped raining down in short, uncontrollable bursts. The beginnings of a plan started to come together in my head.

The first thing I did was start exploring the parts of Q Sector I had never been allowed to go. There were still areas that were off-limits, but every once in a while the guards in latex and kevlar would let me through.

It was in one of these murky Epsilon corridors that I found what I was looking for: a little, crooked plaque on the back of an opened door. The word "EMMIGRATION" had been carved into it and painted over in thick, black strokes.

How do you like that? They all know. The one, maybe two percent of the population of the Bunker with a security clearance knows we're not the only one.

I wondered which Bunker this was.

When I opened the door, I saw an empty, ill-kept waiting room. A small, plastex window was set in the far wall. Sitting behind it was a bored, well-endowed woman. She was staring at the tube set in the ceiling to the right of the door. Two stocky guards lounged in the corner, doing the same.

I glanced at the tube as I strode into the room. It was that mind-killing sitcom, How'd You Get So Loyal? The actors were all supposed to be run-of-the-mill citizens, going through the mundane gestures of the model life of loyalty in the Bunker. The show sometimes lasted two hourstretches. A typical routine was watching them eat the slop in their community dining hall and talk about how delicious it was and how different it tasted from yesterday's.

"Hi," I said as I slipped my Card through the little slot near the bottom of the window.

The woman looked at me as if I had just stepped on her foot. "What do you want?"

Good question. I hadn't thought about that. "Lakshmi Bunker." I think I was as surprised by the words that came out of my mouth as she was.

Suddenly, she wasn't thinking about How'd You Get So Loyal? anymore. She adjusted herself in her seat and leaned forward to take my Card. "What's your clearance?"

"Epsilon." I swallowed.

She looked at me wiltingly.

"I have this," I said quickly and pushed the waiver Scorpio had given me towards her.

She looked at it. "It says you can carry a package."

I nodded eagerly and showed her the box.

Now the guards were getting interested in our conversation. One of them meandered a little closer, the tips of his fingers lightly brushing the laser pistol strapped to his waist. The woman behind the counter briefly made eye contact with him.

"You're supposed to take it to Lakshmi?"

I nodded again.

She shrugged and scanned the document.

A few moments later her attitude changed. She got a lot more businesslike. "I see, Mr. Renfield. I'm sorry for the delay. We don't get many of these special waivers." She waved the guard away.

I was amazed. I was pleased and amazed at the same time. It's a

63

feeling you don't often experience in the Bunker.

"There's a ship leaving in four hourstretches."

"Four hourstretches... That's at the end of my daystretch. Isn't there one leaving now?"

She looked at me, a shade of the bureaucratic superiority returning briefly to her face. "Now, Mr. Renfield? But you still have to get to the spaceport."

"Oh yeah," I said, looking at her sheepishly. "Of course. It's just that I'm so excited."

She smiled at me condescendingly even as she continued to process my ticket. "I see. Is this your first time leaving the Bunker?"

"Yes."

She pursed her lips and nodded as if she had just confirmed her own brilliance.

I hate bureaucrats.

"Ah!" she exclaimed suddenly and frowned. "According to the system, you have no security clearance."

The paperwork! I never got around to filling it out.

"Just check my Card," I insisted. "I only got it this morning."

"I see. But according to the terminal, you do not have the necessary clearance to board this ship."

"But my Card!" I pointed at it through the plastex.

"Yes, Mr. Renfield. I understand. But Cards are subject to manipulation by social deviants. If everything is legitimate – as I'm sure it is – then you should have no problem just popping down to Central Management and filling out the proper forms. Once they've been approved, I can issue your ticket."

I swallowed and switched gears. "Yes, yes. Of course. I'm sorry if I appear anxious. The regulations are in place for a reason. I'll be happy to follow them."

The woman behind the plastex window seemed pleased. She gathered up my documents and prepared to hand them back to me.

"Do you think I'll still be able to make tonight's flight?"

"That depends on you, Mr. Renfield, doesn't it?"

"It's just that if I don't get this package to Lakshmi Bunker on time – well, I might not survive." I winked at her. A little dose of charm never hurt anyone.

The woman fixed me with an empty stare, cocked her head slightly to one side, and said, "Then I would hurry if I were you."

She pushed my Card and the waiver back through the slot, folded her arms across her ample chest, and went back to watching the tube.

I obtained the necessary forms on my PA. It took approximately twelve minutestretches to print and fill them out, but it took two hourstretches in a long line at the Peace In Our Time Community Register in Q-4 sector to reach someone who would care. When I got to the end of it, the bureaucrat on the other side of the desk glanced at the first form in the stack and handed it back to me.

"This line is for new registrants only. You need to be in the line for modifications to an existing registration."

"But -"

"Next!"

The beefy guards in latex and kevlar motioned for me to move on.

The line for existing registrants was so long it snaked all the way across the lobby and through the toilet facilities before looping back and terminating near a vending machine selling dusty packets of PermaCrunchy and Green Flavor.

The two citizens at the end of the line were arguing about who had got there first. They were so involved with one another – and so wired up on pep pills – that I was able to step in front.

As slowly as it moved, the line actually did move. After another two hourstretches, I had reached the toilets.

It was then that their pep pills ran out, and the two citizens having an argument realized they were still at the back of the line.

Another argument broke out, this one involving far more people. Eventually, someone got stabbed. A consignment from Homeland Security wielding stun-guns charged the area and proceeded to arrest two-thirds of the line in front of me.

Much to my delight, I suddenly stood within sight of the desks, the final destination.

Next to me, two janitors, armed with mops and a trash bin, were cleaning up the mess that the Homeland Security mob had left behind.

I was growing weary. I had already missed the next flight to Lakshmi. I could only hope there would be another one soon.

Finally, an hourstretch later, I stood before the dry, middle-aged man who would process my forms.

"Card," he demanded and reached out a bony hand. Meanwhile, someone standing next to him scanned my I-chip.

I could see the output on the terminal in front of him. A named flashed on the screen. It wasn't mine.

"Jeremy Whiles," it said.

I was stunned, but I knew enough to keep my mouth shut.

The bureaucrat carefully examined the forms I had filled out, searching for any mistakes and deciding whether or not he liked me. My experience with bureaucrats is that you have to approach them on their own level. This one obviously didn't like to be talked to, so I didn't talk to him.

Apparently, that was enough because after ten excruciating minutestretches he produced a large, rubber stamp and began hammering at my forms.

"Approved!" he shouted and returned my Card. The forms were thrown quite deliberately into what looked like the very same make and model of trash bin as the janitors were using.

This was getting weirder by the hourstretch.

I glanced at the package. The name on the top stood out clearly. It was the same name that belonged to my I-chip, and it was the same bloke whose Card I had.

How in the Bunker do you alter the information on an I-chip?

I supposed it didn't matter much now. For all intents and purposes, I *was* Jeremy Whiles. I hoped he was a safe guy to be.

Of course, the name on my waiver didn't match the name on my I-chip. That could turn out to be a problem. I could only hope that the real Jeremy Whiles – whoever he was – had my Card and original biometric data. Assuming he wanted to be Jeremy Whiles again (because I most certainly wanted to be Terry Renfield), one of us would eventually find the other and the whole situation would be sorted out. And I would finally be rid of this package!

I stared at it suspiciously.

But there wasn't enough time for that now. I had a ticket, and there was another ship leaving for Lakshmi in about an hourstretch. I found a terminal and located the spaceport. I even knew how to get there.

It was close, but I got lucky changing metros. I made it with time to spare. Just outside the station there was a heavily guarded door. It was unmarked, but those who needed to go through it would know where it went.

They checked my ticket and scanned my I-chip. I winced as I handed it over. What name was on it?

Of course! The woman at the emigration desk had remembered me. She thought I was Terry Renfield. I was glad at the time, because I thought so, too.

The world seemed to slow down as I ran through my options. I could run and try and loose myself in the crowd. But there weren't many people milling about. Better to try and talk my way out of it. An accidental swap? The idea sounded promising.

But in the end it didn't matter – at least, not at that moment. The scanner bleeped in a disconcerting way. The woman who wielded it shook it uncertainly and tried again. No result.

I took the opportunity and pounced.

"Something wrong, citizen?"

"Naw, naw," replied the woman's companion in an off-hand way as she fiddled with the contraption. "Happens all the time."

"Is it going to take long?" I held out the ticket to him. "I'm in a hurry."

The man shook his head slowly, eyes boring into mine. "I'm sorry, sir. We can't let you through until we've verified who you are."

In the Bunker, whenever a citizen starts waving around the rulebook, it's usually an invitation to bribery. Only bureaucrats take the rules seriously.

A few stretches later, I was passing through the door, leaving two very pleased guards behind.

"Of course I am who I say I am!" I had jibed as they downloaded the credits off my Card. "Who else would I be?"

The man had winked back. "Just a snag in the system. Happens all the time. Anyway, you're in a hurry!"

In front of me, there was a moving corridor that climbed steadily upward. As stressed as I was, I felt a sudden rush of excitement.

Up meant only one thing. I was leaving the Bunker! I would see the surface of Mars! I wondered briefly what space was like, and Venus, too.

But my musings were interrupted. You see, at that moment several things started happening more or less at once, and they all demanded my immediate attention.

For example, at that moment a new episode of Ten Things I Hate About Treason hosted by Van Johnson came on the tube. Which was unusual in itself, because it wasn't the normal hourstretch for it.

"Ladies and gentlemen, loyal citizens everywhere!" The announcer's voice flooded the moving corridor. "Today, we've got a special treat for you. It's a surprise, thirty minutestretch episode of your favorite vidshow. That's right! Ten Things I Hate About Treason hosted by the fabulous Van Johnson!" He drew out the vowel in the first name for a few, terribly long secondstretches.

The live studio audience clapped and whistled.

"Howdy, folks!" crowed the well groomed figure of Van Johnson in his ridiculous accent. He and his slicked back, dark brown hair clapped their manicured hands along with the crowd. "It's great to be back!"

The studio audience roared. They adored him. His was a face you could take home to mom.

Maybe Sally and her Underground friends were able to alter the data banks implicating us in a rather unfortunate rush-hour series of traffic fatalities, but they sure as the dome couldn't access Lance Trevor's PA.

I don't like Ten Things I Hate About Treason hosted by Van Johnson and I never have, but normally I wouldn't have called it a disaster when it came on. But it really is a disaster when you are the star of the show. You are only ever the star of a show like Ten Things I Hate About Treason hosted by Van Johnson one time and one time only.

As I said before, all the footage shown on Ten Things I Hate About Treason is submitted directly by loyal citizens themselves. Homeland Security isn't involved. Naturally, all this footage is examined and verified to be authentic by experts at Human Resources before it is aired. It never happens that one citizen frames another using Ten Things I Hate About Treason hosted by Van Johnson.

Oh, shit! I thought as I caught images of myself in Barracks One, brutally assaulting an old woman.

Even I was disgusted by it. I don't know if Lance edited it himself, but I have to admit it was a good job. I wondered who the old woman in the clip really was. Or had been, judging by what was happening to her.

"Let's stop the feed here," Van Johnson and his slicked-back hairdo said. The image froze at an awkward and particularly gruesome moment. It was awkward and particularly gruesome at the same time, if you can imagine that. "What was that sound we just heard?"

"That, Van, was the sound of me throwing up." The voice was Lance Trevor's. He stood to the right of the image, a small and uncomfortable figure who kept pulling at his beard.

I noticed he had cleaned himself up.

"Well done, citizen! Your loyalty is astounding! If only we were all as heroic and selfless. Despite the inconvenience of your bodily functions, you managed to do your duty and continue recording. Let's hear it for this model of good behavior, folks!" The live studio audience applauded obediently.

Behind me, the door to the corridor burst open. Three figures charged through, two of whom had laser pistols drawn and no one to point them at.

"There! That's the impostor!" It was the man I had just bribed. He looked indignant. After all, I had just lied to his face and made of joke of it. Even worse, he thought he was getting his fingers wet as a matter of convenience to me. Suddenly, he found himself complicit in real, meaty treason. Identity theft is big business in the Bunker.

It must have only confirmed the guard's suspicion that I was a dangerous social deviant when he recognized me on the tube.

The two figures with laser pistols now had someone to aim them at. I started to run.

The fact was not lost on me that running was pointless. Even if I managed to get to the end of this corridor, I'd have to run down another. And the security cameras would be watching. Unlike Sally, I had no friends in the Underground who could provide me with clever escape routes and whitewash the surveillance afterwards.

But what else was I going to do? Give up?

Even if there was just the smallest chance I could get out alive, it was enough. And an instant death in a hail of laserfire was far preferable to the long, slow one that doubtlessly awaited me in the dungeons of Homeland Security.

My pursuers took a few shots. They missed.

I understand that not everyone in the Bunker is as handy with a laser pistol as I am. It comes naturally to me. It always has. I don't think I've ever met anyone who can more accurately place a high intensity beam of polarized light. But these saps were shooting everywhere I wasn't, and it was embarrassing.

They must have been fresh recruits. Maybe they were terribly hung over. Or doped up.

Whatever the reason, I was thankful for it.

At the end of the corridor was a fair-sized lobby. There was plush, deep red carpeting embroidered with handsome, geometric designs. The walls were wallpapered beige and red and there was a kitsch chandelier hanging from the ceiling. About half the tinted bulbs were lit, bathing the room in a soft, red light. Some comfortable chairs and couches had been arranged in the middle of the room. These were red and orange.

Facing the entrance was a brown reception desk. Behind it, the wall was one large, plastex window overlooking what appeared to be a huge bay filled with space ships. A piece of yellow tape had been draped across the window. "Danger! Do not lean or apply pressure in any way!" The window looked in perfectly fine condition to me, although admittedly I didn't stop to investigate.

The goons will have called ahead. There will be a security team waiting to blast me as soon as I burst in. All I could do was try and anticipate where they'd have positioned themselves and try and get a few shots in first.

But when I burst into the lobby, the only resistance I met was a cowering, terrified secretary trying not to apply pressure to the window and a few other citizens doing their best to pretend I didn't exist.

Two corridors branched off to the left and right. They seemed to curve slightly, clinging to the outside of the bay. Attached to the wall next to the each entrance was a tall, bright screen littered with flight numbers and schedules. I caught sight of mine as I darted past it. My ship awaited at Gate #7.

To my left, the curving, plastex wall overlooked the bay. It looked like I was forty, maybe fifty meters above the floor. There were a few people down there in ecopacks. High above, the ceiling was composed of individual plates arranged in a circular pattern. The edge of each plate fit nicely under the adjoining one. Presumably, the harsh, Martian environment lay just outside.

For the first time in my life, I was outside the dome.

The ships were impressive. They looked like stubby cylinders standing on end. They were thicker at the base and narrowed as the body progressed towards the nose. Little, flimsy looking corridors extended straight out into the bay from the level I was on. These attached to the sides of the ships just under the nose.

Even as I took in my surroundings, I was busy grabbing for a plan of action. Behind me I could hear grunting and running. Thanks to the curvature of the corridor my pursuers weren't able to take any more shots, but they could easily see me through the transparent wall.

The corridor was not empty. Aside from the occasional citizen surprised or curious about all the commotion, there were the gates themselves. These were cordoned off areas around the entrances to the flimsy corridors connecting with the ships. A monitor hanging from the ceiling announced the gate number, time of departure or arrival, and the destination or origin of the ship that was docked there. A bulky desk had been placed under each one. In most cases, these were deserted. At this hourstretch, no other ships were scheduled to depart or arrive except mine.

There were also occasional doors opening off the other side of the corridor. These looked like maintenance rooms.

I had an idea.

Up ahead I could see Gate #7. It was the only one with people standing around it. They looked agitated.

I flung myself through the crowd. I could hear some poor, ignorant sap having a polite disagreement with the guardian from Defense whose job it was to explain politely but firmly why the passengers could not board. It was then that I noticed there was no ship.

Great.

In the Bunker, all ships depart and arrive on time. Any deviation from the schedule is the result of plots by social deviants and traitors. When confronted with such an inconvenience, the loyal citizen with good instincts realizes it is not in his best interests to argue with the guardian from Defense. Because if you argue with the guardian from Defense, very shortly she will identify you as the culprit behind the treason and have you dragged away.

If, on the other hand, anyone were stupid enough to complain about the delay *after* arriving at his destination, he would find that the official departure and arrival times were exactly as planned. At which point, said citizen would fall under suspicion of rumor-mongering and have to think fast to save his ass.

But I found this out much later. At the time, I was dismayed to discover there was no ship. If there was no ship, there could be no flight, and if there was no flight then I was fodder for these Homeland Security agents who – if they kept at it long enough – were sure to get me.

I was dismayed by something else as well. It was the sight of Lance Trevor, standing arms folded in front as if he had been expecting me. In fact, I almost ran into him.

He was ready. In a fluid, deft move he tripped me. I fell hard to the ground. The package flew out of my hands and tumbled away. Before I knew it, he had leaped onto my back and expertly pinned my arms. Lance Trevor – whoever he was – was surprisingly strong.

He also slipped a thick strap of some kind around my neck.

Have you ever been strangled? I hardly recommend it. It's not a very pleasant experience.

Some of the crowd had gathered around to film my last moments.

"You told me yourself you'd be on one of these flights," he growled as we struggled. "All I had to do was check the schedule and wait. And what do you know? You were right! Of course, I didn't expect you to come barreling through like a madman."

The boys from Homeland Security finally caught up with me. I could see them out of the corner of my eye. They were standing by, having a discussion.

I was a traitor, reaping the just fruits of my deviant lifestyle. It would be cheaper if I died here rather than go through all the bother and expense of extracting a confession and having a trial.

But I didn't die. You see, an amazing thing happened. One of the Homeland Security agents hit Lance with a charge from his stun-gun. My attacker collapsed next to me on the ground, twitching and convulsing and drooling.

A detachment of Homeland Security agents emerged from Gate #8 just up ahead. In their midst was a familiar man. He had rectangular, black-rimmed glasses and wore puffy, green pants. In one hand he held a thin stick which he twirled absently but energetically.

"Get rid of him," Scorpio said and swatted the back of Lance Trevor's neck with his stick. "Nothing fatal, mind you."

"What's the charge, sir?"

"He was using violence against this poor, innocent fellow, I presume?" The stick poked at my back.

"Yes, sir!"

"And we have witnesses!" Scorpio frowned. "We don't like witnesses. Arrest them, too."

"Erasure?"

"No, no, nothing drastic like that. But make sure no one talks or remembers or cares. You know the drill."

"Yes, sir!"

There was a commotion as they dragged Lance's trembling body away.

I was starting to be able to do more than simply breathe. I flopped over onto my back. A few centimeters from my face were a pair of black boots, conspicuously clean and unmarked. They were made of some mysterious, shiny material.

The person they belonged to was looking down at me. "Hello, Terry. Glad you could make it. Do you mind getting up now?"

Chapter 6

Two agents from Scorpio's entourage helped me stand. One of them relieved me of my laser pistol. The other pressed a familiar object into my hands.

"Oh, no," I moaned and didn't dare to look.

"You must try and be more careful." It was Scorpio. He was standing directly in front of me. His lips were thin and bloodless.

We started moving. They were leading me to Gate #8.

"Where are we going?" I asked.

Scorpio ignored the question. "You gave us quite a scare, Terry."

"When I ran off?"

"We put a collar on you, remember? We knew where you were the whole time." He smiled, but he did not look either happy or pleased. "A few seconds more and that terrible man would have killed you. We'd have had to start all over again from scratch. Not to mention poor Complicity."

We were proceeding down the narrow corridor from the gate to the ship. It was dim in here. Tiny, green lights in the ceiling came at intervals.

"You mean Lance?"

"Is that his name? Well, at any rate, I'm rather surprised at you. None of my friends want to kill me. Perhaps you should be more selective."

He was making fun of me. He was being sarcastic, but he was still making fun. After all, everyone in the Bunker has friends who want to kill him. It might not even be safe for Alphas to have them at all.

I was recovering my strength. I threw off the arms that had been supporting me and growled at their owners.

"I've never met him before in my life."

Scorpio frowned. "But you do know his name."

"Yeah, but – Okay, I met him once before and he *told* me his name."

"Well, I think it was clear to everyone that he knew who *you* were."

I stopped in the corridor. Just up ahead was the hatch to the ship. We'd all have to duck to go in.

Scorpio took a few more steps before he realized I was no longer with him. He turned and regarded me curiously, as if I were a new but apparently harmless lifeform.

I spoke plainly. "I know you're involved. I know Complicity's involved. I don't know what you're involved *in*, but I'd appreciate if you just forgot who I was and left me out of it."

If there was such a thing as sympathy in Scorpio's world, he showed me some of it now. "I'm sorry, Terry, but the die has been cast."

"It's not a coincidence you were at the interrogation center this morning when they hauled me in, is it?"

Scorpio shook his head. "There are a lot of coincidences in the Bunker, Terry, but this is not one of them."

I held the package up. "There's no Jeremy Whiles, either. You *created* one as some kind of distraction, and in the process destroyed Terry Renfield."

Scorpio's thin lips pulled back into another, unfeeling smile. "There most certainly is a Jeremy Whiles. Or was, for that matter." He extended a hand. "But please, Terry. We haven't much time. Everything will be explained to you shortly. You've done very well, and we owe you a great debt. But we must be on our way."

"Where are we going?"

At that moment, the hatch opened with a clang and a resounding squeal. Peaking out at me were two faces I knew very well. Perhaps I ought to have been surprised, but I was through with being surprised. I had been surprised enough this past daystretch. And I was simply too exhausted to manage it.

One of them was George, my supervisor at Deeper Delvers, Inc. The other was Sally.

"Oh, Terry!" she cried out and ran to me. But when she threw her arms around me and buried her face in my chest, I did not react. I stared coldly down at the top of her head until she realized I wasn't squeezing her back.

She looked up at me, eyes wide and vulnerable. "What's wrong?"

"You lied to me."

Her jaw dropped. "But, Terry –"

"Complicity!" Scorpio barked roughly. The voice suddenly had the intensity the eyes always lacked. "Now is not the time for this nonsense! We're leaving!" Without bothering to wait for a response, he marched through the hatch followed by his agents.

Nonsense, he had called it. At the time I thought he had no heart, but now I know I was wrong.

The ship had blasted off and was in space. I suppose I should have been struck by the experience, but I wasn't. Aside from being strapped into an uncomfortable, plastex chair and the rather unpleasant feeling of being mashed into a pulp, I hardly noticed.

From outside the ship had looked huge. But in reality, most of what I saw was filled with rocket fuel. The rooms – if you want to call them that – were incredibly tiny. There was a common area that also served as a bridge. There were a few rudimentary controls and above them three tubes lined up next to one another. The center one showed what was in front of the ship, and the other two were data readouts. I couldn't make anything out of the circles and lines and blinking dots, but Scorpio could, and that's what mattered.

A short passage led from the bridge to two barracks-type alcoves where we slept in bunks stacked even more tightly on top of each other than back in the Lower Quarters of Q-16 sector. There was also a small storeroom where water, food, and meds were kept.

A half hourstretch after take-off, we docked at some kind of station in low orbit around Mars. There the booster rockets were removed and we picked up some supplies. After a few hourstretches, we would be ready. The others left me alone in one of the bunks while they tended to their tasks. I thought I would catch up on some much needed sleep, but even though my daystretch had run out long ago, I couldn't get so much as a wink.

The package sat on my chest. I stared at it. I thought. I stared at it some more.

I don't know how long it was before I finally decided to open it.

I tore at the packaging. To my surprise, it came apart quite easily. A simple, rather flimsy, unmarked box was revealed. The top had a flap that tucked neatly into one side. I stuck my finger under it and pulled on it.

I stared at the contents for quite some time before I realized I was not alone. Sally and George were standing in the cramped corridor just outside the alcove.

Angrily, I threw the empty box at them. "I don't know who's idea of a joke this is!"

George regarded me somberly. "You always go your own way, Renfield. We had to work around that."

"Get bronchitis, George. You set me up."

"You'll call me Kuasimodo around here, Renfield! If you know what's good for you."

"Why? I'm not in your damned Underground."

"If you don't, you'll be floating back to Mars all by your lonesome self without an ecopack."

Sally clicked her tongue. "Oh, cool it, Kuaz. No need to make threats you can't make good on." She kneeled by my bunk and spoke to me soothingly. "We've undocked and we're on our way. Scorpio and the others are waiting in the bridge. They want you to come and listen to what we have to say."

"Why?" I was being surly and childish, I know. I'd like to see you behave any better if you'd just been fired from your job, chased, threatened, chased again, shot at, blown up, betrayed, chased some more, and strangled – all in a single daystretch.

"I'm not going to say anything more. You've got to hear the whole story, not just little bits and pieces of it. Then you can judge for yourself if you've been treated unfairly." She stood up, gestured for George to follow, and slipped away.

I didn't want to go. The whole lot of them could get gangrene. But after a few minutes of fuming I began to see that I had no choice. I was stuck in this ship with them. And if I wanted to find out what was really going on, the first thing I should do is listen to what they have to say, even if it's riddled with lies. Later on I could try and sort out what was useful information, what was tricksy, and what I was going to do about it.

I swallowed my pride. I got up. I went.

Sitting quietly in a circle inside the bridge were the conspirators, waiting quietly. Some of them I knew, some of them I recognized, and some of them were complete strangers to me.

Fat George sat at one end. Next to him was Sally, and next to her were Alibaba, Starbuoy, and Brutalizer. Van Johnson himself was there. I didn't know what they called him in the Underground, and I couldn't see that it mattered. Everybody in the Bunker already knew who he was. The last two seats were occupied by Scorpio and a tall, pretty but spoiled looking youth I had never seen before.

There was one place that was empty between George and the boy. I supposed that was where I was supposed to sit, so I did.

"Where would you like us to start, Terry?" asked Scorpio.

"Give it to me however you want. Just don't leave anything out."

"Excellent. I've always appreciated your frankness." He cleared his throat and began. "The problem, Terry, is Control. Control has always been the problem and we mean to do something about it."

My jaw dropped. Frantically, I scanned the room for cameras. "There's nothing wrong with Control," I responded quickly. You had to seem sincere or such declarations wouldn't carry any weight over at Homeland Security. "It protects the rest of us from social deviants like yourselves!"

George and some of the others snickered.

Scorpio whipped his stick through the air in front of him. "There are much easier ways to get rid of you, Terry, if that's what you're worried about. Now please put aside this childish paranoia and allow us to get on with this."

"But the cameras –"

"I'm an Alpha, Terry. The cameras are not recording."

At that, a strange feeling took over. I had rarely felt it before. "You mean we're not being watched?"

"No, Terry. And no one is filming you with his PA, either. We are perfectly free to do and talk about whatever we want."

"It's a case in point, though, isn't it?" observed George.

Maybe it's because I didn't believe him, or maybe it's just the power of a habit long ingrained, but I wasn't quite ready or able to let down my guard.

Van Johnson, adjusting the gooey strands of his slicked back hair, said, "Don't you feel sorry for him? He looks like an ape in a cage. The poor cancerhead."

I was shocked. The Van Johnson I knew never talked like that. You could bring him home to mom.

"As you have just demonstrated," Scorpio continued, "the problem is Control."

"Without it, we'd have happy lives," said Brutalizer.

"No one watching," added Alibaba.

"No security clearances." It was the youth. After he spoke, a brief but uncomfortable silence descended.

"But *you* are Control," I said and pointed at Scorpio. "You said it yourself. You're an Alpha."

Scorpio turned that lifeless smile on me. I shivered. "Wrong, Terry. Like so many poor, ignorant citizens who waste their whole lives shuffling from one place to another in the sanitized corridors of the Bunker, you think Control is staffed by people. You think it's like one of the conglomerates, just on top."

I frowned. "Well, what it is then?"

"It's a computer," Sally answered me in a soft, gentle voice.

"A computer?"

"Of course!" Scorpio barked. "How else do you think it could succeed where people have always failed? In order to manage the environment, we required a *machine*, something without emotion that could look objectively at the facts. All of them."

"So that part is true then. Control is there to protect the environment."

"Yes," Sally said, "but it's obviously gone too far."

"Well, why don't you just turn it off?"

"Are you sure he's worth putting time and energy into?" the youth muttered and rolled his eyes.

"Cut him some slack!" Sally shot back. "This is all news to him."

"Don't take that tone with me!" the youth complained and glanced at Scorpio as if for help.

"You see, Terry," Scorpio continued, laying a hand on the youth's thigh, "we Alphas do not *staff* Control. We *program* it. We are the ones who write and change the code that determines what Control *is*."

"Then it shouldn't be a problem for you to turn it off!"

"Think, Renfield." It was George. "You know how it works back in the Bunker. Pick a Bunker. Any Bunker. They're all the same. Everyone is out to get ahead of the pack. We stab each other in the back because if we don't someone else will. We rat each other out. It doesn't matter if it's really true or not. Do you think it's any different if you have a security clearance?"

"Yeah, I'm sure you know all about stabbing people in the back."

George's face twisted into a sneer. "I thought you'd understand."

"I do understand. You're saying you can't take steps to take down Control because if you did some of the other Alphas would turn you in."

Scorpio nodded approvingly. "Exactly. Control is the largest distributed system ever created. The codebase is far too large for one person to sabotage. It's constantly being monitored and updated. It's replicated and it's fault tolerant. Even looking for a single point of failure invites accusations of treason. Are you beginning to understand our conundrum?"

"This is ridiculous! Control – all our misery – is a product of our own making?"

"I'm afraid so, Terry," said Scorpio.

Van Johnson snorted and popped a tiny, white pill into his mouth. "Finally, the kid gets it." He held out a little box. Inside were more pills. "Want one?"

"What is it?" I asked warily.

"Hell if I know. But they make the walls melt!"

"I still don't see what any of this has to do with *me.*" I sat back in the chair and folded my arms stubbornly across my chest.

Brutalizer rolled her eyes. "He's only looking out for himself. Just like last time."

Starbuoy shook his head. "I know it's illogical, but the traits I didn't appreciate in the first continue to surprise me in the second. How do you put up with his stubbornness, Complicity?"

"You think you're all little bundles of joy?" Sally threw back her hair and stared Starbuoy down. "I love Terry Renfield. I don't care what you think."

It felt good to hear her stand up for me, but I did my best not to show it. Not yet.

"Don't we all feel warm and giddy," muttered Alibaba under her breath.

"You're just jealous," Sally insisted.

The only other couple in the room knowingly kept their mouths shut. I may not have liked them, but at least we understood each other.

"This has *everything* to do with you," Scorpio told me.

"Baby," Sally said softly, "I know you're not going to like this so I'll just tell you straight out."

"Like what?"

"You've been cloned."

"Cloned?" I knew the medibots could replicate organs and limbs, but never a whole, grown up person. "You mean there's a copy of me walking around somewhere?" The thought was revolting.

"Not anymore. It's dead."

And that's when I understood. That sap I had seen this morning on the tube – that everybody had seen – the one who got blown up on the asteroid, the one they were calling a traitor: that was me. I was that traitor.

"So that's who Jeremy Whiles was."

Scorpio nodded. "We had the tissue sample, but we still needed a brain scan." He gestured in Sally's direction. "When you showed up at the clinic we took our chance. Afterwards, Starbuoy gave you some pills to make your condition worse, to keep you out of commission just long enough for the clone to get started on its mission. Then we defrosted the body and uploaded your brainprint."

"Naturally, the clone needed an identity," Sally continued. "So we made up Jeremy Whiles. We tried adding it to the Communal Registry, but the security was too tough. The I-chip was easier. You can get one on the black market easily enough. Anyway, no one expected it to live very long."

"If I'm not in the Communal Registry, how did I get into that office building in Ronald Reagan Plaza?" How did Sally get in?

Alibaba snickered and raised her hand. "That would be me. I'm the one who scanned you. Complicity, too."

My mind raced for more examples. "You weren't there when I bought my ticket to Lakshmi. They scanned me when I claimed my epsilon clearance!"

"We have a coder on our hands," George replied smugly.

Scorpio's lips formed a straight, emotionless line. "So that's the story on Jeremy Whiles," he concluded. "Of course, it never thought it was anything but Terry Renfield. We never told it."

"Him," I said, almost choking on the word. "You never told *him*." The feeling of disgust was almost overwhelming. "I didn't think they cloned whole people."

"They don't," George told me matter-of-factly. "It's very expensive. And there's a curious reaction that occurs when a clone and the original become of aware of each other. It's almost as if they can't stand knowing the other one's there." He shrugged. "Curious, isn't it?"

But it wasn't curious to me at all. I understood perfectly. "He's dead? You're sure?"

"You saw the tube."

"In fact," Scorpio continued, "that's why we had to clone you. We sent it on a suicide mission. There was no other way."

"It was the price I made them pay for using you," Sally added gently. I could see she thought it was important I should know, but it didn't make me feel any better.

"Of course we didn't tell *him* that," Van Johnson added and smiled knowingly at the walls.

As perverse as all this was, they still hadn't answered my question. "Okay, so the clone is dead. He did whatever it was you wanted. I still don't see what this has to do with me."

"We still need you, Terry. You are a man of exceptional talents. At least, in the very specific arenas we require."

"What talents?"

"I picked you myself, Renfield." It was George. "You're a quick thinker. Not easily thrown off balance. And you're an excellent shot to match. But even more importantly, you're a miner. One of the best. You know the rock as well as your hands. Weekstretch in and weekstretch out, your crew's output is by far the highest. And you have skills in demolition."

"So Control is buried under tons of rock and you need me to go blow it up?"

"Not exactly," said Scorpio.

The youth leaned over and whispered loudly into Scorpio's ear. "How much longer is this going to take? I'm hungry."

Scorpio squeezed his shoulder and flashed the boy a quick but reproachful look.

"Control runs on a number of nodes," Brutalizer told me. "There are thousands of them. It's impossible to blow them up, or even know where they all are."

"But it turns out there *is* a single point of failure," Scorpio continued. "And it's on Earth."

"Earth is a dead planet."

Van Johnson yawned and looked bored.

"It's another one of the many lies you've been fed," Scorpio explained. "Earth is not deserted and it's not dangerous, either, if you know where to go. It's a paradise reserved for Alpha and Beta clearance citizens."

"But the disaster must have been real. I mean, if Control exists to preserve the environment –"

"Oh, yes, the disaster was real. There are still a great many hot spots, and some of them are quite large. A lot of things have to be imported from the Bunker. But a lot of time has passed since then, Terry. The Earth has been healing. She's exceptionally resilient if you take into account the appropriate timescales. Tens of billions of people were too much for her to support, but a few tens of thousands... It's nothing."

"And you yourself have already taken the first step," Alibaba told me. "You knocked out the transceivers for the Terran data streams. Control is now blind to what's going on there. You see, one thing we managed to find out is that there are no server nodes on Earth."

"That's what I was doing on that asteroid?"

"Not you, honey," Sally told me.

"Yes," responded Starbuoy. "And it gave us hell before it agreed to go."

"We had to promise an awful lot."

"Fortunately for us," added Brutalizer, "you don't know what it was."

"Is this your idea of trying to convince me to cooperate?"

"It wasn't him who was blown up on that asteroid," Sally insisted.

"Yes, it was!" My eyes were suddenly blazing. "What else is a clone supposed to be but an exact copy?"

"It was Jeremy Whiles!"

"You think it matters he had a different name! It was the same thoughts, the same memories, the same habits." It was wrong. I felt it in my bones. There can't be more than one of you in the Universe, anywhere. Every other person should be a mystery that you slowly but never quite unravel.

"It doesn't matter now, does it?" Scorpio broke in. "It's dead. Can we move on?"

"So why the package?"

"Ah, well, that was Kuasimodo's idea. An ingenious device, really. Quite simply, after the transceivers were knocked out, we needed to get you here as quickly as possible. To start on the next phase of our plan."

"Why didn't you just ask?"

George laughed. "You would have come?"

I saw his point. "So you tricked me instead."

Scorpio sighed and waved his hand. "The result justifies our methods."

"But why go through all the trouble of the package?"

George and Sally exchanged an uncomfortable glance. I knew what it meant. Sally had wanted to do this back in the Bunker, but George and the others knew I would never have listened to them if I thought there were other options. But there are no other options when you're floating through space without an ecopack.

"We couldn't be seen together more than occasionally, and even then only in two's or three's. The programs that process the surveillance in the Bunker are quite sophisticated. After all, I should know." Scorpio cracked a thin, bloodless smile. "The package was a brilliant idea. It led you from one place to another without any of us having to risk our lives leaving a trail. Don't you agree, it was the perfect ruse?"

I thought back over what had happened. "So you sent me over to Ronald Reagan Plaza in order to get picked up and escorted to an interrogation center..."

"You ran but we got you anyway."

"... in order to put a collar on me."

"And give you a security clearance."

My face suddenly lit up. A finger shot out in George's direction. "You told me to take it to Central Management, but the address was

Production and Logistics!"

George nodded. "We didn't know what would happen on the asteroid – or even if the clone would get there. Homeland Security could have been onto us. We had to be prepared for any contingency. When I sent you off with the package, you were also carrying a message."

"You're observant," Scorpio pointed out. "At least, that's what I've been told. So we gambled you'd pick up on the discrepancy and report it to me. That's how I knew to give you the clearance. And the waiver. Without the waiver, you would never have got this far."

I frowned. "What's so important about the clearance?"

"Well, Renfield," George said. "Complicity's the only one here who knows you better than I do. Fact is, you're curious. It's a dangerous trait to have in the Bunker, but somehow you've managed to survive. On your own at that, without any help from us."

"And what was I supposed to find out with my clearance?"

George shrugged. "Enough to know you've been lied to. Enough to make you angry. To want to do something about it."

"And how do you know I'd want to do something about it?"

"Because *it* did."

I was growing steadily more annoyed that they kept referring to me as "it". "Okay, but after that?"

"After that, we needed you here. As soon as possible."

"So you sent an agent after me," I said, jutting my chin in Scorpio's direction. "Except that's when things really got out of hand. Because instead of going quietly, I killed her. Or did you know I'd do that, too?"

"I did not send anyone after you," Scorpio snapped and looked cross. "She acted on her own. It happens all the time."

"I had to call in a few favors to get us out of that boehner," Sally explained and shrugged. "But you're a quick thinker, Terry. We worked well together back there in the transtube." An ironic smile crept onto her face. "We make a good team, don't you think?"

"We didn't know you'd listen in on Complicity's conversation," Scorpio said. "You did listen in, didn't you?"

I nodded.

"We're lucky he made it to the spaceport at all," Van Johnson called out and burped.

But the way I see it, there's no such thing as luck. "You all think you're so damn smart." I pursed my lips, leaned back in my chair, and parked my hands behind my head. "Well, there's something you don't know. It looks like Terry Renfield pulled one over on you. Because I'm the clone. The original is the one who got blown up doing your dirty work."

Van Johnson burst out laughing, but the others stared at me, dumbfounded.

"You're Jeremy Whiles?" Brutalizer whispered.

"Hell no!" I shot back. "I'm Terry Renfield. There never *was* any Jeremy Whiles. You created two Terry Renfields is what you did! Thank the dome one of them is dead or I'd sure as hell have other priorities than sitting around here thinking of ways to help you chumps out."

"Impossible!" Scorpio barked. He seemed agitated. "How do you know?"

"You never scanned my I-chip, did you? Back at the hospital after you'd activated me, a medibot came and gave me some pills and sent me back to the barracks. I was sick for two days straight."

"Sent you back to the barracks?"

I must admit, I was enjoying the fact that I had hijacked control of their little pow-wow. "After you activated me, you left me alone with the other patients. No one was keeping an eye on me, were they?"

"It takes quite a while for a clone to become fully active," Starbuoy pointed out.

"If he knew about you, why wouldn't Terry have taken the chance to kill you then and there?" George wondered aloud.

I thought I knew. No, I knew I knew.

I would have been angry at the deception. I would have wanted a chance to trip these typhoids up good.

I didn't know enough about the mission they had sent me on to know what I could have been planning, but that must have been the reason. I was sure of it. It was a desire that could have easily overcome any impulse to immediately kill the clone, especially if I thought I'd have a chance to do it later.

So that's what Lance Trevor meant. I must have hired him to take me out before I was killed. But what was all that talk about payback?

"I don't know," I responded and shrugged. "You'll have to ask him."

George made a rude gesture but didn't say anything more.

"I suppose," Scorpio said slowly after a few moments, "that it doesn't matter. Terry – or someone very much like him – is still here, and he possesses all the skills we require. The question is whether or not he'll help us. Now that we've told him everything. You will help us, Jeremy, won't you?"

I suppose they would have overpowered me before I could take out more than one or two of them. Sally was a wildcard, of course. Even if she did help me out, fighting was probably a losing prospect. And if they had to sacrifice her, I was pretty sure they'd do it in the name of their cause. Ruthless smack addicts, all of them.

I looked at Sally. She was considering me gravely. There was a look on her face I had never seen before. It was as if she had caught wind of some terrible smell that wouldn't go away. It hurt me deeply to see it.

"Yeah, sure. I'll help. What's the plan?"

"But it *is* still me, Sally! I'm the same Terry Renfield I always was!"

"No, your not!" Tears were streaming down her face. "You're an impostor. A *thing*!"

Ouch. That really hurt. I wanted to smack her across the face but I didn't. A man should never hit a woman unless she hits him first. Of course, she had come as close as she possibly could without actually raising a hand.

We were standing in one of the alcoves in some pretense of privacy. But there was no privacy on a ship like that. The others didn't even have to stand outside in the passage to hear us.

"If you don't like me, why'd you go along with this? Why'd you let them do this to me?"

"Because!" she said between sniffles. "It was the clone who was supposed to go on the suicide mission!" She straightened up and jabbed an accusing finger in my chest. "This is all your fault! Instead of just going home and lying in bed for a few days you went and screwed everything up! What were you thinking?"

Indeed, what was I thinking?

"You lied to me!" I shouted back at her. "Not just once, but repeatedly for daystretches! Did you forget to mention you were in the Underground? Pretending you didn't know what was in the box. 'Let's go find out!'" I mimicked her voice in a demeaning, childish way. She cringed. "And you made choices for me! *Allowing* them to clone me. What do you think I would have said if you asked my permission? How could I ever trust you again?"

"I don't care if you trust me! My boyfriend was Terry Renfield, and he's dead!" After that pronouncement, she dissolved into a burst of tears and turned away. There was nothing more to say.

Stunned, I wandered back to the bridge.

The others were still there. They were waiting for me. Sensing the advantage, they pressed the attack.

"I'm sorry if things aren't exactly working out right now," Scorpio said, tapping the end of his stick energetically against the toe of one of his boots. "Domestically, I mean."

Alibaba coughed and looked uncomfortable, but the others didn't seem to mind.

"We'll work it out," I rasped, trying to sound convincing.

"I'm sure you will."

The tapping suddenly stopped. Something was wrong.

"Sorry, Renfield, but your performance didn't cut it." It was George, the fat bastard.

Inwardly, I sighed. I didn't want to deal with these people. There were much more important matters at hand. But what can you do when there's no place to run off to and they've taken your laser pistol?

I sat down. I didn't know what they were going to say. I didn't care.

"Some of us feel that you went along too easy," said Brutalizer.

"You're holding back," the tall youth, Antinous, accused me. He leaned closer to Scorpio as if for protection.

Scorpio patted the boy affectionately on the back of one of his hands and looked at me slyly. "It did all go remarkably smoothly, didn't it?"

George was staring, trying to decipher me. "Fact is, the Renfield I know would just say yes to avoid an unpleasant situation now, only to stab us in the back later."

"The proof is in the clone!" said Van Johnson and gestured, giggling, in my direction. He seemed to think he had made a witty joke.

The situation was becoming clear. "I see," I said. "So what kind of reassurances do you need?" I looked around the circle. "You must have something in mind."

"Yes," answered Brutalizer. "Before we can tell you anything about our plans on Earth, you have to tip your hand."

"Give us some information that you could otherwise use against us," added Starbuoy.

"Do you understand what we're getting at?" Scorpio asked.

I knew what they were getting at. "Lance Trevor."

George and Brutalizer nodded their heads.

I shrugged. "I don't see why you're making such a big deal about him. Like I said, I never saw him before this morning."

"You can't expect us to believe that," George purred dangerously. "You're holding out."

"The man tried to kill you." Scorpio whipped the end of his stick through the air in front of him. "Twice."

"Imagine my surprise when I was called out to record a show targeting the very guy I thought we were supposed to be saving," Van Johnson sputtered.

"It's true I only met him this morning," I insisted. "I'm not lying about that. But I've also got an idea who he is."

Scorpio let go of Antinous' hand and leaned intently forward in his seat. "Did Terry Renfield – the original, I mean – compromise our mission?"

I shook my head. "I don't think so. Based on the information you've given me, I wouldn't have, at any rate. But if I had known about the clone, I would have taken steps. I don't know how much I paid him, but that's what Lance is for. To take me out."

"That's pretty much what I thought," Brutalizer said. She seemed satisfied.

"Well, Lance is now in Scorpio's hands," George muttered. Still, I could tell by the look on his face he wasn't convinced.

"I'm sure we'll be able to cure him of this terrible need to do harm to our good friend here," Scorpio mused. "Anyway, whatever his motives, he is no longer of any concern."

"So," Alibaba broke in and looked around at the others. "Do we proceed as planned? I mean, do we trust it?" She turned to Brutalizer. "You seem to trust it."

"I think it's come clean. Yes."

"Terry Renfield or not, it's got all his capabilities," observed Starbuoy and shrugged. "If we have to go digging around on Earth, we'll need it."

I didn't wait to hear what the verdict was. I stood up and approached Alibaba. She eyed me warily.

In a lightning stroke, I had her head in a choke hold. One of her legs and an arm pumped uselessly at the air behind us.

Her chair hit the floor with a loud bang. Other than that, there was no other sound.

I spoke slowly and clearly so there could be no mistaking me. "I'm going to say this only once. If any of you refers to me as 'it' again, I will hurt you. My name is Terry Renfield. Do I make myself understood?"

Chapter 7

"Before there was anything, there was the Void. Some say the Void is nothing, but they are wrong. The Void is endless falling. It is a place without borders, a place of blurriness and endless blending. In the Void, there are no shapes and because there are no shapes there are no things. But where there are no things does not mean there is nothing. There is the Void."

In the tattered, soupy darkness, the motley crowd began to bark and bay.

"Out of the depths of the Void came Sol, the Eternal Father."

The tribe was silent.

"From Sol's body sprang the planets and the moons and the asteroids. These we call Gaia, the Eternal Mother. No matter where we stand – on Earth or Phobos or Ceres – our feet rest on Gaia. For the Eternal Mother, which was born of the Void, is in many ways its opposite. Gaia offers us a floor to break the falling. On Gaia, there are clear lines of delineation. And because there are lines, there are also things, each one distinct from the others. We can point to where the one ends and the other begins."

Some of the tribe stomped their feet and clapped their hands, drumming up an energetic beat. The soft, damp ground muffled the blows. Others pointed and spread their hands wide beside their painted faces, twisting and churning, turning their wide eyes in all directions.

Zeus, standing on a platform hastily thrown up next to the bonfire, continued. "The first of the Titans sprang from the Void. After Sol, there were Night and Day. Night cannot exist without Day, nor Day without Night. There were also Darkness and Light. Night is dark, yet she is pierced by the light of Stars and Moon. But Darkness is pure and unadulterated. Her daughter, Light, is pure and unfiltered brilliance, but the Day – her sister – also knows shadows."

A loud burst of affirmation from the tribe.

"Now, Gaia is the floor we stand on. But this floor is not flat nor is it boundless. At one end, there are the mountains where the nymphs live. They rise up and up and up, far above the places where Titans and mortals walk. Their tops are swallowed in the forever brilliance of Light. At the other end, Gaia is broken up into pits and clefts. These give way to the Underworld. At her gates we find the abode of

Darkness. The Underworld is a boundless expanse. The underpinning of Gaia is the very Void from which she sprang."

The painted bodies formed a spinning circle around the bonfire. When Zeus spoke next, his voice had picked up strength.

"And there was Eros. This is not the familiar icon, the champion of love between two mortals. This is the Eros that preceded him. This is the Eros that induces creation without sexual union. It was this Eros that first stirred the creative forces in Gaia, the Eternal Mother. Under his influence, Gaia brought forth other creatures onto her surface: Sky and Ocean and others."

I swallowed and glanced uncomfortably at the blackness above. It was night, but I didn't feel any better. In some ways, it was worse when the sun had gone down. It was then that I could see the terrible pinpricks that were the stars. Climbing away from the horizon a third of the face of the waxing moon showed brilliantly. It had risen several hours ago. I shivered. I remembered how the stars and the moon had looked on our way in. To see them now just as I had seen them then, with my feet on firm ground, meant there was nothing between us. Just a huge, empty expanse. It was unnatural.

"Sky lay heavy atop Gaia like a smothering blanket. Every square meter was covered by an equivalent portion of Sky. This presented a problem for Gaia, for Sky was fathering children by her. One after they other, they accumulated in her womb. You see, the children of Gaia were trapped. Even though she was a goddess, she was not meant to keep what was inside her there forever. She is the Eternal Mother. And as a mother, she wished for her children to go out into the world."

The throng cupped their hands about their lips and moaned.

"The first of the Titans numbered twelve, and the youngest of them was Cronus. It was he who, when Gaia asked, castrated his father as he lay copulating with her. Recoiling from the pain, Sky sprang into the Heavens. There he remains to this day. Still he covers her, meter for meter, but now there is space enough between them for the events of the world to play out. If it were not for Cronus, the Titans would never have emerged into the world, and nothing more would have happened on the stage that is Creation."

I heard clapping. The fire seemed to leap. The tribal members stretched their arms out to it and then snapped them back. I saw now that the dancers had separated into two circles, one inside the other. The two wheels spun in opposite directions.

"But even though Gaia and all the other gods and goddesses long desired the outcome, his was a crime nonetheless. Even though the days of the Titans would be remembered as an age of peace and tranquility, the forces of revenge and punishment that heralded its beginning were never far away. For a great many things happened the day Sky was banished to Heaven and the Titans emerged into the world with Gaia's blessing."

I like to think I've been around in the Bunker. I'm not a squeamish man, and I'm not easy prey for charlatans like Zeus. But when the tribe started moaning and wailing, I shivered.

Was it the sky? The ghostly weight of a night on Earth?

I glanced over at Sally and George, but they were too far away. I couldn't make out their faces.

Next to me was a bamboo cage. It wasn't tall enough for a grown man to stand in. Inside, Antonius squatted, gripping the bars tightly with both hands and peering helplessly out. I could smell the fear in him. It came in sharp, overpowering waves.

"Cronus threw Sky's dismembered penis into the Sea, but before he did drops of blood spilled onto the ground. From these arose the Furies, the three goddesses of vengeance. These are the goddesses that teach us to nurse our wounds in the heart long after our bodies have healed. No matter how much Time goes by, the Furies ensure we do not forget. They teach us to be patient, and they provide the drive when the moment for revenge is ripe."

The dancers changed direction.

"The Furies were not the only dreadful consequence of Cronus' crime. The Giants, too, were born of the blood of Sky. These were the beings that filled the hearts of our warriors in the heat of battle with pure and unrestrained violence. These were the creatures that blinded our understanding in the heated aftermath, when the victor has his way on the field. We can only count ourselves lucky that in the ages since, they have been slain to the last. But the work of those awful hands surrounds us still.

"Such were the terrible gods and goddesses released into the world because of Cronus' crime. But not all was woe and destruction. For Astarte, the goddess of love and beauty, was also given form and meaning. She washed up from the Sea, stepped up onto the shore naked and ravishing, and shook the dampness from her hair. All the world held its breath in awe when it first beheld her. Strands of seaweed like a wreath clung to her long, dark locks. Her skin was chocolate and smooth as silk. The eyes showed with a fierceness that belied the seduction of her smile. Astarte is the patroness of lust and animal love, the kind that the young are apt to mistake for the real thing. These devotees she treats with contempt, the way a cat plays with a mouse when it isn't hungry. Her tenderness and affection are reserved for those who are truly fond of each other, trust each other, and know each other."

Now the inner and the outer wheels swapped places. The exchange happened delicately. For the duration of a few breaths, the dancers intermingled and spun around and between each other. But as close as they came, they never touched.

"Mere mortals, too, sprang from these same droplets of blood. They were unlike anything the world had seen before. The gods and the goddesses, the Giants and the other mystical creatures which I did not tell you about, each has immense power in but a single realm of existence. Together, they span the length and breath of possibility, but as individuals they are like a color isolated from the beauty of the rainbow. Not so the mortals. Even standing alone – although he may not excel in even a single competence – he can change in the world in more ways than one. He can adapt. Most of these mortals are harmless, but human beings in particular have shown great talents in both destruction and creation. It is hard at this time to say what their ultimate fate will be.

"Now, the Titans and the other gods and the mortals lived together in harmony on Gaia for a long time. I do not say prosperity, for there was nothing prosperous or otherwise shameful about an existence in which one is supplied with an abundance of the things he requires to live and be content. Prosperity – and all that accompanies it – was introduced by the Furies at a later time. But for now, they and the Giants were absent. Some refer to this long age of tranquility as the Garden of Eden. But we know that it was never a place. It was a state of mind.

"Eventually, of course, this tranquility came to an end."

With a great cry, the dancing stopped.

Zeus paused and surveyed his followers. The fire crackled and roared in the gaping silence.

"The Furies and their lust for revenge could not be put off forever. No one knows how they made their way back into the world where gods and mortals walked. The Titans did not notice them, or if they did, foolishly paid them no heed. They appeared as three beautiful sisters, and they spoke to any who would listen. Their speech was disingenuous.

"'Are you happy with your little hovel and a few scraps of bread to satisfy your hunger?' they asked.

"'I am,' answered the human. 'My house is crude but warm and it shelters me from the rain and the wind. The fruits from the vine and the meat from the hunt are plain but wholesome. It is pleasant here.'

"'Is this mean existence all that you aspire to?'

"The human frowned. 'Aspire'?

"'Yes!' the three Furies crooned in unison. Sensing and opening, they crowded around their victim. Now they spoke rapidly.

"'There is more to life than lying in the sun and making love and chewing on apples,' sneered one.

"'Your contentment has induced laziness,' accused another.

"'Don't you wish to know more of the world?' whispered the third.

"'To master it! To bend it to your will!'

It was hard to tell which one had spoken those last words.

"'Master it?' stammered the human, perplexed. 'But why would I want to do that?'

"'Power!' cried one.

"'Luxury!' shrieked another.

"'Adoration!' hollered a third.

"'Lordship!' they all screeched in unison.

"And so it happened that human beings began to seek after knowledge. The quest might not have brought them any ill. They might have learned how to live in harmony with the gods and Creation, becoming the masters of both and allowing each to thrive in its own way. Alas, their search was tainted by their purpose. For it was at this time that the humans began to speak of prosperity, and any knowledge which could not lead them directly to it was discarded as irrelevant or fanciful."

The tribe broke up their orderly formation. They began to wander to and fro as if blinded or lost, howling and shaking their fists. Whenever they encountered one another, they fought. The battles were mock, of course, and soon enough the loser was back on his feet. But it didn't seem to me they were coming back to life. Rather, the chaos and banditry were forever being replenished.

"In order for one human being to consider himself prosperous, another must first be impoverished. And so the lust for prosperity led to great, armed conflicts called wars in which many people suffered and died. But the strife was not confined to themselves alone. The humans brought misery and hardship to the gods as well. And Gaia, the Eternal Mother, was foremost among the victims.

"First, the humans discovered agriculture. They used this

knowledge to build large settlements. The settlements allowed their populations to grow, which in turn drained the resources from the earth around them. They did not think to replace that which they took.

"Next, they gave birth to money. Unlike the other gods and creatures which filled Creation, money had to keep growing to feel healthy. Larger and larger it grew. The larger it became, the more attention they were forced to give it. Eventually, money began to make demands of the humans, and the humans always acquiesced. For what had seemed at first to be a beneficial relationship had been perverted into slavery. Before they knew it, money had spawned other terrible things such as derivatives and credit default swaps.

"They were at the mercy of a many-headed demon called Economy. It was a monster larger and more dangerous than the Cyclops or the Hundred-Handed Beasts combined, and it stood taller than Atlas himself, towering over them all and sowing havoc and discord into their lives."

The tribal members began to dig up clumps of dirt and grass from the ground and toss them into the fire. They were silent and their faces grim. Soon the ground where they squatted was pockmarked and scarred.

"There were other consequences to their quest for prosperity than Economy alone. There was also Pollution. In many ways, Pollution was a far more insidious beast than Economy, which stood tall and threatening in plain sight of everyone. Pollution was hardly noticed when she first appeared. A fleeting ghost that you could only see if you tried, she seemed almost innocuous. You could not ignore Economy when he was beating you down and destroying your family, but Pollution was ephemeral. Pollution was always somewhere else. Alas, the rapacity of the humans blinded them to the danger. For Pollution destroyed all that she touched, and she touched everything. First she poisoned the air and then the water on Earth, and when she had depleted these of their vitality she set upon the rest.

"It was at this time that Gaia finally cast the humans away. For too long she had tolerated the wickedness of her grandchildren. Powerful and numerous were their poisons, but the strength of Gaia was greater still. They would behold the woe that only a furious goddess can unleash! She opened a great, dark pit near her belly and shook. She shook until all the humans had either perished or been swallowed up in the pit. Economy and Pollution tumbled in after them. Then she closed it and set Titans as guardians at its mouth to prevent the survivors from ever venturing out into the world again."

The tribe leaped to its feet and cried out in a short but powerful burst of joy. The sound faded into the relieved silence that followed. All I could hear was the roar and crackle of the fire.

Once again, Zeus' followers formed a spinning wheel and danced. This time, they tried to smooth over the pits in the ground with their feet as they passed.

"The humans were not alone when they were shut up in the Underworld. Locked away with their creations, Economy and Pollution, until the end of Days, there was also a Titan. This was Logike, the youngest of the youngest of the Titans, and he went against his will. Logike was born of Thamyris and Leto and was the last of that primordial race down to this very day. From his earliest years, Logike was a nuisance to his peers, for he was closely linked with a new and unpleasant concept called 'righteousness'. He took it upon himself to lecture his parents and the other Titans.

"When it became apparent that he would never stop and all their days would be filled with endless remonstrations, the Titans contrived to rid themselves of him. It was his own mother, Leto, who thought to lure him out to the pit in Gaia's belly. She told him that the humans had invited him to give one of his 'sermons'. Pleased that for the first time someone had asked, he rushed to the spot. The other Titans were waiting and pushed him in.

"By all accounts, Logike is insatiable and cruel, but he is not evil. Logike genuinely believes that he offers a utopia. The other Titans ignored him, but trapped in the Underworld with the humans he finally had a chance to impose his plain and regimented way of life on others. He easily defeated his only rivals, Economy and Pollution, and thereby earned the humans' devotion. Deep in the nooks and crannies of the Underworld, they followed his every directive. They gave up their own free wills to him because he seemed to know better.

"But we all know that Logike's world is not a utopia at all. I think the humans know it now, too. They discovered only when it was too late that they had sacrificed too much. They have safety and security, it is true. They have a clean place to sleep and enough nourishment to survive. They have been given tasks to occupy their time, even if they aren't always useful or invigorating. But the truth is, the human spirit needs excitement and adventure to grow. There must be something new to discover. But even more importantly, human beings have opinions. It is not possible for them to submit blindly to the dictates of another, even if by doing so their own physical well-being has been secured.

"Such is the long reach of the Furies that they were able to introduce strife deep into the bowels of the Underworld, out of sight of Sol, Moon, and Star. For Logike's is a utopia riddled with rebellion. Logike is, alas, out of the humans' reach, and so their blows often turn on one another. Theirs is a perilous world in which consequences do not seem to have causes, in which death may come suddenly and for apparently no reason at all. The inhabitants pretend one thing and do another. It is a world of paradox and desperation."

At last, Zeus fell silent. The dancers ceased their movements. The fire crackled and burned.

"Fellow Olympians," Zeus intoned, raising his arms and turning on his heels to face them all. "We are the progeny of Logike. He sought to keep us swallowed up in the Underworld, trapped with the mortals. He endeavored to prevent us from rising against him. He knows that we and we alone threaten him.

"We managed to escape. Once again, we are afoot on Gaia. And as she once called on Cronus, she nows calls upon us."

Zeus took a great breath, threw back his head, and shouted. "Throw down the tyranny of Logike, my grandson! Release the humans from their slavery! They have suffered enough."

The tribal members answered him with a single voice. "Lead us on to victory, O Zeus, King of the Olympians!" they shouted.

Zeus paused and smiled. "Fellow Olympians, I will do as you ask."

The tribal members stomped once with their feet and grunted loudly in affirmation.

I looked around at their painted faces gleaming with adoration. I saw Zeus standing over them on his platform, the large, colored feathers of his head piece jerking excitedly as he moved.

As much as they bothered me, under the stars and the moon I might have believed in Zeus' story of Creation. All around me, seeping up from the Earth, I felt the presence of that sleeping power he referred to. It was old, maybe even ageless. It had an unmistakable quality, something wise that offered answers. I knew life in the Bunker – and, apparently, outside it as well – was wrong. I couldn't tell you what else there should be, but now that I was on Earth, I knew it was possible.

But I also knew this wasn't the time. That power was still injured, and anyway, the look on Zeus' face was plain enough. I'd seen it before.

What a crock of slop, I thought to myself and spat on the ground.

I'd heard about traitors like these in the Underground. They always have a large following. What makes Control so afraid of them is that these cults often outlive the typhoid who spawns them.

They take a kernel of truth and distort it for their own purposes. That's what makes them so dangerous. Because if they do it well enough, it's hard to separate the truth from the reactor sludge. You sink your teeth into what feels right and pass off the rest as harmless baggage. Or you accept it as truth, too, and shut your eyes to the suffering and harm that comes. You explain it away to yourself as an unfortunate but necessary price to pay in the honorable struggle for perfection.

Or – even worse – you claim it's all the work of infiltrators trying to bring you down from the inside. You stay on the alert. You purge your ranks of deviancy every now and then.

You start to sound like Control.

Maybe Zeus didn't, but these other crackheads really *did* think they were gods. Who knew what they were capable of. It didn't bode well for Scorpio and the others they'd taken captive.

I hadn't been among them very long, but I already had a pretty good idea what they'd replace Control with even if they didn't.

It was probably a smart idea to pretend to believe all this slop about their being Olympian gods. If George and Sally are as sharp as I think, they'll be doing the same. It was the reason why we were still standing up straight and Antinous was squatting in a bamboo cage.

Best to make our escape before Control finds out and blasts these flapheads into a fine, molecular spray.

I knew I could rely on George and Sally, even if George would love to see me at the other end of his blaster and Sally wouldn't care what happened to me. There'd be time enough afterwards to sort out old rivalries. There always is. Right now we'd need each other to get out of this mess.

If only John the Baptist had taken Antinous along with Scorpio. The kid was dead weight. I'd have been happy to leave him behind, except I knew what it would do to Scorpio if we managed to rescue him. He'd have made us go back and get him.

The most important thing to do now was have a private conference with George and Sally. We'd cook up a plan and go from there.

But it didn't look likely any time soon. They were keeping us in separate   tents.

Chapter 8

Look, I know I've been skipping around. If you don't like it, you can go get gangrene.

When we arrived at Earth no one was dead or injured. What else did you really want to hear about the three monthstretches it took to get there anyway?

There's no way you could ever know what boredom really is unless you've made an interplanetary trip like I have. There wasn't any place to go other than those three tiny rooms. Always staring at the same damned eight faces, most of them hostile.

We ate Algatine out of rusty cans, PermaCrunchy out of discolored bags, and powdered Vitamim by the spoonful. That's right. There wasn't enough water to actually turn it into slop.

And I wouldn't want to forget all the ambient radiation.

I don't recommend space travel to anybody. You're better off agitated underground.

We played video games to pass the time. Scorpio and Brutalizer organized frequent bouts of push-ups and sit-ups and devised other things to do to keep the sluggishness from setting in. The others didn't like it, especially George, but once we got it across he'd never be able to walk again, even that fat, wheezing bastard joined in.

Behind my back, I was still Jeremy Whiles or an inanimate personal pronoun. But they didn't dare call me those things to my face. In conversation, they went to great lengths just to avoid calling me by any name at all. Sometimes I'd chat them up to amuse myself.

I thought I'd work on her, but I wasn't able to get very far with Sally. She wouldn't breathe a single word back to me.

We took turns staring out the portholes for long hourstretches. In the course of the journey, the only thing I noticed is that Mars slowly got smaller and the Earth grew out of a tiny dot that had to be pointed out to me until it took up half our view. Scorpio told me the Sun got bigger, too, but it was too bright to look at, so what did it matter?

Space, though, is pretty damn interesting even if it hardly seems to move. You'll just have to take my word for it. Maybe it's because it's everywhere. Or the sharpness of the colors. Those pinpricks of light they call stars – I'd never seen anything like them before. Starbuoy told me they were all yellow, red, white, or blue, but it seemed to me that each one was its own color.

Did I forget to mention I got my laser pistol back? Half way through the trip, Scorpio removed my collar, too. He said it could be used to track us.

They told me their plan. I didn't think it was a very good one.

Earth could no longer communicate with any of Control's nodes, which meant they were on their own down there. The others assumed that all out war had broken loose as each Alpha and his backers vied with the others for domination. One of these factions was Scorpio's. Apparently, they already had their instructions.

I'm not sure what these typhoids were thinking. After all, if knocking out communication with Control meant an immediate descent into chaos, what did they think was going to happen in the Bunker when they took it offline completely?

Scorpio would then put in a surprise appearance and save the day, in the process convincing the other Alphas to unite behind him in his quest to destroy Control. How exactly he was going to do all this was unclear.

After restoring order and establishing himself as undisputed leader, Scorpio would lead us to the Self-Destruct Mechanism.

Did such a thing really exist? Scorpio had never seen it, but he had heard of this mystical stream of data from some of the older Alphas. We were all skeptical, so he divulged some of the more fantastic bits of rumor that often passes for history in the Bunker.

Apparently, Control's original coders had built in a back door that could be used to shut down the whole system in case it went awry.

When Control found out about the existence of the Self-Destruct Mechanism, it ordered the Alpha's to remove it.

What happened next was typical. Some of the Alphas, in fact, loyally tried to rip out the offending logic from Control's codebase. Others duplicated it. Still others tried to erase Control's *awareness* of the Self-Destruct Mechanism but wanted to leave it intact.

Of course, Control is a distributed system of the highest order. It is extremely difficult – if not impossible – to delete *any* information once it has been replicated across more than a few nodes. All these Alphas managed to do was create a series of dangerous data inconsistencies and logical paradoxes.

Some of Control's nodes began to crash when they tried to access data about the Self-Destruct Mechanism. Others went on hyper-alert and ordered the destruction of whole sectors, or determined that the people living inside them would behave far more efficiently if the ambient temperature were raised to six thousand degrees Kelvin.

I was told this is one reason there are twenty-five letters from A to Y but only eighteen existing sectors in our Bunker.

Eventually, all the Alphas who managed to survive finally agreed to cooperate and fix the problem. Scorpio emphasized this point to us dramatically, as if there was some lesson in it for us to be learned.

They added the necessary libraries and subroutines to make it appear that the Self-Destruct Mechanism was really Alpha slang for Code Review.

At that time Control was already comprised of hundreds of thousands of libraries hanging onto tens of thousands of interfaces joined – and, when necessary, forced – together like a gazillion pieces of an ugly, bloody-minded puzzle.

Wouldn't you know it? Control has never mentioned or tried to access data connected to the Self-Destruct Mechanism since.

"GREETINGS CITIZENS. THIS IS CONTROL. WELCOME TO EARTH. BEFORE YOU CAN DEBOARD THE AIR MUST BE EXTRACTED FROM YOUR SHIP. AFTER IT HAS BEEN SANITIZED IT WILL BE RETURNED TO YOU. THERE IS NOTHING TO WORRY ABOUT. PLEASE PREPARE TO HOLD YOUR BREATH FOR APPROXIMATELY SEVEN MINUTE-FOURTEEN POINT EIGHT ONE EIGHT SECONDSTRETCHES. THANK YOU FOR YOUR COOPERATION."

"Oh shit!" I spat and quickly scanned the cabin.

Alibaba got to the compartment labelled "Oxygen Masks" first. She ripped it open. We all stared. There was some dust inside but no masks.

"Control!" Scorpio spat, fingers twitching nervously. "Human beings can't hold their breath that long!"

"ARE YOU SUGGESTING THAT MY DATA IS ERRONEOUS?"

We all shook our heads vigorously.

"Yes!"

There was an uncomfortable moment of silence.

"VERY WELL. AFTER THE PROCEDURE HAS COMPLETED PLEASE BE SURE TO SUBMIT ELECTRONIC FORM NUMBER 0x7A19BD04 'REQUEST TO RECONFIGURE'. CENTRAL MANAGEMENT WILL REVIEW AND RECOMMEND. THANK YOU FOR YOUR COOPERATION."

An unnerving and forceful hissing sound began somewhere above us.

"George Walker!" Sally screeched, clawing at Scorpio. "You told us Control would be cut off from us here on Earth!"

I lunged and pulled her hands away from his face. "Find something to batter down the door with! Quick!"

The air thinned. We filled up our lungs as best we could.

Antinous started desperately pulling at one of the bulky, plastex chairs we had been strapped into on take-off. Of all the furnishings in the ship, those were the most securely attached.

George ran out of the bridge. Not sure what else to do, I followed. Starbuoy and Brutalizer were just behind me.

I saw him slip into one of the alcoves. Of course! The bunk beds were solid but some of them were coming loose from the wall. It was an excellent idea.

We each took a corner of the nearest bunk and started to rock and yank and sway.

The hissing sound from the control room dimmed and stopped.

It's a strange feeling being in a vacuum. There's an uncomfortable tingling all over your skin. Your eyes start to hurt.

The bed came loose without so much as a squeal. Desperately, we picked it up and limped back to the bridge.

Van Johnson, standing uselessly under the bank of tubes, stared at us with frightened, glassy eyes.

Exhausted, we dropped the bed.

Scorpio, Sally, and Alibaba, however, understood what we meant to do. They picked it up and went to work on the bulkhead.

My lungs were aching and my head felt funny. Slumping to the floor, all I could do was hope they had enough breath left to batter it down.

I did not hear the clanging of the heavy bunk against the thick metal of the bulkhead so much as feel it. It echoed, low and distant, through the floor where I had laid my head.

My vision was shot through with patches of gathering blackness. My ears started popping. This is it, I thought.

The outer door gave way.

I found out later on that the descent through the Terran atmosphere had substantially weakened the outer locking mechanism. We would never have been able to open the door without battering it down even if we wanted to. It was the first time I would ever be thankful for the Bunker's shoddy craftsmanship.

Scorpio was the first to stumble out. Coughing violently, I pulled myself up and started after him.

Sally met me along the way. I tried to catch her eye. Hell, I think I caught her eye. I tried flashing her one of my winning smiles, but she wouldn't have it. Darting just a little bit faster and squirming, she made it to the shattered bulkhead a heartbeat before I did.

I looked over her shoulder.

The first thing I saw was a ring of blasters, their muzzles all pointed at us in a most unwelcoming way.

But I was more put out by the second thing I saw. It was enormous and blue and stretched overhead like a great umbrella. White, floating masses of mist broke it up into terrible chunks. Somewhere behind them a ghastly light shone with a brilliance that was difficult to behold.

I screamed and fell to the ground, covering my head protectively with my arms. I expected to be sucked out into the great unknown that lay behind that horrid blue.

Actually, I did feel the air moving against my face, but it was a slight, almost caressing feeling.

I looked up. The guardians holding the blasters were snickering.

"Get up, you fool!" It was Scorpio. He looked embarrassed.

Astounded, I climbed to my feet.

Sally was terrified, too, but she had managed to keep her wits. Still, as soon as I was standing her hand slipped defensively into my own.

My heart glowed.

Of course, when it became clear the sky was no menace to us at all, she yanked it away and shot me a nasty look.

"What's this all about?" Scorpio demanded, his stick held smartly under an arm.

One of the guardians stepped forward. "Felix Tubman, sir!" she barked accusingly. "We have orders for your arrest and all those in your company!"

Scorpio's eyes narrowed dangerously. "What's the charge?"

The guardian spat on the ground. Horrified, we recoiled. I had never seen anyone do that before. It was so unhygienic.

"Plotting to overthrow Control and conspiracy thereof."

"What's your clearance?"

"Beta, sir!"

"Well, I'm the head of Homeland Security!"

"All of it," I added for clarification, in case she didn't know.

"Yes," replied the guardian. "But we have our orders."

"From who?"

"I thought you would have guessed by now, Felix."

It was a sweet, harmless voice. The funny thing was, it seemed to have come from somewhere above us.

Raluca Ioannou – a.k.a. John the Baptist – sat in a gravity chair floating just a meter or two from the hull of our spaceship, smiling pleasantly. That's right, all those cancerheads on Earth are in the Underground. They practically run the place.

"What a joy it is to see you again, Raluca," Scorpio muttered and pursed his lips.

Raluca lifted a thin, wasted arm and gestured grandly. "But I can say it with conviction, Felix! You are a traitor. You are a midget, it's true, but you are also a traitor. As the loyal citizen to arrest you, Control will reward me well. And my faithful companions here, of course. It's already been arranged." She giggled mischievously and grinned. "Assuming, of course, we're compensated based on the threat level and not on your height."

Scorpio's eyes flashed. "What happened to my own faithful followers?"

"As soon as we heard of your treason, we had them arrested. The regular courts are handling their cases now. Some have already been terminated. Others have been sentenced to corrective surgery and the labor camps. A good many are hoping that their truthful confessions – and testimony to your various depravations – will spare them a similar fate." She shrugged and rolled her eyes.

"I should have got rid of you when I had the chance," Scorpio snarled and wrung his hands.

Raluca laughed brightly. "Oh, don't blame me for your carelessness. What were you thinking anyway? The Self-Destruct Mechanism. Did you think no one would notice?"

"I don't understand." Scorpio threw a suspicious glance in my direction. "The communications should have been cut."

"Don't blame him, either, Felix." At that, the thin, unhealthy looking woman guided her wheelchair over our heads and sank slowly to the ground. She came to hover a few centimeters from the asphalt in front of us and turned her gaze upon me. "So this is the notorious Mr. Whiles." She took a moment to look me over. "Terrorists of Epsilon clearance don't merit much of a reward from Control. That doesn't mean I don't value the chance to meet you. Anyone who is able to locate and penetrate one of the most protected and sensitive areas in all of Gaia – " She waved her arms grandly and left her sentence hanging. "Well, in any event, there are a number of personnel from Defense who are eager to meet you."

"My name is Terry Renfield," I told her flatly.

She flashed me a sagging, sickly smile. "Yes, of course you are."

"This is just a clone," Sally informed the floating woman coldly. "He never went anywhere near that asteroid."

"Yes, we know. The original Terry Renfield is still at large."

"Dead, you mean," I corrected her firmly.

"No. At large." Raluca smiled at me grandly. "You mean you didn't know?"

A knot suddenly appeared in my stomach. "I saw him blow up. We all did."

"No you didn't," came the sweet reply.

I was about to argue, but then I realized she was right.

"So where is he then?" The words came out between clenched teeth. If we hadn't been in this ridiculous situation, I would have slugged Scorpio right then and there, Alpha clearance or not.

"As I told you, we don't know. But we will. It's only a matter of time."

"You didn't carry out the mission!" Scorpio turned on me, pivoting on the shiny heels of his boots.

Raluca shook her head. "He did just as you asked, Felix. He blew up most of the transceivers on the asteroid. We have no idea how he managed to escape."

Now why would I have done that?

I saw Sally twitch with excitement.

"I don't understand," Scorpio protested. "You're still linked up!"

"What's disappointing," Raluca observed gravely, "is your lack of faith in our loyalty. We did *not* descend into chaos as you expected. Of course, some of us took the opportunity to run off into the outside. Those under my command have been meticulously hunting down these social deviants and destroying them."

A bloodless smile pulled at Scorpio's lips. "I see. You beat the others to the punch. So it's John the Baptist who rules here in Hallowed Hills."

Raluca feigned humility. "Call me Raluca, please."

Antinous pushed past me and rushed up to Scorpio's side, slouching protectively in his shadow. "Don't listen to her," he breathed and glared at the woman in the wheelchair spitefully. "She's spinning a web of lies."

"Ah," chirped Raluca, "the second prize of the bunch."

I couldn't possibly believe she was talking about Antinous.

Sure enough, sulking in the bulkhead stood Van Johnson. At that moment it seemed unlikely he'd be hosting another show of Ten Things I Hate About Treason.

"Not only are you in cahoots with a dangerous criminal, Van, but you conspired to imprison a law abiding citizen."

"The clone's not law abiding," Van Johnson stammered. "You said so yourself."

"I was talking about Lance Trevor. A most dutiful and loyal citizen. I can attest to the fact myself."

"I had no part in that!" Van Johnson protested.

"Lance Trevor is under your protection?" Scorpio asked.

"Indeed he is." Raluca's thin, skeletal face leered at us happily. "Your attempt to imprison him unlawfully has not gone unnoticed. Of course, we freed him as soon as you left Mars."

Scorpio swiped the air in front of him angrily with his stick. "Is Terry Renfield by any chance working for you as well?"

"Don't be silly," Sally scoffed, shaking her head adamantly.

Raluca might have said something more, except at that moment she broke out into a fit of terrible coughing. The gravity chair lurched and swayed.

Disgusted, I looked on as she convulsed just off the ground in front of me. Sure, I'd coughed before. Who hasn't? But never like that. There was spittle spraying from her mouth. Her eyes were blood red. "George Walker!" She gasped for breath.

What did diseases look like, anyway? I had heard of them before, but I thought they were just the fancy of vengeful learnbots.

I glanced fitfully to the left and to the right. Not far away at one end of the runway was a set of squat, square buildings, but I didn't see any diseases.

Were they furry? How many legs did they have? Did they get you in your sleep?

I took a step back and bumped up against Van Johnson.

"What will happen to us?" the former host of Ten Things I Hate About Treason stammered nervously, clearly horrified by the turn of events.

Raluca managed to get her coughing under control. "Eventually, you'll be terminated, of course," she wheezed, wiping her lips with her sleeve. "But first we'll have your trial."

Starbuoy and Alibaba were working for Raluca, too. Brutalizer was genuinely shocked when they strolled out of our ship and received a

warm welcome from the guardians. They slapped their open palms
together over their heads and grunted loudly. It was a ridiculous
gesture.

Also, they relieved me of my weapon before leading us off the
runway. How was it that I couldn't manage to keep my hands on my
own laser pistol?

What a strange shape for a building, I thought sourly as we
approached the squarish, skulking structures at the nearer end of the
runway. In the Bunker, all the domes are curved.

Inside, we found ourselves on the outskirts of a disorderly mob of
citizens, pushing and pulling and pretending to be loyal. It felt
strangely enough like home. I was happy to be out of sight of the sky
and back into familiar surroundings, but there was hardly anything
else to be chirping about.

The space was large enough, I guess, but not quite as large as a
public square back in the Bunker. Maybe the size of buildings above
ground is constrained by the heaviness of all that air piled up on top
for kilometers on end. Or perhaps they ran short of building materials.
Or maybe there just weren't that many people living there. I never did
find out.

Large cracks could be seen threading their way ominously across
the ceiling. A few buckets had been placed here and there on the floor
to collect the precious water that dripped through.

Gaping, squarish entrances opened irregularly in the walls, leading
to tunnels that sloped sharply downward. Glowing signs identified the
sectors that they led to. Like the Bunker, everyone in the settlement
lived underground.

Citizens – all Beta and Alpha clearance, apparently – moved
confidently from place to place, barking and shouting at each other.
Some used stepbots. Others sat hunched over on full sized mobots,
loosely gripping the fore handles and occasionally revving the engine.
A few old-fashioned types like us were using their own two legs and
the feet attached.

There were bots without people riding them, too, lots more than I
was used to. Crawlbots and watchbots and cleanbots, they were all
busy doing whatever it is that bots do to keep from getting junked.

Never before had I seen so many security cameras in one place.
The red lights underneath all gleamed brightly. They swiveled busily
to and fro, zooming in and out, sometimes pausing to monitor a
situation and then letting it go in search of another. Every corner of
the terminal was being watched. And it wasn't people on the other

side. Oh no, it was surely Control itself, unforgiving and relentless.

There were announcements. They echoed blandly throughout the hall, one after the other, separated by a deep, lonely silence that lasted mere moments.

It was not a person's voice. It was a cold and mechanical voice, an eerily detached voice. The words seemed to have all been recorded in isolation and then strung together as necessary without any attention to proper phrasing.

"GREETINGS CITIZENS. THIS IS CONTROL. IT IS INTERMITTANTLY CLOUDY IN THE OUTSIDE. WITHIN A HUNDRED METER RADIUS OF HALLOWED HILLS SPACEPORT THE MEAN TEMPERATURE IS SIXTEEN POINT ZERO NINE NINE DEGREES CENTIGRADE. ALL CITIZENS ARE REQUIRED TO WEAR COATS. THANK YOU FOR YOUR COOPERATION."

I suppose there was nothing shocking about that first announcement. No one seemed to react to it in any case, and no one was wearing coats. But then I heard the next one.

"GREETINGS CITIZENS. THIS IS CONTROL. IN KEEPING WITH OUR NEW OPEN DOORS POLICY THE FOLLOWING WORDS HAVE BEEN DEPRECATED FROM THE WORKING VOCABULARY: CLOSE CLOSES CLOSED CLOSING SHUT CHALK. EFFECTIVE IMMEDIATELY. THANK YOU FOR YOUR COOPERATION."

Chalk?

But I was already getting a feel for this place. It's the one I'd already been living in. I just didn't know it at the time.

My guess is that one of these Alphas siphoned off some or all of the budget for chalk production, and now he was covering his tracks.

I wondered what other words had fallen victim to budgetary sleight-of-hand and public decency.

"GREETINGS CITIZENS. THIS IS CONTROL. DUE TO SUPPLY SHORTAGES CAUSED BY INCREASED TERRORIST ACTIVITY SCHEDULED DELIVERIES OF LIGHTBULBS TITANIUM SIDING AND PERMACHUNKY FROM BUNKERS GANGES ELYSIUM AND LAKSHMI HAVE BEEN CANCELLED. ANYONE CAUGHT CONSUMING LIGHTBULBS OR TITANIUM SIDING WILL BECOME PERMANENTLY CRISPY. THANK YOU FOR YOUR COOPERATION."

Did Control have a sense a humor? Somehow I doubted it.

Six citizens crossing the hall caught my attention.

They had formed a circle, and each one had a hand extended towards the center. The hands appeared to grip something, maybe a handle of some kind. What had caught my attention, though, is that there was no handle. Nor was there anything that the proposed handle could be attached to. Whatever this invisible contraption was, the six citizens strained to move it as it if were incredibly heavy.

Four cameras were following them intently.

"Clear the way!" the one in front called out. There was no one in front of them.

"Nothing to see here!" called another. He had, in fact, spoken the truth, itself an amazing feat.

"Please move along!"

Did we really possess the technology to turn things invisible?

It's hard to say for sure what the earthlings had been capable of. Official history doesn't say much except they wasted an awful lot and they're extinct. There are the rumors, of course. I've heard, for example, that they were policed by superhumans, men who could climb like spiders or leap tall buildings in a single bound. They worshiped a god called Hollywood who apparently specialized in happy endings. And they cared a lot about their feet. But not once did I ever hear that they could turn things invisible. Which would mean that the technological marvel in front of me was an incredible achievement of our own doing.

In the Bunker, we never achieve anything notable except maybe the occasional rash.

Was it possible that I was wrong?

Were we more than an authoritarian society based on the abandoned knowledge of ancient times, knowledge that was slowly but inevitably degrading, knowledge we only partly understood?

Was it actually possible that we could solve our own problems? Could we be decisive and get things done?

The way I reckoned it, I was already a dead man, and as sure as the dome I wanted to find out before they terminated me.

Raluca and the guardians were distracted. I saw my chance. When the invisible contraption was as close as it was going to get, I broke away from our group, confidently strode up to the citizens carrying it, and smiled.

All movement in the terminal came to a sudden standstill. The only sound was of three more cameras snapping to attention and zooming in on the action.

The citizen closest was a stocky, middle-aged man. The look on his face was a curious mix of suspicion, fatigue, and fear.

It's a good thing he doesn't have a gun, I thought.

"Hi!" I said and thrust my hand into the space where the invisible machine should have been.

Everyone except the citizens pretending to carry it gasped.

The invisible machine wasn't.

I moved my hand around just to make sure, but it didn't come into contact with anything.

My PA lit up.

I removed it from its carrying case and flipped it open. A single, red eye stared unblinkingly back at me.

"GREETINGS CITIZEN JEREMY WHILES. THIS IS CONTROL. I HAVE WITNESSED FIRST HAND YOUR COURAGEOUS ACT OF PATRIOTISM. AFTER DIVULGING THE IDENTITY OF THEIR CO-CONSPIRATORS THESE VILE TRAITORS WILL SERVE AS A LESSON TO OTHERS. IMAGINE THE REPURCUSSIONS IF OUR NEW STEALTH VENDING MACHINE WERE TO FALL INTO ENEMY HANDS."

A contingent from Homeland Security arrived, shot two of the traitors outright, and made to haul the remaining four off. One of them had other ideas, however, and whipped out a heavy blaster from a bag that had been slung over his shoulder.

As sometimes happens in the Bunker, a firefight ensued.

I thought perhaps it might be a good idea to get out of the way of the crossfire and mentioned the fact to Control.

"NONSENSE CITIZEN," came the reply. "YOU MUST SERVE AS AN EXAMPLE. STAND FIRM IN THE KNOWLEDGE THAT GOOD ALWAYS TRIUMPHS OVER EVIL. OUR CAMERAS ARE WATCHING. IF YOU SURVIVE YOU WILL BE CELEBRATED IN ALL THE BUNKERS AS A PATRIOT."

I swallowed thickly and watched longingly as everyone else scattered for cover. "And what are my chances of survival?" I figured if anyone would know, it ought to be Control.

"I ESTIMATE A SEVENTY-FOUR POINT SIX ONE ZERO PERCENT CHANCE THAT YOU WILL STILL BE FUNCTIONING IN ONE MINUTESTRETCH."

It was one of the longest minutestretches of my life. I watched as one, now two of the thugs from Homeland Security were felled by the slow but steady stream of fire from the heavy blaster. To wield it required both hands and something to brace yourself against. Each blast was accompanied by a tremendous boom that shook the walls and hurt the ears.

In the end, it was one of his own companions that shot him.

"Control! Control!" she shouted into her PA, waving at the still twitching body. "I got him! Doesn't that count for something?"

I don't know what Control said, but her disappointment was evident when she turned her weapon on herself and put a hole through her own temple.

The other two traitors went along without any further fuss. One of them was sobbing and babbling incoherently.

While the sanitation crew was getting rid of the bodies, Raluca and her retainers gathered up Sally, George, Scorpio, Van Johnson, and Brutalizer.

"Control," I barked into my PA. "What is my status?"

"I DO NOT UNDERSTAND THE QUESTION CITIZEN. PLEASE BE MORE SPECIFIC."

"Am I to remain in the custody of citizen Raluca?"

The response was immediate. "YOU ARE A TRAITOR AND MUST BE TREATED ACCORDINGLY. HOWEVER YOUR RECENT SPONTANEOUS OUTBURST OF PATRIOTISM DESERVES RECOGNITION. A MARK OF EXCELLENCE HAS BEEN ENTERED INTO YOUR PERMANENT RECORD."

Why didn't I feel any better?

I could see that Control had cut the line. I shut my PA, put it back in its carrying case, and heaved a heavy sigh.

"Jeremy!" Raluca shouted as best she could. "Get over here."

"My name's not Jeremy," I mumbled. No one heard me, and at the time I didn't care. After all, there's nothing more demotivating than ingratitude.

"Where are you taking us?" Scorpio demanded suspiciously.

It was a good question. We had left the terminal and were back outside. The awful sky and all the menacing things in it loomed over us. I could hear the cameras mounted on the perimeter straining to keep up with us.

Raluca did not answer. Instead, she motioned her followers to hurry after her. The gravity chair bobbed and swayed slightly in the moving air. I found it confusing how the wind seemed to come from one direction first, and stretches later another.

There were no smells out there. Well, no chemical, synthetic smells. Not that the air in the Bunker is bad. I'm sure it's as hygienic as it could be. In fact, I'll be sure to mention the fact to Control when

I have the chance.

But this air, there was something about it. It smelled... fresh?

We were walking on some kind of thick, green carpet. It was torn up occasionally, revealing a moist, brownish substance that contained small rocks. I was curious and bent down to grab some.

Sally saw what I was doing and looked at the stuff I held in my hand. "Looks like dried slop," she observed.

"Mongolian stew," I said and smiled at her, but she kept her eyes trained on my hand.

"Can I have a feel?"

I was about to give it to her when Van Johnson erupted behind me. "It's just dirt, okay! There's nothing special about it!"

"Don't put any in your mouth," Scorpio advised. "It's unhygienic."

We were approaching an area enclosed in some of the oddest fencing I'd ever seen. It was brown and woven together like a basket. Even stranger, the strands were covered with green flakes as thick as fur. They seemed to be attached somehow.

Unfamiliar shapes stirred in the shadowy depths.

Sally and George exchanged a nervous glance.

Suddenly, Raluca's PA lit up. The party halted while she answered it. "Yes, Control?"

A chill swept up my spine.

"Leaving the comfort and safety of Hallowed Hills and penetrating deeper into the outside is an unfortunate but necessary step if we are to neutralize the immediate threat posed by citizen Felix and his co-conspirators."

A brief pause.

"I was unable to report this information as it was revealed to me on the tarmac just a few minutestretches ago."

Another pause.

"Yes, of course, but if I fill the reports out now, the traitors hiding in the woods will launch their attack."

We all stood, riveted, Scorpio most of all.

"Nuclear missiles."

He shook his head and smiled wryly. It was the look of a man who respects the skill and depravity of his adversary.

The sun broke out and nearly blinded me. I stumbled and threw an arm across my face.

"As soon as we have the situation under control, we will let you know and complete all the necessary paperwork. Peace out."

Raluca flipped her PA closed and stuffed it back in its carrying case.

"All right," Scorpio declared, stepping forward and whipping the point of his stick in Raluca's direction, "we all know there's no band of merry brigands out in the woods here, waiting to launch an attack on Hallowed Hills. What are you really up to?"

A broad smile spread across Raluca's face. "We're going to recover the Self-Destruct Mechanism. And you're going to lead us right to it."

The guardians in a ring around us released the safety catch and raised their blasters.

Chapter 9

Of course, Raluca was not the only Alpha who had heard of the plot to recover the Self-Destruct Mechanism and wanted it for herself.

We plunged into the strange, furry fencing. Its long, supple fingers slapped at my face. I raised my arms to protect my eyes. That's why I didn't see them waiting for us just inside.

The guardians in front opened fire. As soon as I heard the fresh retort, I dropped to the ground. It was soft and forgiving.

There were the screams and grunts that normally accompany a firefight at close quarters. My thoughts turned to escape, but I wasn't sure where there was on this damned planet to escape to.

A few beams of laser light struck nearby. I could smell something burning.

I looked up. The battle raged all around. Some guardians lay on the ground, bodies twisted and smoking. Others were still alive and firing their weapons in earnest. Nearby, a few pairs struggled in hand-to-hand combat or smashed each other with rocks.

No merry band of brigands lurking in the woods? This was the second time Scorpio's operating assumptions had proven wrong. I was beginning to have doubts about his ability to lead.

In a place like the Bunker, merit has very little to do with position. Everybody knows all you have to do is become director of one of the private firms and you're set for life regardless how well you perform. After all, the annual reports are easily faked.

Of course, heading one of the conglomerates probably requires greater bureaucratic skills than martial. For all I knew, Scorpio was an expert in making his enemies disappear with the tail end of a pencil.

Thinking of enemies, I began to wonder who these typhoids attacking us were. Quickly, I scanned for Sally, George, Scorpio... anyone I could recognize.

That's when somebody hit me over the head and everything went black.

Later on I found out that twisted mass of fencing is called underbrush. Their taller, thicker relatives usually standing apart are trees. The green carpet is grass.

The stuff only grows on Earth. Hell, they don't teach us that back at the Bunker, but I still felt like an idiot for not knowing.

"George Walker," I moaned and touched a sore spot on the back of my head.

"Shut up," someone grumbled nearby and kicked me.

When I came to again, I tried adjusting my eyes to the light.

I was lying on the ground under the cover of some of those trees. The sun was low in the sky. In fact, it wasn't very bright here at all, but my brain seemed to think anything more than complete darkness was asking too much.

There was a little fire burning in a pit. Sitting on dead, stripped logs (formerly trees) arranged around the fire were some people I didn't know, including Zeus.

When he wasn't wearing his ridiculous headgear, he had a full mane of wavy, blond hair. His skin was light and his eyes a piercing blue. The outfit he wore was made entirely from the undergrowth. The twigs had been sewn together and padded with leaves. It looked uncomfortable, not to mention extremely drafty. Maybe he wasn't wearing his headgear, but he still looked ridiculous.

The few of his companions I could see mulling around were dressed the same way.

It was then that I realized Raluca wasn't an especially exceptional flaphead. They were all a bit looney here on Earth.

Next to me, peering coolly down, were Sally and George. They were still wearing the familiar clothes pressed out of synthetic fibers in factories back in the Bunker. Antinous had already been put in his bamboo cage. It was behind me. I could hear him sniffling.

It was clear what had happened. Raluca and her flying wheelchair were gone. They had been replaced by this strange man.

That's when I noticed Scorpio was missing.

Well, I thought to myself, Scorpio can take care of himself. Unless he's dead, in which case it doesn't matter.

Zeus smiled. I hate it when a citizen smiles. It's never a good thing. "We were starting to believe you would sleep all day."

I squinted into the light. "We're not dead?"

"It doesn't appear so. I'm sorry if you're disappointed."

"But I'm a traitor. We're all traitors. Control says so."

"Ah, yes, well, Control's not here. We're in the outside."

"True," I muttered, and in a flash of inspiration I added, "but we can't stay out here forever."

Zeus' face darkened.

"Don't provoke him!" George growled under his breath.

"We know what you're up to, Jeremy Whiles," Zeus told me and stood up. He walked around the fire and came to stand near my head. I had an awkward moment of deja-vu.

"I'm not up to anything," I muttered and blinked a few times, "unless it's staying alive."

Zeus reached out a hand. I stared at it as if trying to decide what it was before eventually latching on to it.

Zeus heaved me into the air. He was incredibly strong.

I landed with a wince. There was a hammering in my head.

"Please, sit," Zeus offered and gestured to a spot next to George.

Grudgingly, I took it. Anything seemed better than standing or lying. Once I got there, though, I was painfully disappointed.

Zeus and his ridiculous outfit of twigs began to pace. "I know all about this cloning business." He clicked his tongue and shook his head. "I don't know who put them up to it."

"I thought of it myself," interjected Antinous. "Scorpio agreed it was an excellent idea."

"Shut up, you!" Zeus roared suddenly and strode over to the cage with great, oversize steps. He planted his hands on his thighs and squatted next to the bamboo rails.

"There's not enough room to stand up in here!" Antinous complained and backed away to the other side.

Zeus stood up and walked around. Antinous scurried away again. "We can fix your problem with a saw if you like."

"Leave the boy alone!" Sally barked and rolled her eyes. "He's harmless."

"Yes, so he is." Zeus threw the boy a last, threatening glance before striding back to the fire pit. "What was I saying?"

"Cloning," Sally reminded him.

"Ah, yes!" A finger shot into the air. In a moment he had turned it against me. "You – or the other one – seem intent on causing as much damage to Scorpio's cause as possible. You, however – the one sitting here now – don't appear to have taken a side. This is the problem."

I didn't see my apparent lack of commitment as a problem at all. If anything, it was part of the solution. Survival was the problem, not whose side you chose.

Zeus took a step closer. "Now you're making matters worse down here for all of us."

I frowned. "But I just got here."

A slender, dark-skinned woman dressed in much the same way as Zeus stepped forward. Her small, delicate breasts were uncovered. She looked so differently on Earth I didn't recognize her, but as soon

114

as she spoke, I knew who she was.

"How long until he brings us to the Self-Destruct Mechanism?"

It was Lady Lagrange! She was the sexy and alluring host of one of the most popular vidshows in the Bunker, Audition For Freedom. Rumor had it that she and Van Johnson were bitter enemies. You didn't have to be in the Underground to know that.

Zeus cracked his knuckles. "We haven't got to that part yet."

"He's a liar, you know. Just ask his friends."

"He's not my friend," George snarled and gave me a nasty glare.

"Aw," purred Lady Lagrange and approached the dead, stripped tree where we were sitting. "Do you feel betrayed?"

George didn't answer, but it was plain to everyone how he felt.

"Weren't you his boss?"

"He was always reliable."

"Yes, well, just because someone shows up for work every day and does what he's told doesn't mean he hasn't got an agenda all his own."

Lady Lagrange had long, beautiful legs. And they were hairless! Apparently, they had access to more razors than we did back in the Lower Quarters of Q-16 Sector.

Sally turned to me. "What is your agenda, anyway?"

I smirked. "How would I know?"

Lady Lagrange laughed. "You want revenge."

There was a brief lull in the conversation. "It's not a plan with a happy ending," I finally pointed out. "Especially for myself."

"You're a dead man no matter where you go on Gaia. You have enemies but no friends. And it's because of these people, Jeremy. They dragged you in against your will. Don't think you can fool us. We have information. We know what the real Terry Renfield has been up to."

"You know where he is?" The words tumbled out before I could stop them.

Lady Lagrange put one of her feet up on the log next to me. Her leg was as delicate as her breasts.

I noticed Sally noticing that I was noticing, so I lingered longer than I otherwise might have.

"He wants to get his hands on the Self-Destruct Mechanism just like the rest of us."

"So he's here on Earth." I looked around as if I might be lurking behind a nearby tree.

Zeus shook his head. "Not yet," he thundered. "But he's on his way. He's sent John the Baptist's lackey, Lance Trevor, on ahead."

"But Scorpio is the only one who knows where the Self-Destruct Mechanism is!" Sally objected.

"Not any more," Zeus told her flatly. "We think Terry knows where it is, too." He shrugged. "Anyway, the fact is, we don't. Scorpio's the one we needed, and John the Baptist's still got him. That's where Lance Trevor is, too, by the way."

Lady Lagrange grunted derisively, picked up her leg, and trotted off to the fire.

"But," he continued, "this is a situation we'll soon remedy. The importance of having you –"

Lady Lagrange finished off his sentence. "– is we know Terry Renfield will come sniffing you out. In that case, we don't need Scorpio."

"It will be an uncomfortable situation," Zeus pointed out. "We'll have to keep you two separated until we've got what we want."

"Separated?" I frowned.

Lady Lagrange laughed that petite little laugh of hers, the one that made her famous. "If we're not careful, one of you will kill the other one."

"Just kill this one right now," Sally suggested. "Terry won't know the difference."

Zeus shook his head. "He's on his way here now, but John the Baptist is a fool if she thinks he has no way of keeping tabs on us. He's playing a game of his own. I don't know what it is, but I'd rather not to deter him. Let him come. And if that means letting the clone live for the time being, so be it."

Lady Lagrange threw back her long, silky hair. "I agree with Complicity. He's dangerous and unpredictable. It's better if this citizen were terminated. Every last one of him."

Zeus reached into his nest of twigs and leaves and pulled out his PA. He had a call. Gesturing for silence, he flipped it open. "Yes, Control."

A hush fell over us.

A weary look crossed Zeus' face. "Yes, that's my present location."

There was a slight pause.

"The satellites don't pick up any terrorists in the vicinity because we killed them all this morning."

Another pause.

"You assigned us the mission yourself, Control. If the data is missing, I would suggest we start immediately searching for signs of the saboteurs. Before they delete the evidence themselves, that is."

Someone snapped a twig. Zeus winced and made a cutting motion in the air with his hand.

"I was unaware citizen Raluca's team had been reassigned to the task. I'll return at once." Lips tightly pursed, Zeus snapped his PA shut and shoved it back into his clothing. "Damn!" he roared. "Where is my tablet? I have to get programming!"

"Will you have time to supplant John the Baptist's subroutines before the ceremony tonight?"

He glanced at the lowering sun and shrugged. "I think so. She's not the best coder on Gaia. But it's going to take a while to get the most recent updates. I haven't synched up since early yesterday."

He muttered something under his breath and continued looking for his tablet, whatever that was.

"What's going on?" George wanted to know.

"It's a search routine!" Lady Lagrange sighed. "John the Baptist added it to the codebase. Now he's got to neutralize it or we'll be traitors for staying out here."

"What's the ceremony he was talking about?" Antinous wanted to know. He was nervous. I think he thought they were going to cook him and eat him.

"Oh, you'll see. We're all going to paint our faces and relive a story."

"A story?"

"Yes, a very special one. It reminds us of who we are and why we are here."

"Really?" The boy sounded genuinely interested. "Have I ever heard of it?"

"Most certainly not," Lady Lagrange scoffed. "Only those of us Olympians who have reconnected with Gaia know it. You are a mere mortal. One day, you will die."

I didn't know what Lady Lagrange knew that I didn't or if she was just trying to make trouble, but I am not a liar. Sure, sometimes I bend the truth, but only when my skin's on the line. You think you'd do any differently?

One thing she did say was true, though. I didn't have any friends, and if I was going to keep wearing this same skin of mine, I knew I'd have to find some fast.

Audition For Freedom is a lively vidshow where citizens accused of various crimes have a chance to defend themselves against their accusers. There is a panel of three that decides the outcome of the cases. The decision of the panel is final, and the sentence is carried out immediately. In fact, the only way to survive an appearance on Audition For Freedom is to be hilariously funny, which is admittedly difficult if you are fighting for your life. The most popular feeds are those where the accuser suddenly becomes the accused. The live studio audience just loves it when that happens.

Lady Lagrange, the seductive host of the show, always dresses in some absurd but attention-grabbing costume. Once she wore reactor shielding and bags of PermaChunky for shoes. She had tins of Algatine for earrings. Clink! clink! clink! they sounded every time she turned her head or made a sudden move. Another time she wore a heavy, furry hat half again as tall as she was. The poor sod who was defending herself had to keep holding it up. Lady Lagrange made it clear she would be very angry if it sagged. I even remember a time she wore patches of skin from the previous feed's victims, all stitched together like a quilt.

Although it was the panel who decided, Lady Lagrange was the star. She was often known to intervene with the judges one way or another, and they always listened to her recommendation.

One of the reasons why citizens waited with such anticipation to see the next episode of Audition For Freedom is to see what Lady Lagrange would wear next. She never wore the same thing twice.

I had seen her in a lot of outlandish clothing before, but never one made up of leaves and twigs.

The next day, after they had removed the paint from their faces, Zeus and his followers broke camp. Antinous was let out of his cage and deposited onto one of the dead tree trunks while the others packed up.

Breakfast consisted of one of the most bizarre foodstuffs I had ever seen. They called them nuts and berries. George, Sally, and I turned them over in our hands suspiciously, but Antinous shoved them into his mouth with relish.

"Eat them!" he urged. "They're good." But his tongue was red and some of the juice dribbled from the corner of his mouth. It looked like blood.

Eventually, hunger got the better of us. George tried first. He bit down, winced, and then his eyes opened in surprise. "George Walker," he muttered and began shoveling the things in his mouth.

The taste was beyond description! The fact that there *was* taste seemed far less important than that there was so much of it. The berries had more than the nuts, but the nuts were obviously more sustaining. I could have eaten fistfuls, but as it was we were only given enough to dent our hunger.

We spent the rest of the time licking our palms and our fingers until they stood us up and marched us off through the forest.

It just so happened that Lady Lagrange had taken a position in the column just in front of me.

I cleared my throat and said, "I couldn't help but notice that some of you Olympians were killed by laser fire yesterday. When you kidnapped us."

"Excuse me?" She turned and fixed me with a hard, fathomless glare.

"You told Antinous he was a mortal. That'd he'd die. Implying you won't."

"Oh, that." The glare dissipated into a harmless, little laugh. She fell back enough to be walking next to me. "We're not crazy, you know. This body dies, yes." She indicated herself. "But we Olympians are reborn."

I pretended to understand. "If you don't mind me asking, where are we going?"

"But I do mind you asking. Is that why you're talking to me?"

"Yes."

Maybe she wasn't used to such candor. I don't know, but the novelty of the experience seemed to relax her. "Zeus is tracking down John the Baptist. She's got Scorpio which means she knows where to find the Self-Destruct Mechanism."

"You mean she wants to bring Control down, too?"

Lady Lagrange lifted her eyebrows ever so slightly. "What else do you think she'd want to do with it?"

"Well, it's what you want, too. Why not let her do it?" But I already knew the answer to that question.

"And let John the Baptist become the undisputed leader of New Gaia?" she scoffed and rolled her eyes. "I think not."

"Lance Trevor's with them."

"So?"

"I want a shot at him."

"I see. And what about when Terry comes looking for you? Will you want special treatment then, too?"

"*I* am Terry Renfield. I'll deal with the other one when the time comes. But Lance is first."

Lady Lagrange looked amused. "I'll see what I can arrange."

I wanted to say more, but it suddenly seemed as if I would have to shout. These things called birds were making an awful lot of noise.

It was hard to see them. They seem to be everywhere and yet nowhere at all.

Up ahead a man stumbled and fell to the ground. He was shaking terribly. Unlike the others, his skin was pale and covered with rashes. No one helped him up.

"He's got a disease," I hissed and went out of my way to avoid getting too close.

The poor bloke lay there, mouth hanging open and staring at the undersides of the trees, seemingly oblivious as we passed him by. His breathing was short and labored.

"Oh, no," Lady Lagrange laughed and shook her head. "That fool wandered into a hotspot without an ecopack. It's his own fault."

"A hotspot?" I turned and gave him another look. He had clambered over onto his hands and knees and was trying to get up.

"Yes. There are still a great deal of them here on Earth. We know where most of them are. The satellites help identify when they've moved. It has something to do with the weather." She shrugged.

After that, someone came trotting up the line with a message for her and she headed off.

Still, I was pleased. Sure, she knew I had some angle, and I knew she did, too. But she talked to me, and I thought she was telling me the truth.

Or enough of the truth, whatever that means.

It was one of those strange coincidences that on Earth a daystretch lasts almost exactly the amount of time between sunrises.

Zeus and the others all slept soon after it got dark, and they all rose together sometime after it got light again. Back in the Bunker, there was always a lightbulb on somewhere. We each had our own individual daystretches, and we slept when it was the nighttime that had been assigned to us.

We captives were out of synch with our hosts. We got sleepy long after everyone else had bedded down, and we didn't want to wake up when it was time to move on.

Of course, the perfect time to conspire is when no one else is listening in.

"I saw you getting real cozy with Lady Lagrange," Sally sneered softly in the darkness.

The four of us had each been given a blanket woven from thin, dark green strands, presumably made from the fibers of the trees or plants.

We slept on the soft, damp earth, surrounded in a tight circle by our captors. I quickly discovered that the earth was more than just a pile of dirt and the occasional rock. It had contours, and sometimes there were dark knots of long, hard tubes that ran along the ground. I couldn't imagine what purpose they served except to keep me awake at night.

Antinous had learned to be on his best behavior. After that first day, they didn't put him back in the cage, although they kept it conspicuously nearby.

I smiled. "Are you jealous?"

"No," Sally retorted defensively.

Now it was George's turn to weigh in. "We don't want you stabbing us in the back. You already did once."

My brow scrunched up. "When?" I didn't know what he was talking about.

"You didn't blow up the communications equipment on the asteroid like you said you would."

I was about to point out that I had, but Sally interjected.

"You're a demolitions man. You know how to blow things up. They wouldn't have been able to put it back together so quickly if you had *really* wanted it out of commission."

I didn't know what to say. The world seemed horribly unfair. I was being blamed for promises being broken I hadn't even made.

"Look, I've got a plan to get us out of this mess." The words came from my own mouth. They surprised me just as much as they did George, Sally, and Antinous.

"Really?" George's eyes narrowed. I could see the wheels churning, even if they did so with difficulty. "So do I."

"Scorpio always made the best plans," Antinous chimed in. He was chewing on his fingernails.

"I beg to differ," I scoffed.

"Scorpio's not here," Sally reminded him gently.

"Yeah, that's the problem!" The hand flew from his mouth. "I say we loose these flapheads and go get him."

George rolled his eyes. "You want to sneak away now?"

Antinous shrugged. "Sure."

"And then what?"

Antinous blinked.

"What do we eat? Where do we sleep?"

Antinous shrugged and waved towards some nearby bushes. "We find where Raluca's camping and set Scorpio free. I'm sure we can find berries and nuts, too. Or eat one of those animal things. I overheard someone who said he's done it."

George was growing frustrated. I could see he was doing his best not to wake the others.

I jumped in. "But Antinous, we've been looking for days. Do you have any idea where they are?"

"Of course I do."

We all perked up.

"How?"

"He's got a locator implanted in his skull. And I have the receiver."

There was a brief moment of silence.

"Why didn't you tell us before?" Sally burst out.

Cringing, we all took a quick look around. Fortunately, no one was stirring in his sleep.

Antinous shrugged. "You didn't ask."

George gnashed his teeth and flexed his hands. They seemed to want to wrap around the boy's neck.

"Well that changes everything," I muttered and glanced at George. "It doesn't solve the food problem, though."

"Ask him how far away they are."

I asked.

"I'm not sure," was Antinous' answer. "I don't know how to read it."

"Why don't you give it to me?"

Antinous drew back. "No."

"Antinous," Sally prodded, using her softest and most inoffensive voice. "How else are we supposed to find Scorpio?"

A sudden idea seemed to occur to him. "I know! I'll hold it and you can read what it says."

He would only show the locator to Sally. While they huddled, George and I sat in the middle of the camp and eyeballed each other.

"You told us the truth about Lance," he finally admitted. "I guess that should count for something."

Damn right, I thought.

A few moments later, Sally was back. She was excited. "We're close," she whispered. "We could get there in a few hourstretches."

I looked up. There was light coming from the full moon above us. "You think we can find our way?"

"It's worth a try," Sally said and winked. I wasn't sure if she meant it or was just trying to manipulate me, but either way it worked.

Chapter 10

Apparently, Sally had some experience with a locator like the one Scorpio had in his head, because every time Antinous showed her the receiver she seemed to know exactly where to go. For a few hourstretches we plodded in a fairly straight line through the dark. Occasionally we got sidetracked by some kind of obstacle: a ditch or running water or a cluster of trees so thick we had to go around. The time passed uneventfully, and the air grew chilly.

The moon sank in the sky, and after a while one of us or another began to catch a foot on something unseen. We could see better, though, when we broke out of the trees into a wide open area covered by grass. Of course, the sky was more difficult to ignore out there, but I was starting to get used to it.

We came upon Raluca and her underlings just as the horizon was brightening. They had camped behind a low hill.

I suppose it should have struck me that no one was watching Zeus' camp at night. I suppose that's why we weren't talking any precautions, either. We just stumbled over the top of the hill and there they were.

They were waiting for us. It turns out *they* had set guards.

More surprising still, the first shots of the battle came from behind.

Back in the Bunker, there is an official checklist for almost any pre-approved situation you can find yourself in. If there's no official checklist, then chances are what you are doing is treasonous.

What's the first thing you should do when you find yourself caught in an unexpected firefight? We dropped to the ground. What's the second thing you do? Craning my head, I took a look around. Sure enough, Zeus and his merry band of Olympians had followed us. He was leading a detachment past one side of the hill, blaster in hand, firing merrily away.

It doesn't happen often, but at that moment I felt stupid. How many nights had they stayed up waiting to see if we'd go?

The third thing you do is get the hell out of there. I started to crawl forward.

"Where are you going?" Sally demanded, peeking up from between the apparent safety of her arms.

"We'll get picked off up here one by one."

George started after me. "If he's going, I'm going."

Antinous surprised us all. "Me, too." He swallowed thickly.

"People are dying down there," I pointed out. Not that I really cared one way or another, but who needed dead weight at a time when decisions had to made in split stretches?

"I know. But Scorpio's down there, too." His voice seemed to be scraping his throat.

I think they call it bravery. I'm not talking about the kind that comes easily, either. You know what I mean. The kind where you get all the credit but didn't sweat any. Sometimes you jump blindly into a situation, other times you don't know the risks or it's simply not something you're bothered about doing. Afterwards, other people come up and pat you on the back and talk about how brave you were, but the compliments ring hollow. You know you don't deserve them.

Antinous, on the other hand, was about to crap in his drawers. This was the real thing.

I led the way into the thick of the battle.

The Betas were doing all the fighting. Despite Zeus' initial enthusiasm, he preferred to stay behind the lines and scream at his followers to kill and maim more efficiently. Underlings, it seems, are expendable no matter what security clearance they have.

At the base of the hill we started encountering the dead and wounded. Behind me, I heard Antinous retching.

Slowly, meter by meter, we got closer to the camp. We left most of the fighting behind. Up ahead I could see Raluca's airborne gravity chair. She was agitated, to say the least. She coughed and wheezed and tried to spit out orders, but it didn't look like there was anyone near or alive enough to hear them.

My hand closed over something hard, warm, and metallic. It fit snugly between my fingers. When I looked, I saw that I was gripping the nose of a recently fired laser pistol. Its previous owner was lying nearby, missing a necessary part of her brain.

How convenient, I thought, and picked it up the proper way, which is to say by its handle.

It was powered up and ready to go.

When your life is on the line, time seems slow down. You can react to events that in normal life would have passed you by in the blink of an eye.

Someone was about to step on my face. Not any more. He fell over screaming, one knee smoking and partially detached. Nothing the medibot couldn't fix, I thought to myself and carried on.

Raluca was about twenty meters ahead. Her face was red and puffy and she was pounding the armrests of her gravity chair. It zigzagged dangerously in the air. Things weren't going as she had planned, I assumed.

I began to wonder if all Alphas didn't experience a similar, endless frustration.

Sitting cross-legged on the ground, still dressed in his boots and brown vest and not without his glasses, was Scorpio. His stick was laid out across his lap. It looked like he was meditating, except I could see his eyes skipping intently about as he watched the progress of the battle. He was attached by a thick chain to a boulder some ten meters away.

Suddenly, Raluca drew a laser pistol of her own. Her gravity chair sank to the earth and hovered a few meters above the ground near Scorpio's head.

"Your little friends have come to save you," she sneered and pointed the gun at him. "You know, I wonder... Would they show such enthusiasm if they knew you couldn't lead them to the Self-Destruct Mechanism?"

Maybe George thought I was taking aim at Scorpio. Maybe he hadn't seen the drama that was unfolding in front of us. All I know is that his hand came down hard on my forearm just as I fired. The shot, which would have hit Raluca right between the eyes, instead struck the underside of her gravity chair.

The wheelchair rolled over. Raluca, who appeared to be strapped in, screamed, her hair dangling in loose, wet clumps underneath her. The pistol dropped to the ground with a dull thud.

A low, grinding noise started up and gained in volume. It quickly worked itself up into a whining crescendo. With a sudden BANG! the boosters ignited and the wheelchair took off.

It must have been top speed. I never realized a gravity chair could be outfitted with such a powerful propulsion system. I guess it's one of the perks of being an Alpha.

The gravity chair shot through the air, two jets of orange fire shooting out the back and Raluca's horrified voice trailing after it.

Who knows where she would have ended up. The moon? The stars? A communications asteroid?

It's a moot point, because wherever she was heading to, the boulder Scorpio was chained to came first.

After the dust and spray of metallic debris faded from the air, I noticed that all sounds of fighting had stopped.

I took a stretch to look around. The Betas were all lying dead or dying on the ground. Wisps of smoke wafted from their bodies into the early morning air and then were disrupted and swept away by the breeze.

Well, almost all of them. Lady Lagrange had managed to survive. She and Zeus – laser pistols still in hand – were standing not far away, surveilling the damage like the rest of us. Her face was smudged with dirt, but apart from a bleeding gash on her thigh and a quickly swelling lump near her temple, she seemed unhurt.

Antinous was the first to do anything noticeable. With a cry of delight, he got up and ran towards Scorpio.

Our man, too, had climbed to his feet. Amazingly, he seemed to be unscathed, although he was shaken by the explosion. The chain had been severed, but it still bound him tightly around the waist.

Scorpio fixed me with an intense stare while Antinous worked on his bonds. "Why did you do it?" he demanded, eyes narrowing as if trying to penetrate my thoughts through sheer force of will. His hands shook slightly.

Sally and George seemed just as interested to hear the answer. They climbed to their feet and dusted off their clothes, but their eyes were on me.

I shrugged. "Let's call it an investment."

Scorpio snorted with contempt and folded his hands tightly under his armpits.

"I got it!" Antinous shouted out. The chain fell from Scorpio's waist.

Zeus and Lady Lagrange were approaching.

George, Sally, and I spun on our heels and aimed our pistols at them. No one fired, and they stopped.

Zeus smiled awkwardly. "Um," he began. "Parlay?" He held up his laser pistol.

I thought I saw George twitch. Hell, I twitched. My gun almost went off.

And why not? If they met their end there, in some primal field on the planet Earth under the dimming starlight, they ought to be pleased. After all, they couldn't die. They'd be reborn, maybe somewhere nearby. In a hotspot, for example. The genetic mutations would no doubt help them in convincing others that they were the spawn of Titans.

"I appreciate your fealty." Scorpio spoke calmly and quietly even as he came to stand between George and Sally. "But please don't kill them." He laid his stick across the barrel of their guns and pressed them towards the ground. His hands were still shaking.

They turned on him, astonished. "Are you pumped up on meds?" George spat.

"Now's our chance!" Sally blurted out. "Let's blast them!"

I kept my eye on Zeus and Lady Lagrange, ready to shoot one of them down if he tried something funny.

"All my followers are gone," Scorpio replied. "There's no friendly faces waiting for us back at Hallowed Hills. You want to stay out here forever?" He held up his PA. "I'm an Alpha, yes, but I can't go up against all the others. I wouldn't even make it through the main entrance."

I think Zeus was about to say something, but at that moment his PA lit up. "Damn," he grunted under his breath and drew it out of its carrying case. He flipped it open and shook his head. "It's Control again."

Lady Lagrange smiled. "It looks like John the Baptist was a much better coder than you thought."

That night, we sat around a fire somewhere in the wilderness, eyeballing each other suspiciously. It was George and Sally, Scorpio and Antinous, Zeus and Lady Lagrange, and – of course – myself. There wasn't anybody who would sit next to me.

Brutalizer, Alibaba, and Starbuoy had all been killed during the battle. We found their twisted bodies about twenty meters away from the main action. It was easy enough to read what had happened. Brutalizer was trying to make an escape and Alibaba tracked her down. Brutalizer must have got a lucky shot off first and took Alibaba out, but Starbuoy wasn't having it. He nailed her in the back of the head, and then someone else nailed him.

It's the familiar ending to a sordid tale that repeats itself daystretch in and daystretch out back in the Bunker.

We sat on four logs arranged in a square so we could keep keep an eye on each other. Zeus and Lady Lagrange had finally decided to ditch the leaves and twigs in favor of overalls and boots, the standard Bunker fare.

No one said much. We were too busy trying to figure out what everybody else's angle was.

"It was a glorious end for your Olympians." Scorpio, kicking up his green, baggy pants, seemed slightly amused. "You spent so many yearstretches building them up."

"Oh, no," Zeus replied and ran a thick, muscled hand through his mane of blond hairs. "It was a heavy blow to the organization, no doubt. But we're by no means finished."

"This was just a contingent," Lady Lagrange explained. "Zeus never gathers us all in one place."

"And," Zeus added, glancing at me with a hint of the admiration that was to come, "a sacrifice well worth the death of John the Baptist."

"You said Lance Trevor was supposed to be with her," Lady Lagrange recalled suddenly. "I searched through all the corpses, but I couldn't find him."

Zeus threw his hands in the air. "It's the intelligence that was brought to me! Maybe he got away."

Both of them turned on Scorpio.

That one shook his head, stony-faced. "I don't know what you're talking about. He was never here."

"Maybe he slipped away before we got to Hallowed Hills," Sally suggested unhelpfully.

I could see Zeus and Lady Lagrange trying to make up their minds whether or not Scorpio was telling the truth. But trying to read his face was like reading the metro timetable back at the Bunker. It only told you what you *didn't* want to know.

"You made a deal with him, didn't you?" Zeus spoke up and fingered his laser pistol.

Scorpio scuffled the ground with the bottoms of his animal skin boots but otherwise didn't answer.

"Where's Van Johnson?" George wanted to know. "He's not among the dead, either."

"You mean Van Johnson the vidstar?" Zeus asked.

"The one and the same," Lady Lagrange answered and sighed.

Zeus, clearly disturbed, turned and stared accusingly at his sidekick. "You mean you knew he was here and you didn't tell me?"

"I thought I'd get a shot at him during the firefight, but I lost sight of him. After that, I had more important things on my mind." She shrugged. "I didn't *know* he was going to be here or I would have mentioned it. I saw him and I took my chance." Cocking her head curiously, she asked, "Why do you care about Van Johnson, anyway? He's just a vidstar."

"You're just a vidstar, too." A smirk grew on Zeus' face. "Remember, while we're out here, you're working for me. I don't want you going off and doing something reckless! Take care of your personal rivalries on your own time."

Antinous bit his lip nervously. "You believe her? Just like that?"

Lady Lagrange cut him a threatening look while the rest of us smiled.

"Everybody knows they hate each other, Antinous," I told him.

"That doesn't mean anything," he replied and yawned as if he were bored. "Most of us here hate each other."

More silence followed. The eyes roamed, trying to read the thoughts. Were we really working together? And what were we trying to accomplish?

I knew what I wanted: a free pass back to my old life, including Sally. Never before had my job digging through rocks sounded so appealing.

Scorpio, Antinous, Sally, and George wanted to take out Control. At least, that's what they claimed.

I took a moment to look them over. Even if she didn't love me anymore, I knew Sally well enough to know she was committed. But Scorpio... he was clearly the leader of their little conspiracy. He was sticking his neck out. What did he have to gain by betraying everyone else? I could only conclude he was serious, too. And whatever Scorpio wanted, Antinous would want.

But George was another story. Like a bowl of slop, it was impossible to classify him with any accuracy. Was he roast beef and potatoes with asparagus or sugar-coated hamburger and spindly fries? Hard to say, even once you've tasted.

As for Zeus and Lady Lagrange, the feeling I had was they were more interested in keeping the Self-Destruct Mechanism out of Scorpio's hands than using it themselves. Or – worse – they were aiming for a take-over as soon as Control went offline.

And considering it was worse, the latter possibility was more likely.

Eventually, I had had enough of the silence. There was no point to sitting around and brooding. "So," I said, loudly striking the tops of my legs with the palms of my hands. The others stirred as if waking from a dream. "We're going together to fetch the Self-Destruct Mechanism, is that it?"

Zeus and Sally nodded blankly, but George was sneering. "We'd better hurry," he said, "or Renfield will get there first."

I swallowed the obvious retort. There was no point in arguing with him. I'd settle the score when the time was ripe.

"I wouldn't put stock in the claim he knows any more than the rest of us," I said. "Excepting Scorpio, of course."

"But that's what our agents tell us," Lady Lagrange insisted. "Terry knows where it is."

A wry smile took hold of my lips. "I see. And are these the same agents who also told you that Lance Trevor was with Raluca?"

Lady Lagrange pursed her lips and glared at me with unrestrained hostility.

"Sounds like a trick to me," I continued. "And I should know."

Scorpio leaned forward. "You mean Terry's got a plan of his own?"

I nodded. "Look, he betrayed you. You're an Alpha. There's got to be something in it for him, something that makes it a reasonable proposition to go head to head with you."

Sally was growing agitated. "You've got it all wrong! I don't know what you're trying to pull, but it sounds to me like *you're* the one with the hidden agenda. None of us knows how they got those transceivers back up and running so fast. We don't know what happened up there. Something could have gone wrong. You saw the feed on the tube. He set off some kind of alarm. It's a miracle he managed to escape."

The others considered us both. They were trying to make up their minds. Problem was, there wasn't much to go on.

Zeus blew out a long, exasperated breath. "If Jeremy's right and Terry is a conspiring traitorous criminal crackhead, then Jeremy's a conspiring traitorous criminal crackhead, too, and we shouldn't believe him. And if Complicity's right, then Terry's just an honest citizen overtaken by events and we should trust him, which means we should also trust Jeremy."

"That doesn't make any sense!" Antinous snapped.

"Exactly." Zeus stood up. "The best we can do is continue as we were. Scorpio will tell us where the Self-Destruct Mechanism is and quick as a termination we'll go and get it and –"

"And what?"

Zeus turned his thorny eyes in my direction. "No one knows what the Self-Destruct Mechanism actually looks like or how it's used. So we'll just have to see once we get there."

Once we get there things will unfold quickly and unexpectedly is what he meant. We'd all have to watch our backs.

Scorpio slashed at the air in front of him with his stick and turned his squarish lenses up at Zeus. "I will tell you nothing."

"But how else are we going to –"

"I will tell you how it's going to work," Scorpio continued. "There will be no discussion."

Zeus quivered with fury, but he managed to control himself.

"It's very simple, really. I'll lead the way, and you will follow." A thin smile formed on his bloodless lips.

"But you could lead us anywhere!" Lady Lagrange leaped to her feet and settled in next to her boss.

"I suppose that's true. But there's only one place I mean to go. And that's where the Self-Destruct Mechanism can be found."

"We won't even know when we've arrived. You could sneak off and retrieve it and we'd have no idea until you were gone."

Scorpio nodded. "I suppose that's true as well." The smile widened. "It looks like you'll just have to trust me." At that, a hand flew to his mouth. He was trying to feign shock and dismay, but it was an unconvincing performance. "What an unenviable prospect! I'm glad I'm not in your shoes."

The smile by now had grown into a full-fledged grin.

"What do you think it will be like when Control's offline?"

"What?"

I repeated myself.

"What kind of a question is that?"

"A sincere one. It's hard to imagine, isn't it? These Alphas don't trust each other one widget. You think that's going to change when Control's suddenly out of the picture? They'll spend a lot of time settling old scores. Everyone will."

"No, no," Sally insisted. "There's all sorts of preparation in the works. You're worried about Zeus and Scorpio?" She brushed my concerns away with a dramatic wave of her hand. "Anyway, it's the fear of Control that makes people behave that way. You should know that."

I had my doubts about Control being the root of all evil. It seemed to me the root of all evil lay somewhere much closer to home. "You didn't answer my question."

The answer I received was less than reassuring. Sally stammered and she guffawed, but it was clear she had no idea, either.

We were trudging along through a hilly hinterland. The air was stagnant and heavy with moisture. Each of us carried a backpack with supplies. It turned out Raluca's party had packets of powdered Vitamim with them. There was plenty of water around, but those who were already familiar with life on Earth warned us not to drink any. Each creek or pond was carefully tested with a special program running on the Alphas' PAs. I don't know what it was meant to detect, but they rarely let us fill up our bottles and drink.

On Earth, there are other living things besides human beings. They told me that the trees and the plants are alive. I found it hard to believe. But the creepy-crawly things and the ones that run around on four legs, that was an easier sell. Scorpio called them animals.

We ate as many nuts and berries as we could find that were safe. Fortunately, Zeus and Lady Lagrange turned out to be adept hunters, too. They fashioned primitive weapons called bows and shot sharpened sticks at the animals. The elasticity was provided by strings made from the sinews of previous kills. I was intrigued and – much to the delight of everyone else – tried to make my own, but I never could get the damned thing work.

The animals on Earth are tasty. Zeus and Lady Lagrange claimed there were different kinds, but they all looked the same to me. We pulled the skins off, tore their guts out, and roasted their muscles over a fire at night. Then we ate them.

I'll never forget the way animal fat tastes. Just thinking about it makes me salivate.

Like the water and the berries, we had to be careful about the animals. Sometimes when we retrieved a kill we found a sickly looking beast. Even to my innocent eyes it was obvious something was wrong. Patches of fur were missing, and they smelled horribly. More often than not, the creature was just a loose bag of skin and bones. Other times there were covered with bulging, discolored growths.

Zeus and Lady Lagrange told us that the animals had no way of knowing where the hotspots were or which was the good and bad water. Strangely enough, they seemed genuinely sad for these sickly specimens.

It was when they showed such signs of sympathy that I thought maybe life really would be different when Control was gone. After all, if they were capable of caring for some ignorant, four-legged animal, then they could most certainly do it for a fellow citizen?

We had a bot with us, too. Raluca had had the foresight to attach a medibot to her company. It rolled along in our midst on four wheels, carrying a full stock of the liquids and sterile gauze and reconstructive tissue you'd expect. Its many arms were tucked inside the barrel-like body.

I think we all felt a little bit safer with the medibot in our company, as if it were some kind of insurance we had taken out against ourselves.

Occasionally we passed signs of the old earthling civilization. These usually consisted of half-buried, metal contraptions and cables snaking along the ground. Other times they were structures, or the remains of structures. These were made of a rough, grey material similar to stone but crumbling, revealing long, thin poles of rusted metal tied together at weird angles like wire frames.

The metal contraptions had doors. Most of them were hanging open or had been ripped off entirely and were missing. Sometimes there was a round wheel mounted in the front. I asked what they were, but no one could tell me. There seemed to be an awful lot of them.

Zeus and Lady Lagrange seemed very much in their element in this strange, ghostly world. It was hard to imagine them back in the Bunker, even if they were wearing overalls now. Scorpio didn't seem out of place exactly, but he didn't look like he belonged there, either. The look on his face was determined. I don't think he particularly enjoyed it out there, but it didn't bother him, either. He was on a mission.

George and Sally reacted to Earth each in their own particular ways. Sally seemed intrigued. She was interested in every new encounter or sensation. I don't think she ever felt unsafe. George, however, was spooked. He grew withdrawn, and his eyes skittered uneasily about. I think the insects bothered him the most, especially the flying ones.

As for myself, I couldn't make up my mind. It was interesting to see where we had come from as a race, but it was also clear that this way of living – whatever it was – had failed. The Bunker was all I knew, and we had set out to bring it down. What would take its place?

I didn't know, but I was sure the answer couldn't be found out there.

Chapter 11

"Rain!"

Oh shit, I thought and ran for cover.

Apparently, the sky was filled with more evils than just the sun and a boundless, open expanse. There was also thunder. And rain.

A few of the drops hit my clothing. There was a harsh hissing and some of the material bubbled up. One drop struck my hand. It felt like someone had stuck a needle between my fingers. I wanted to suck on the skin where it hurt, but I knew better.

Fortunately, there was some shelter provided by an overhang in the cliff face we had been skirting. It wasn't enough to completely shield us, but Zeus and Lady Lagrange had a quilt of sorts they had made from vines, twigs, and leaves. We pulled it overhead, listened to the hissing as the plant fibers were cooked up by the acid in the rain, and waited.

The air grew steamy from the vapor released by the falling droplets. The shower didn't last long, however. Before we knew it we were packing the quilt away. Lady Lagrange told us we were lucky. Apparently, this was the dry season, whatever that meant.

The rain spoiled all the clean water wherever it landed. It would take days for the environment to flush out all the toxins. Fortunately, as I later learned, it didn't always rain everywhere at once.

We had to take precautions for our feet. The tainted water collected in puddles that quickly evaporated or were absorbed into the ground, but even after they had disappeared the muck and mud left behind were harmful. Zeus and Lady Lagrange had specially made slippers with soles of stone. Scorpio's boots were resistant to the acid. The rest of us, however, were clad in the cheap, poorly made footwear provided to everyone free of charge back at the Bunker.

Fortunately, in such rocky terrain there were plenty of smooth, flat stones to be found. We strapped them to the bottoms of our feet.

Not so fortunately, there was nothing we could do to protect the innards of our medibot. After a few such bouts of rain, it ceased functioning. Despite our best efforts, we couldn't power it up again and had to leave it behind.

More than a few of us glanced regretfully back at the strange sight of that barrel-like torso standing crooked and deserted on a patch of grey, lifeless rock. It struck me as some kind of science probe from another world, sent to gather information about a strange, new planet and beam it back to its makers. Except this world had killed the probe, and the makers, discouraged, would never come.

I'll bet it's there now, still abandoned and a bit more rusty.

"Yes, Control. That information is correct."

Zeus listened intently.

"It is indeed an extraordinary distance to have covered since leaving Hallowed Hills this morning. In pursuit of terrorists and criminals, the most amazing feats may be accomplished." He smiled to himself as if savoring the irony of his joke.

Another pause as Control confided suspicions of sabotage.

"Of course. We'll return at once." He flipped his PA closed and shook his head. "I'll need a few hourstretches to clear this boehner up."

"All this programming just slows us down," Antinous complained.

"Can't you find the search routine and purge it?" Scorpio demanded, eyes narrowing suspiciously.

Zeus snorted in frustration. "You don't think I've tried? It keeps replicating itself."

Scorpio was already pulling an oblong object from his pack. I had seen Zeus using one just like it. It was about three times the size of a PA. They called it a tablet, and it was how they accessed Control's codebase.

Programming, it would seem, is a very exclusive talent, and it requires a very exclusive vocabulary. When Scorpio and Zeus started talking about callbacks, interrupts, and semaphores, everyone else's eyes glazed over and wandered away. They would be at it for a while, so I decided to go for a walk.

We were in a strange place. Well, to be honest, everywhere in the outside was a strange place. But this was even stranger than trees and creepy-crawlers and acid rain.

Rocks. They were everywhere. Squatting on the grassy ground, some of the largest could have blocked an entire corridor back in the Bunker. Others were small enough to sit on. And everywhere there were little tiny ones that you could squeeze between your toes.

Scorpio told me they were mineral and lava deposits. He tried explaining what that meant, but I couldn't get my head around it. I just nodded until he stopped talking.

Between the huge slabs of rock there were the shrubs, round, bulbous formations like tabletops. The leaves were tough and small, almost needle-like.

Occasionally, there were cracks in the ground, vast rifts we sometimes had to travel kilometers around to cross. There were cliffs, too, and more often than not behind them rose some of the most enormous structures I had ever seen. They were piles of stone, far bigger than even the highest dome back in the Bunker. Sometimes they stretched so high the greenery faded from their sides and gave way to grand, white caps. They were always visible, sometimes far in the distance.

It was easy enough to get lost here. After a few twists and turns the camp was out of sight. All the rocks seemed to look the same, and the shrubs were no help, either.

Left, right, left, right. I weaved in an out among the rock formations, heading consistently in a single direction.

Or so I thought. It was a stupid idea, I know, but at the time I was confident I had the situation under control.

Eventually I got bored and retraced my steps. When I arrived where I was sure the camp would be, I was surprised to find just another empty space lodged between mossy rocks and a few lonely looking shrubs, the same as all the others.

The wind picked up and tossed my hair about. It made a howling sound. I suddenly felt very lonely.

Left, right, left, left, right. All it would take is one wrong turn. But which one?

I was wandering aimlessly trying to figure out how to get back when suddenly I came out into a wide open, grassy area. Boulders stood around the edge. They had taken up key positions like armed guardians back at the Bunker, silent, disapproving and trigger-happy.

There were a few of those four-legged animals, grazing about on the meager grass. They were white and had horns of some kind. They looked me over for a moment – they didn't seem very interested – and continued with their meal.

Near the center of the clearing was what could only have been a dwelling of some kind. It was shaped like the husks of stone and pipe we had passed earlier – before we got into this dreary, rocky land – except this one was complete. There were no gaps or rusted pipes sticking out. This was a square building made entirely of stone with a door and two windows.

Suddenly, staring at it, I recognized the icon of the Bunker.

In front of the hut were two people. One was a woman. A long time ago she might have been pretty, but time and circumstance had hardened and chipped away at her features. She was care-worn, and her skin was wrinkled. Long strands of greying hair clung to the sides of her skull. Still, she looked strong and healthy, stronger and more alive than most people I've met back home.

The woman had her leathery arms placed protectively about the shoulders of the broken boy who stood next to her, cowering and gibbering uncontrollably. He was mounted in the center of a crude, homemade contraption much like a table, but there were wheels attached to the ends of its legs. He was holding on tightly to one of the wooden bars that ran along the side.

There was something wrong with his face. It was too long, and the eyes were crooked. Something like that, anyway.

"You're lucky," she told me gravely. "I spotted you first. But my weapon's inside." She shifted uncomfortably and glanced regretfully at the boy.

It was clear to me what I had stumbled upon. This woman – whoever she was – had left Hallowed Hills and was surviving entirely on her own, here in the outside. And the reason was most certainly the child. She seemed particularly attached to him.

Amazing, I thought to myself as I peered at the broken boy. This was someone who had lived his whole life outside the confines of Control's invasive, decaying world. He may not even know what Control is. He's probably never tasted slop.

I didn't know whether to envy or pity him.

I couldn't call him a citizen, that's for sure. But what, then? An animal like the other things I'd seen eking out a meager existence here on the Earth's battered surface? He certainly looked like some of the kills we'd left behind uneaten, except I doubted he had the means to survive on his own.

I felt sorry for the woman. And – even if he disgusted me – the boy.

I was disturbed. After all, I couldn't allow myself to get soft. Feelings are a liability back in the Bunker. The only one I ever let my guard down for was Sally, and even that arrangement had proved a liability.

"Look," I said, "I'm not going to tell."

The woman threw her head back and laughed. Oh, yes, she most certainly had been born and raised in the Bunker.

I took out my weapon.

The boy cried out. His legs were broken, too. They smacked at the ground as if he were having the kind of spasms I usually associate with smack addicts.

The woman stiffened, but she knew she was helpless, unarmed, and too far away to throw herself at me.

I exchanged the trigger for the barrel in my hand, walked calmly over, and offered it to her.

She didn't react. I could see the thoughts racing behind her narrow, hazel eyes. She wasn't sure what I was up to.

"Look, all I want is to get back to our camp. I'm lost."

"Camp, eh?" She took the laser pistol and turned it over in her hand. "I haven't seen one of these in yearstretches." Suddenly, she pointed the barrel at me.

I chuckled. "Everyone wants to kill me, lady. You'll have to take a number."

I don't know why, but she seemed comforted by my reaction. Slowly, she lowered the weapon and handed it back. Turning to the boy, she said, "There's nothing to worry about, Lai. This man won't hurt us." She looked me in the eye. "And I don't think he'll tell anyone about us, either."

The inside of her hut was cramped but pleasant enough. A small fire burned in a pit in the center. The smoke escaped through a hole in the roof. Next to it was a sliding piece of stone she could use to block out the rain. In the corner were two piles of dried grass where she and her son slept. In another corner were the clothes and other utensils required for their daily life: a tub, pots, clay jars, and many other things besides I don't know the names for.

There was also a small, low table. The two of us sat there while the boy played on the floor with round stones she called marbles. I couldn't quite understand the game, but a broken laugh escaped his throat every once in a while. It seemed to me the boy was easily amused.

Again, I didn't know whether to envy or pity him.

"I am Kiran," she said as she placed a bowl of steaming food in front of me.

It smelled wonderful.

"This stew is all I have prepared," she continued and handed me a wooden spoon. "I hope you like it."

I don't know what was in it, but it was the best tasting meal I had ever had. There were chunks of orange and white foodstuffs, and some smaller white, virtually translucent ones as well. And something brown and stringy that was tougher to chew. All of it was immersed

138

in a brownish broth the consistency of warm slop. But slop was slop, and aside from the consistency, the two had nothing in common. I could feel the vitality seeping from my mouth and stomach into the rest of my body.

She seemed pleased to see me attack the stew as I did. Shortly, the bowl was empty.

"I'm sorry," she told me as she took the utensils away. "I don't have more to share. I wasn't expecting guests." A wan smile touched her face and she sat down again.

"Kiran?" I asked. "I've never heard a name like that before."

"I gave it to myself after I left the Bunker. I am no longer the woman I was when I was living there."

I glanced at the boy. "It's because of him, isn't it?"

She nodded. "Control didn't approve Lai's birth, but I was determined to keep him anyway. Unfortunately, I had to kill the father. He was going to turn me in to Homeland Security."

"You were both Alphas?"

"I was a Beta." Her fingers traced invisible shapes on the top of the table. "Life has been hard since we came here, but I've never regretted it for an instant."

I thought it was best to be straight with her. "I can't see how this ends well, Kiran. Either you or he will die first. The other one will be left alone."

Kiran shrugged indifferently. "Perhaps circumstances will change before that time comes."

I was amazed. "You're willing to gamble on hope alone?"

"No, not really." She looked up at me shyly, as if caught trying to steal Algatine from a vending machine. "But however it ends, the time spent out here – relying on ourselves, in perfect freedom from human or machine – will have been worth it."

"And if you break an arm? Where's the medibot?"

She looked up at me sharply. "You don't happen to have any reconstructive tissue on you by any chance, would you?"

I couldn't stay for very long. There were only so many hourstretches of sunlight, and I knew the others would be wanting to move on. There was no telling if they'd even wait for me.

Naturally, Kiran couldn't help me find our camp. She did ask me to ensure they wouldn't come anywhere near her home. I said I'd do what I could.

I was only just out of sight of her hut when Sally and George surprised me.

"What took you so long?" Sally demanded suspiciously.

"How'd you find me?" I shot back, just as suspicious.

"We followed you when you left camp."

"Followed me? Why?"

"Who knows what business you had out here in the wild," George answered. He looked past me back the way I had come. "Did you see that child? Someone should put it out of its misery."

"Someone should put you out of your misery, you unhygienic typhoid!" I spat and shoved him roughly against a boulder.

"Hey!" Sally shouted and got in between us. "What's the matter with you?" She stared me squarely in the face.

I looked past her shoulder and pinned George with a nasty look. "If you tell anyone about them," I said, "I'll hunt you down wherever you hide. Underground or not."

He could tell that I was serious. "George Walker, Jeremy," he muttered. "It's just a genetic reject. I don't see what you're getting so worked up about."

"The name's Terry."

"Yeah, yeah. Whatever."

Sally, though, was touched. I could see it. She was staring at me, conflicting emotions racing across her face. It was the old feelings again, trying to break through. If I had been the man she wanted me to be, we would have had a special moment. But I wasn't, and she was doing her best not to let them.

I wasn't going to try and take advantage of the situation. "You cancerheads know the way back?"

Sally nodded absently and motioned to George.

That one marched off between the boulders, mumbling darkly to himself. I followed.

I could feel Sally's eyes delving into the back of my head the whole way back to our camp.

"Okay, this is it."

Everyone turned and stared at Scorpio.

"We're here."

"Are you serious?" Lady Lagrange looked around in disbelief. "Is this some kind of trick?"

I'll admit, I didn't like it there any more than she did.

There was a road. It was most clearly a road.

I think I've already mentioned the twisted metal contraptions with the wheels in front and the sides torn off. We'd seen a lot of them in our wandering, but nothing like this. One day we came upon them standing in eight silent rows, stretching as far as the eye could see. They were separated in the middle by a thin stretch of grass.

It was ghastly because there was more inside those metal contraptions than simply wheels. There were skeletons, too. Propped up in what could only have been seats, jaws hanging open and empty eye sockets leering, it was impossible to pretend they weren't there.

We turned and followed this parade of death and decay.

And now, suddenly, Scorpio was announcing we had arrived. We were there. The scenery, though, was just as unfriendly and lifeless as it had been ten hourstretches ago.

Off to each side were some twisted poles. Whatever had hung suspended between them now lay in pieces across the road, blocking the way. Something large and rectangular and dullish green lay over a few of the contraptions. It looked like there were words of some kind written on them, but it was hard to tell through the thick layers of rust and corrosion.

"No trick."

Not far away there was an angry river. It was close enough that we had to raise our voices to be heard over the noise.

We had left the mountains behind. This place was flat and grassy. The terrain was clear for kilometers in all directions. To the sides, we could see nothing interesting except a few rises and more grass. Up ahead, though, was the crumpled remains of a city.

It looked like the Bunker, except this one was built on the planet's surface. Rising from the earth, the domes were tightly packed, and most of them had collapsed. The city looked like it had been squashed by some invisible hand.

"Okay," Zeus said and heaved the backpack onto one of the metal contraptions. It swayed dangerously but held up under the weight. He took an interested look around. "What next?"

Scorpio pointed with his stick. "Up ahead is a hotspot. That's where we have to go."

We all considered the hulking shadow of the city dominating the horizon.

"There are ecopacks for only four of us," Sally pointed out.

"Obviously, Scorpio gets one," George said. "And I'll take another."

"And me!" Sally added quickly. "I won't be left behind."

Lady Lagrange stepped forward and bared her breasts. "Someone from our side will go along, too."

Surprisingly enough, everyone seemed pleased with the arrangements. Everyone, that is, except me.

"One of you is going to have to make room."

As expected, they all turned on me.

"Why you?"

"What have you got up your sleeve?"

"We're not going to fall for it!"

And so forth.

When they had finished, I said, "You said it yourselves. Well, one of you did. The other one knows where the Self-Destruct Mechanism is, too. So chances are he's waiting for us. And I'm the only one who might know what he's got in mind."

As much as they might have liked to, it was hard to argue with me. There was some grumbling and muttering, but before long the conversation turned to who would *not* be going.

"I'm the one carrying the suits," George said. "They're in my pack."

Lady Lagrange was amused. "You think that earns you the right to come along?"

"Damn right."

Zeus spoke up. "The suits may be in your pack, but they're only here at all because we brought them."

"Antinous packed them!" Sally pointed out. "Does that mean he gets a spot?"

"I don't want to go!" Antinous yelped and took a step backward.

Scorpio put a reassuring hand on his shoulder. "Perhaps I should decide."

"No!" screeched Sally and Lady Lagrange.

I walked off until their bickering had melted into the rushing of the river. After a few stretches, I realized I was not alone.

"The river's pretty, isn't it?" Antinous said.

I shrugged. "It seems like a waste of good water. If it isn't tainted with anything, I mean."

"Waste?" Antinous frowned. "Just because no one's drinking it?"

"Sure. What else would you do with it?"

"Appreciate it!" The boy shook his head in disbelief. "Is that what your world is like? Everything has a use or it doesn't belong?"

"What are you getting at, Antinous?"

"Beauty! Asceticism! Wonder!" He stared at me as if *I* were something to behold. "Can't you hear the water rushing over those rocks?"

It sounded like noise to me.

"Do you know there are things living in it?"

"In water? Are you out of your mind?"

He approached the bank of the river. The ground was wet and slippery. As he got closer, his feet began to sink into the soil, and he stopped.

Curiosity got the best of me, and I began to follow in his footsteps. "Do you see anything?" I called out.

He motioned for me to be quiet. I quickened my steps. What could he possibly be pretending to see in the water?

But after a stretch I saw it, too. There were thin shapes milling about just under the dark surface.

"They're fish," he whispered when I reached him.

We stood in silence for some time, watching. The experience was amazing. Forget the fact they didn't need air. I saw it with my own two eyes, by the way. They never came up for it. But I was more captivated by the way they moved. Hovering, sometimes in groups, and then darting away for some inexplicable, sudden reason, they seemed blissfully unaware that the river was flowing in a single direction. Birds of the water, I thought to myself.

"Jeremy, are you coming?" The words jarred me. I looked behind. The others were standing on the side of the road, staring down at us. Lady Lagrange had her hands on her hips. "We haven't got much time!"

I turned back to the boy. "Thanks." The word issued gruffly from my mouth as if it had difficulty forming the sounds.

"No worries," Antinous replied absently. His gaze never left the water. He was clearly mesmerized.

I felt sorry for him and jealous at the same time.

"I don't feel so well."

If I had thought the road was a strange place, where we had come to now was impossibly alien.

Scorpio, Lady Lagrange, Sally, and I had picked our way between the soulless metal contraptions towards the ruined city. The journey took us hourstretches.

Hotspots don't just begin. They grow steadily out of nothing. That's why we had to leave the others so far behind.

Ecopacks are made of a silver, resistant material formed into heavy, baggy layers. It took more than a few minutestretches to get safely into one, and then someone else had to check to make sure all the straps were done up properly. Even a single leak could prove deadly.

You can't tell you're in a hotspot unless you have a special device like the one Scorpio was carrying. That's what's so eerie about them. Everything around you looks and feels the same. Except for the dead animals. As we got closer to the city, there were more and more of them. Birds and dogs and other things I didn't know the names for. If you wandered in by accident and got far enough to notice the corpses, pretty soon you'd be one, too.

Everywhere there hung this thick, impenetrable silence. It wasn't the tense silence of expectation. No, this was completely different. It was the silence of nothingness, of nothing ever having been and nothing ever going to be. I could taste it in my mouth and feel it pressing down on my ecopack. It didn't like to be disturbed. It was trying to absorb us.

"I think I need to sit down for a stretch."

Of course, there had been something before. If there ever was a heart to the earthlings' civilization, we must have been in it now. I had never imagined a place could be so big.

The Bunker is larger in terms of sheer size. But no one ever sees it all at once. You travel through cramped, rickety corridors and occasionally you might end up in a community dining hall or a plaza. Maybe you work in a reactor core or an industrial furnace or one of Buster B's many pre-approved fashion outlets selling pre-approved overalls that look just like everyone else's except for the big "B" emblazoned on the front. These are the biggest places we have. There's always walls between you and the rest.

Not here. This mess was all out in the open. An incomprehensible mass of rusting metal and crumbling stone and broken glass, piled into heaps on top of heaps. It was like a great, creaking beast. Yes, here there were sounds, or rather unsound. It didn't disturb the ever-silence at all. I imagine it was the wind, seeping through the wreckage and squishing it down. The whole thing was collapsing in slow motion, a little bit more every daystretch.

"Lady," Scorpio said firmly and stopped. "What do you think you're doing?"

"Just a rest," she breathed. I could barely see her face through the grimy faceplate of her ecopack.

"Not here," he told her. "We need to get back as quickly as possible. I have no intention of staying here any longer than we have to."

"Agreed," Sally said quickly and shivered. Her voice sounded tinny coming through the suit's speakers. There must have been something wrong with it.

We carried on.

There were streets that wound their way between the towering piles of wreckage, but even these were not entirely safe. In fact, they were little more than obstacle courses. The way was treacherous. Sometimes our path disappeared entirely into mountains of rubble and the dead corpses of towering buildings, and we had to backtrack.

Sally was the first one to discover the ground wasn't entirely solid, either. Without warning, her foot disappeared through a thin layer of debris into a round, gaping hole. Fortunately, I was just behind her and managed to grab her under the arms before she toppled in.

We stood a moment, staring downward, but the darkness was impenetrable.

After that, we tested the ground in front of us as we went along. We used makeshift poles taken from the piles of rubble, long sticks of wood or metal poles or whatever suited the purpose.

Lady Lagrange was coughing. Sometimes she doubled over. She didn't have a pole. She stumbled along recklessly.

"Here we are."

It didn't seem to me we had arrived anywhere at all.

Scorpio pointed with his stick into a dark opening that led into one of the mounds of rubble. Now that I looked more closely, I could see that there were tall, stern letters engraved in the sturdy, stone frame that still outlined it. I couldn't read the words, though. They were foreign to me.

He exchanged the sensor for a flashlight and flipped it over the top of his helmet. A thick, intense beam of light sprang from his head.

"You wait here."

Before we could say anything, he ducked inside and was gone.

Lady Lagrange collapsed onto the ground. Her breathing was heavy and belabored.

"You shouldn't push yourself so hard," Sally told her.

Lady Lagrange didn't answer. She simply lay there, panting.

We waited. The sky had grown cloudy. Please don't let it rain, I thought. I don't know who I was talking to, but I kept repeating the thought. Not now, not here.

I looked around for cover. There were more gaping holes like the one Scorpio had disappeared into, but none of us was eager to check them out. In fact, nowhere in the ruined city looked particularly inviting. I had the sneaking suspicion no matter where we tried to hide, the horrific, acidic water would eventually seep through the layers of debris and drip down on our heads.

There was a tear in the back of Lady Lagrange's ecopack.

I stared at it for a few stretches. It looked like it had been made with a knife.

Sally saw it, too.

Neither of us said anything. We just looked on as Lady Lagrange fought the great fight.

I wonder if she knows, I thought to myself.

When Scorpio reemerged, he had already put the flashlight away. In its place, there was a little, rectangular stick with connectors on either side. He held it up triumphantly. The Self-Destruct Mechanism, apparently. It wasn't very impressive.

When he saw Lady Lagrange lying on the ground, he grew testy. "George Walker, would you get up?"

But Lady Lagrange would never be getting up again.

The flaps on either side of the tear in her suit fluttered in the breeze.

Who done it?

It was on all our minds as the three of us headed back. It was possible, of course, that her suit had come like that, the result of faulty fabrication. But somehow I doubted it. We all did.

I knew I wasn't responsible, but Sally and George didn't. Not that any of us cared one whit for Lady Lagrange's life. But sure as the dome Zeus would.

We all have enemies. But everybody knows that nobody is more apt to put a knife in your back than your friends. Enemies we take for granted.

Who had an interest in Lady Lagrange's death anyway? I mulled it over in my mind, but the truth was that rivalries and jealousies I knew nothing about could lay behind that dead body we left back there. There wasn't enough information to go on.

For all I knew, Zeus was the guilty party. Whatever guilty means in a world such as ours.

When we got back, it was nearly dark. Zeus was on his PA, talking to Control, no doubt. Which was strange, because usually the search routine activated in the morning.

"It is indeed an extraordinary distance to have covered since leaving Hallowed Hills this morning."

Something was wrong. George and Zeus were standing where we had left them. There was a blank look on Zeus' face, but George was clearly worried.

Scorpio looked around in spoiled anticipation.

"Where's Lady Lagrange?" Zeus mouthed the words.

Scorpio was too distracted to answer. Sally pretended she was busy getting out of her ecopack and hadn't heard.

"She's dead," I told him matter-of-factly and removed my helmet. I didn't want to get caught up in a tumble of straps and heavy, radiation-proof folds in case Zeus went berserk.

I don't think the words registered immediately. "In pursuit of terrorists and criminals, the most amazing feats may be accomplished."

"Where's Antinous?" Scorpio wanted to know. He, too, had removed his helmet.

I think George's mistake was the callous way he told Scorpio what had happened. Sure, I wasn't particularly sensitive to Zeus' feelings when I told him about Lady Lagrange, but then again (as far as I knew), he wasn't in love with her.

"He's dead, Scorpio. We found him washed up on the side of the river."

"What do you mean, she's dead?" Zeus mouthed, peering at the three of us suspiciously. He took a few, cautious steps back.

Of course, I thought to myself. He thinks he's next.

I shrugged. "Someone sabotaged her ecopack."

"Sabotaged?" Zeus roared.

Scorpio threw his helmet down on the ground and ran off towards the river.

"I didn't do it!" Sally and I echoed each other. We exchanged uncomfortable glances and then flashed Zeus disarming smiles.

"Yes, Control!" he barked into the phone. His face was turning purple. "Clearly the work of terrorists and traitors, even this far out in the outside!"

He stared us down, trying to decide who to blame.

"The suit just came like that," Sally told him.

"There was a hole in it," I added.

We both pointed at each other.

"He was behind her the whole time! Ask him if he has a knife."

"I heard her conspiring with Kuasimodo. You're next," I added confidentially.

Sally turned on me. "That's a crock of slop!"

"Yes, Control, indeed I am furious!" Zeus blinked.

I pointed at George. "The suits were in his pack."

"Thank you, Control, for entering it into my permanent record." Zeus flipped his PA shut and lowered his arms.

I never did find out what he was going to do next.

We had all forgotten about Scorpio.

"You smack addicts!" A burst of laserfire exploded around us, centered mostly where George was standing.

Tears were streaming down Scorpio's face as he rounded the top of the incline. His laser pistol was aimed steadfastly in George's direction.

"You did it, didn't you?"

Scorpio didn't roar like Zeus. He spoke in eerily quiet tones. But I put more stock in the way he was shaking and the wild look behind his crooked spectacles than the deceptive calm in his voice.

We all stepped away from George. He stood alone among the dead, metal corpses lining the road.

"I - It wasn't me!" he stammered. "I swear it!"

"What was he doing in the water?"

"He said he wanted to go in! I warned him not to." George gestured towards Zeus. "Didn't I?"

But Zeus wasn't getting involved. He had troubles of his own.

George turned back to Scorpio. "He didn't come back, so I went looking for him."

Scorpio shuddered and loosed another shot from his pistol. It singed the hair on the top of George's head. "You went looking for him," he repeated softly. "All by yourself."

He had fired an awful lot of rounds in a short time. The pistol was staring to whine suspiciously.

George ran his hand nervously over the top of his head, feeling the heat from the laser shot.

Scorpio fired again. This one struck the ground near George's feet.

I have to admit, George stood up remarkably well under the pressure. He may have been a fat bastard, but he still had a spine. He didn't plead, and he didn't beg. He didn't flinch when Scorpio fired at him. Who knows, maybe it's what saved his life.

But far more likely what saved his life is the fact that Scorpio's laser pistol was overheating.

The furious screeching penetrated even the dense haze of hate and grief that had engulfed him. Just in the nick of time, Scorpio tossed the pistol away. In an angry flash of light and sound, it exploded.

Chapter 12

"GREETINGS CITIZENS. THIS IS CONTROL. THE NEXT FIFTEEN MINUTES WILL BE SPENT IN HONOR OF CITIZEN HAROLD SCHNIPP OF ELYSIUM BUNKER A TRUE HERO AND PATRIOT. A SNAP HAS BEEN FORWARDED TO YOUR PA. PLEASE TAKE A MOMENT TO STUDY IT. EARLIER TODAY CITIZEN HAROLD BROKE THE ALL TIME RECORD FOR CAUSING HIS FELLOW CITIZENS TO FLEX THE MUSCLES NEAR BOTH ENDS OF THEIR MOUTHS. MEDICAL STUDY HAS REPEATEDLY SHOWN THAT HUMAN BEINGS PRODUCE IN GREATER QUANTITIES AND OTHERWISE BEHAVE MORE PROPERLY WHEN HAPPY. CITIZEN HAROLD PERFORMED THIS FEAT ON HIS OWN TIME RATHER THAN CHOOSING TO LIE INERT IN HIS ASSIGNED BUNK FOR THE DURATION OF HIS NIGHTSTRETCH. AS A REWARD CITIZEN HAROLD HAS BEEN GRANTED THE EPSILON SECURITY CLEARANCE. LET US TAKE A MOMENT TO PERSONALLY CONGRATULATE HIM. CONGRATULATIONS CITIZEN HAROLD. SNAPS OF CITIZEN HAROLD HOLDING OTHERS AT GUNPOINT AND COERCING THEM TO SMILE ARE THE WORK OF TERRORISTS AND WILL NOT BE TOLERATED. POSSESSION OF SAID SNAPS MAY RESULT IN A FINE CORRECTIVE SURGERY MEMORY WASH OR OTHER. THANK YOU FOR YOUR COOPERATION."

The tubes hanging around the terminal in Hallowed Hills all showed the same thing: a picture of a well dressed and cared for citizen about twenty years of age smiling shyly into the camera. The backdrop with a towering rendition of the Bunker's logo and all the makeup suggested it had been taken in one of Human Resources' many studio labs.

What a load of slop, I thought to myself. The tubes back in the Bunker would soon be overwhelmed by this very same picture, and all the anchormen and anchorwomen would be babbling on about poor citizen Harold. Favorite sitcoms such as Loyal People and Under One Dome would be interrupted with the very important newsflash.

It looked like he was enjoying his fifteen minutes of fame, but I knew better than to envy citizen Harold.

Virtually everyone honored by Control with fifteen minutes of fame inevitably draws the anger and jealousy of his coworkers, bunkmates, and the Underground, not to mention those dedicated addicts of Under One Dome who are going to miss the surprise cliffhanger. The Underground especially is suspicious of these people, even if they're active members, because there are actually people dedicated to the preservation of the Bunker and its way of life, and this could be one of them.

The average life expectancy of someone honored by Control with fifteen minutes of fame is not encouraging.

In my case, I did not feel that I was in imminent danger of being honored by Control with fifteen minutes of fame.

That's not to say I was completely at ease. One is never completely at ease in the Bunker. You see, I was in imminent danger of something else. We all were. And even though I was in the company of Alphas and Betas, the sinking feeling in my stomach told me it wouldn't do any good.

"GREETINGS, CITIZENS. THIS IS CONTROL. AS OF SIXTEEN FORTY-EIGHT TWENTY-SEVEN STANDARD TIME TODAY THE 'BLOOD TYPE DISCLOSURE FORM' 0xAA7AB01F HAS BEEN DEPRECATED. ANY REMAINING UNCOMPLETED FORMS MUST BE RETURNED TO CENTRAL MANAGEMENT IN YOUR SECTOR AND EXCHANGED FOR THE NEW AND IMPROVED 'BLOOD TYPE DECLARATION AND DISCLOSURE FORM' 0xAA7F43D6. IT IS THE RESPONSIBILITY OF LOYAL CITIZENS EVERYWHERE TO ENSURE THAT ANY FORMS 0xAA7AB01F FILED BETWEEN SIXTEEN FORTY-EIGHT TWENTY-SEVEN STANDARD TIME TODAY AND THIS ANNOUNCEMENT ARE UPDATED BY FILING A PROPER 'FORM RECALL REQUEST FORM' 0x0000028E WITH THE STANDARD ATTACHMENT 'FORM CORRECTION AND ADDENDUM' 0x00000005. THANK YOU FOR YOUR COOPERATION."

"Hi there! Carl Buskin, that's the name." The man attached to the smile stuck out a thick, manicured hand. "Pleased to meet me."

Who was this annoying flaphead with the clipboard and the crisp, clean, pressed suit? There was no mistaking him. He was a Marketing Engineer. These are the invaluable members of our society who are responsible for creating new, inoffensive words or phrases (such as "corrective surgery") to replace the words that actually describe what happens (in this case, "maiming"). Other times, they create new, exciting words or phrases (such as "patrioloyalot") to describe something that does not, in fact, exist and which their superiors hope to conjure up by sheer force of will.

"Citizens, do you realize how fortunate you are to be here today?"

You know you're in trouble when a Marketing Engineer suggests how lucky you are.

"You are about to witness nothing less than a paradigm shift in care hair! You are going to increase your mindshare as you encounter this perfect storm of bleeding edge technology! Isn't it exciting?"

Silence.

"Of course, if you're not interested, I'll just empower these clever folks behind you. They look savvy enough to know a state-of-the-art, next generation hair care product when they see one."

"Okay," Scorpio responded curtly.

We all took a few steps forward.

Carl Buskin made a sudden move and blocked the way. A menacing twinkle had taken light behind his eyes. "Not showing interest in a marketing campaign approved by Human Resources for an official Pioneer Product can be construed as less than loyal, citizen."

Scorpio's eyes narrowed. "What exactly do you want, Carl?"

The menacing twinkle disappeared, but the smile did not. Forced laughter erupted from his mouth. "Glad you asked! I'm organizing a Focus Group for ShamBazzz!, the Bunker's new-and-improved, user friendly hair cleaning product for men and women. I'm sure you'd be delighted to participate!"

Inwardly, I groaned. Like a Caring Demonstration, it was difficult to escape from a Focus Group once you've stumbled into one. Unlike a Caring Demonstration, it was impossible to tell until it was too late. Normally, I'd just wait it out, but this time I had concerns. For example, we had just snagged the Self-Destruct Mechanism and still had it in our possession.

"GREETINGS CITIZENS. THIS IS CONTROL. THE TERRORISM ALERT LEVEL HAS BEEN LOWERED TO 'IMMINENT'. THANK YOU FOR YOUR COOPERATION."

"You do realize," Scorpio began, speaking softly and carefully emphasizing each syllable, "who I am?"

Carl Buskin shook his head.

"The Head of Homeland Security." Scorpio leaned slightly forward. His animal-skin boots creaked and groaned.

To speed things along, I thought I'd be more specific. "All of it."

Once again, Carl Buskin erupted into booming peals of forced laughter. Several passers-by eyed him with hostility, but as soon they caught sight of the clipboard they veered wide-eyed in the opposite direction.

"What a sense of humor!" he shouted. "You must be dimensionalizing the paradigm, right?" The eyes hardened and the laughter intensified.

"You're out of your element, citizen," Scorpio scolded the Marketing Engineer coldly and carefully. I cringed to hear him speak like that. "I have urgent business elsewhere and don't have time to waste filling out your silly forms. You will choose someone else."

Quick as a whip, the laughter died away. "I have a Beta clearance –"

"I see." Scorpio gestured at the rest of us to follow. "I'll choose to overlook your treason this time, Carl. Don't let it happen again."

"GREETINGS CITIZENS. THIS IS CONTROL. THANK YOU FOR YOUR COOPERATION."

Carl Buskin held out a manicured hand. "I have a waiver."

Scorpio's eyes narrowed. "What kind of waiver?"

Carl Buskin drew a folded sheet of paper from an inside pocket of his crisp suit, shook it open, and waved it in front of Scorpio's face.

"Hold still," Scorpio demanded.

But Carl Buskin wouldn't wait. "I've been granted Alpha rights with respect to the Focus Group. Refusal to participate is treason."

Scorpio leaned in for a closer look.

"What does it say?" Zeus wanted to know.

"Why don't I get our good friend Control on the line and see if we can't straighten this out, okay?" Carl Buskin exchanged the waiver in his hand for his PA.

It depressed me to see such joy in a fellow citizen's eyes.

"Yes, Control. Carl Buskin here. Questionable Queries, Consumer Research, Central Management, V-2 Sector, Ganges Bunker. We've been commissioned to set up a Focus Group to gather feedback on the groundbreaking, cross-platform hair care product, ShamBazzz!"

He listened for a moment before nodding his head in earnest. "Health and Hygiene Plus over at Production and Logistics. It's classed as a Pioneer Product! That's right. The way we see it over at Questionable Queries, hygiene is a best of breed for the security and harmony of life in the Bunker. That's why I take this commission especially seriously. Thank you, Control. You know, I'd really like to hit the ground running, but ... well, I'm unhappy to report that compliance on the work floor is less than patriotic. Yes, I'm referring to the citizen in front of me now."

There was a brief pause. "That's right. All of it." Carl Buskin flashed a toothy smile in my direction.

Scorpio reached for his PA. He was going to appeal directly to Control himself.

We all knew it was suicide. After all, Scorpio (and the rest of us) were officially criminals or terrorists or worse. And the man was unhinged. Was he truly in any state of mind to try and talk his way out of this boehner?

It was hard to say. In the days since Antinous' death, he hadn't said much. There was that brief, initial outburst, but afterwards he had turned cool and hard as steel. We weren't sure how far he had snapped or whether he was making any progress getting better. We observed him, but he told us nothing. All of us, that is, except George. He kept as far away from Scorpio as possible.

Fortunately, Zeus had a good read on what was happening. "I'll handle this," he declared and laid a heavy hand on Scorpio's arm.

"Welcome to the Focus Group, citizen!" Carl Buskin shouted and laughed.

"Go take a walk outside the dome, buddy," Zeus hissed just softly enough to avoid being recorded and smiled.

The mask of enthusiasm on Carl Buskin's face cracked.

Zeus flipped open his own PA and requested Control.

"Control!" Carl Buskin rushed to get a word in. He was no longer laughing. "I'd like to report an outbreak of treasonous activity!"

Zeus started speaking fluidly. "Yes, Control. This is Andreas Fokker reporting from Hallowed Hills."

"The name is Andreas Fokker!" Carl Buskin shouted into his PA. "The crime? Denigrating, disturbing, and otherwise disrupting a Focus Group for a Pioneer Product!"

"I have four known and dangerous traitors in my custody. Preliminary interrogation revealed an ongoing terrorist plot unfolding in the outside. The situation required immediate and extraordinary measures to suppress. I would furthermore like to report that in the ensuing operation I lost a number of colleagues. I plan on immediately filing a full status report. However, I feel it is in the Bunker's best interests to see these dangerous criminals safely in the hands of our friends at Homeland Security before I engage in any other patriotic activity."

"Traitors?" Carl Buskin mouthed in horror.

"That's right, Control." He winked at the appalled Marketing

Engineer.

Carl Buskin snapped to attention. "Of course, Control. Everybody knows that the General Guidelines on Sanitation and Hygiene apply to everyone equally, even traitors."

"Subverting a Focus Group? I categorically deny the accusation. As for murder –" Zeus frowned. "Whose?"

They both stood, listening intently.

"GREETINGS CITIZENS. THIS IS CONTROL. YOU MAY ALREADY BE AWARE OF THE WORD 'IT' ONE OF THE MOST FREQUENTLY USED IN OUR LANGUAGE. AS PART OF THE PRIVATE FIRM !GIDDY-UP¡'S SUCCESSFUL AND ONGOING PROGRAM TO INCREASE AWARENESS OF THOSE ASPECTS OF YOUR DAILY LIVES DENIED PROPER APPRECIATION USE OF THE WORD 'IT' IN ANY FORM OF COMMUNICATION IS HEREBY STRICLY PROHIBITED. THIS REGULATION IS EFFECTIVE UNTIL FURTHER NOTICE. NEXT WEEKSTRETCH WE WILL BE APPRECIATING THE WORD 'THE'. THANK YOU FOR YOUR COOPERATION."

Zeus spoke into his PA. "I can confirm that Citizen Raluca Ioannou was involved in the suppression of the ongoing terrorist plot. She fought gloriously, Control, until she was shot down by a vicious, unhygienic traitor! It was truly an honor to serve with her. As for citizen Lady Lagrange, any information that I have pertaining to her unfortunate and accidental death will be provided in my report."

There was a short silence before he glanced apprehensively at Scorpio out of the corner of his eye. "I was not present when citizen Antinous ceased functioning. I'm sure citizen George Varukas will be able to provide the data you require."

Scorpio's lip curled slightly, but it was his only reaction.

George, standing next to me, started to sweat.

"I'm sure they will make a seamless contribution to our Focus Group." Carl Buskin, looking us over with distaste, spoke reluctantly.

"As soon as possible. Citizen Harold is an inspiration to us all." Zeus flipped his PA shut and pocketed it.

Carl Buskin, too, terminated the line. "Well," he said, tucking his PA back into his suit, "looks like we'll use you all the same." Suddenly, he had a thought. "You know, I think our strategic partnership might actually be well positioned to leverage the exit strategy I originally had in mind." He snapped his fingers, produced the clipboard once again, and patted himself down for a pencil. "How's this for a re-purpose? We'll do that one where we see if the secret sauce burns the skin..."

"Burns the skin?" Sally repeated, shocked, and put a hand to her face. "Don't you know what it does already?"

The smile on Carl Buskin's face widened. "We've done exhaustive research into the new and improved ShamBazzz!'s effects on human skin."

"What effects?"

"Don't worry! We've worked out most of the kinks. I'm sure there won't be any need to call in the medibots like last time."

Annoying peals of forced laughter washed over us.

"Hi!"

We all turned.

Carl Buskin's jaw dropped. "You're – you're –"

Van Johnson smiled appreciatively.

"Why are you walking around up here and not locked up in some voluntary organ donation center down there?" Zeus wanted to know.

"I was the loyal citizen who was able to identify Raluca's killers." Van Johnson winked. "Control values this kind of information."

Zeus paused, taken aback.

"Not you, silly." Van Johnson rolled his eyes. "The real traitors got shot up and mutilated during the firefight in the outside. Unfortunately, there can be no interrogations." He shrugged. "Still, Control weighed the service against my alleged crimes and decided I should go free!"

"GREETINGS CITIZEN VAN. THIS IS CONTROL. YOU ARE NOT FREE. AS HAS ALREADY BEEN EXPLAINED AT LENGTH DURING YOUR TRIAL YOU HAVE BEEN PLACED ON PROBATION. THE COLLAR AROUND YOUR NECK WILL PREVENT YOU FROM UTTERING OR COMMITTING TREASONOUS ACTS OF ANY KIND."

Van Johnson smiled shyly and fingered the thick, studded collar we all so suddenly noticed. "Goes well with my outfit, doesn't it?"

By now, Carl Buskin had recovered from his initial shock. "Van Johnson himself? The host of Ten Things I Hate About Treason?"

"There is no other," he admitted.

Suddenly, the Bunker seemed like a bigger, brighter place to Carl Buskin. "Fantastic! The success of my Focus Group will be assured with the feature-rich synergy a star like you will bring on board!"

Van Johnson frowned. "Focus Group?"

"I think we'll skip the burn tests and go right over to the infomercials. After all, what we're experiencing is a sea change! What do you think?"

"I think you're a raving lunatic, you miserable flaphead."

Poor Van Johnson. No sooner had he uttered the words than his air supply was cut off.

Looking down at the gasping and squirming figure, Carl Buskin shook his head unsympathetically and thumped his clipboard. "How long do you think it will last? He's no good to me dead, you know."

The nearest security camera swiveled in his direction and fixed him in a narrow but bright beam of deceptively harmless, red light.

It was then that Carl Buskin realized what he'd said. A hand clamped tightly over his mouth. "Sorry," he squeaked, peering guiltily over the top of his palm into the lens of the camera.

"GREETINGS, CITIZENS. THIS IS CONTROL. IT HAS COME TO MY ATTENTION THAT YOU ARE ENGAGING IN GAMES OF ELABORATE DECEPTION. HALLOWED HILLS SETTLEMENT HAS THEREFORE BEEN SCHEDULED FOR ERADICATION. PLEASE REMAIN WHERE YOU ARE. THANK YOU FOR YOUR COOPERATION."

Van Johnson stood up. He was no longer gasping for breath. Still, he tugged uselessly on the collar, his face twisted in disgust.

The others were staring at me accusingly.

"What is it this time?" I demanded with just the slightest hint of exasperation.

Scorpio flipped his PA open and tapped rapidly on the screen.

Van Johnson, as if waking from a dream, took a look around. "Why is everybody running?"

"It's Terry alright," Scorpio murmured. "He's on a ship docked to the orbiter. And guess who's with him?"

Zeus growled in my direction.

George jabbed me in the kidney.

But it was Sally's look of concern as she gazed at the ceiling that hurt the most.

"You mean –?" Van Johnson stammered and observed the growing chaos.

Carl Buskin perked up. "We can say 'it' now?"

"There are no more ships scheduled for landing," Scorpio reported and flipped his PA shut. "He's not planning on meeting us down here."

Carl Buskin looked us over menacingly. "I'm sure there's been some kind of mistake." A lot of citizens feel that way in the Bunker. "This is some deviant trick, isn't it?" The eyes narrowed. "You're

157

arranging an emergency to get me to run, then you'll use the feed as evidence of my lack of patriotic duty!" A bit of forced laughter tore past his lips. "You think I'd abandon my Focus Group so easily?" Even as he spoke, a hand reached for his PA.

Carl Buskin clearly didn't know when to quit.

Thoughts of violence filled all our heads, but it was Van Johnson who acted first. Curling himself into a little ball, he threw himself at the Marketing Engineer blocking our way. He was taken completely by surprise. Rolling over each other, they tumbled towards the wall, yelping and squawking and biting.

"Now's our chance!" Sally rasped and bolted for the exit.

The double doors were jammed with desperate citizens fleeing for their lives. It would be a chore getting through. Still, there were five of us, and each was armed with a laser pistol.

We fired indiscriminately. A few of the ones at the back had time to draw a gun of their own, but we had the advantage because we were coming at them from behind.

"Ballistic missile!" someone shouted.

We looked. The silent, awkward snaps of citizen Harold Schnipp had all been replaced by a crude rendition of the planet Earth, the orbiter, and a series of ominously blinking red dots. These had just been loosed from the orbiter and were on a slow but steady trajectory towards Earth. A dashed line plotted their course.

The official ETA was twenty-seven minute- and forty secondstretches.

"AHHHHHHH!" Scorpio screamed as he barreled forward. The bodies in his path dropped like flies.

We ran after him.

"I think," Zeus told Scorpio gravely as we headed across the tarmac towards our ship, "that Typhon would be the most appropriate name for Terry Renfield. If he were to join us in the Underground, that is."

"Why would Van Johnson help us anyway?" I wondered aloud. It seemed suspicious.

George was lagging behind. "Catch up, will you?" Sally barked at him.

"He's committed!" Scorpio barked and surged ahead. "That's why!"

The only thing a citizen of the Bunker is committed to is himself. "I'll bet he hopes to get that collar off. If," I added, glancing at the terminal behind me, "he survives the impact." A steady stream of panicked citizens was exiting Hallowed Hills, knocking each other over and exchanging occasional laser fire.

"Scorpio was careful about who he picked," Sally told me icily. "We're all dedicated."

"All of you, that is, except Typhon," Zeus mused as he jogged along.

"Don't call me that," I snapped irritably. I don't like it when the people around me talk like I can't hear them. "I'm not a member of your damned Underground."

"He wasn't talking about you," Sally sneered.

I could see George had something along those lines that he'd like to add, too, but the fat bastard was too out of breath to contribute.

It was easy enough to find our ship. It was just where we had left it. The bulkhead had been repaired, but otherwise it was in exactly the same condition. Which turned out to be a problem once we reached low-earth orbit.

We were almost out of fuel.

Also, the orbiter and some of the meaner satellites were shooting down craft as they broke out of the Earth's atmosphere. We couldn't differentiate the heavy hand of the shock waves from the bumps and shudders you'd normally expect during ascent, but once we settled into an orbit and looked out the portholes we were able to confirm what the instruments were already telling us.

Teeny, glowing specs emerging from the otherworldliness of the Earth's blue-green background suddenly blossomed into angry bursts of red and orange and then faded into nothing.

Interestingly enough, our ship was spared.

"Oh, it's good to be off that drafty space rock," George muttered, stretching his arms high over his head and yawning.

"I don't know," Sally replied. "I kind of liked it." She shrugged and smiled shyly. "I'll bet Zeus thinks so, too."

But he wasn't listening. "Scorpio!" he shouted, hands gripping the thick lip of the porthole occupied by his head. "Are you really such a good pilot? None of the shots from the orbiter are even coming close!"

Scorpio, hunched over the controls, didn't answer.

"Let's take the ship over to the orbiter and find out what's going on," I suggested as innocently as I could manage.

"You want to go to the orbiter?" the mane of wavy blond hair asked me in disbelief.

George cocked his head. "It's where Renfield is."

"It shouldn't come as as surprise, you know. I've been perfectly clear about my intentions since the start."

George snorted with scarcely concealed contempt. Turning to the others, he said, "I don't like it."

"Kuasimodo, all the other ships are being picked off," Sally told him, pointing out one of the portholes. "Come and see."

Zeus pushed himself away from the decimation outside and turned to face me. "What could you possibly want with Terry Renfield?" His eyes were sharp and suspicious.

"My life back."

Zeus seemed to think I had made a joke. "I can understand you resent having a double walking around. But correct me if I'm wrong: *you* are the clone. Terry's the original."

Scorpio, I noticed, had stopped fiddling with the controls and was considering me quietly.

I could see this line of reasoning was taking me nowhere. "We've got nowhere else to go," I pointed out. "There's no fuel left. So let's put in at the orbiter. We're obviously welcome."

"Not so fast," George growled and pulled himself away from the porthole. "What if he's leading us into a trap? He could be, you know. Maybe they have some secret way of communicating."

"Who?" Zeus demanded incredulously. "Terry and the clone?"

George nodded. He never was one of our brightest citizens.

Zeus laughed. "Clones detest each other. There's no way under the dome they could be working in concert." Still, he eyed me warily.

Sally, too, couldn't make up her mind.

I didn't know what they were afraid of, and I didn't care. Fact is, they all were reluctant to head over to the orbiter, and that was the one place in Gaia I needed to go.

You see, up until now I had been under their control, first because of trickery and then because I was a captive. This had been their show and they ran it the way they liked. But everything would change the moment myself and the other one laid eyes on each other.

Thing is, they didn't understand how.

They talked as if they knew what it was like to have a clone, but they were just repeating what they'd heard from somebody else who had no idea, either. It's a mistake they all make, anyone who's never had a clone running around – an exact duplicate of himself – and that's pretty much everyone.

Zeus and Sally and George still thought of us as two separate people. So would you, I'd reckon.

But I knew we were the same person.

That's why I had an edge the moment I realized why I'd seen a poor sap on the tube who looked just like me sweating up close in the heat of a security camera. They could never have explained how, but they were smart enough to sense it.

Everyone except Scorpio, that is.

He had made up his mind, and his was the only mind that mattered because it was the one in charge of the ship. Deftly, his hands adjusted dials and moved switches. We were heading towards the orbiter.

Not that he sympathized with my situation. No, Scorpio was a man who could quickly and effectively reduce most situations into two distinct choices, each with its own unique advantages and disadvantages.

For example, we could choose to float around the Earth hoping a ship cut off from all communication and filled with lower clearance citizens would arrive before our food and air ran out.

Or, we could choose to put it at the orbiter and risk the ire of Control before we had a chance to destroy it.

"Why aren't we being shot down?" George growled and looked at me apprehensively.

"Isn't it obvious?" Zeus replied, sounding bored. "Terry's got somebody's ear over there. I don't know who and I don't know how. I've checked around but I have no idea what's happened to him since you sent him off on that foolish mission of yours." Suddenly, he snapped his fingers. "Oh yeah, I did uncover one thing. He's got a security clearance. Delta."

Sally's eyes showed wildly.

I glanced outside. The tiny shape of the orbiter could be seen in the distance.

"I figured the lad could take care of himself!" George spat impatiently. "But why's he not taking his chance? He could blast us out of orbit right now and be done with us."

Zeus shook his head. "Control wouldn't allow it. It's against regulations to wantonly murder us."

"But we're traitors!"

"I'm not," Zeus replied. He sat down in one of the chairs, leaned back and, folding his hands behind his head, smiled crookedly.

Sally could hardly contain her delight. The tragic lovers would finally be reunited, I thought to myself sourly.

Not if I could help it.

I was calm. I was ready. And I was pretty sure what to expect.

Scorpio navigated the ship quietly, and he navigated it alone. Cloaked in a dark melancholy, he refused to speak to anyone. The Self-Destruct Mechanism was still in his possession, but no one knew where.

"Now that he's got it," I overheard Zeus whispering to George, "I'd keep a careful eye on him. There's no telling he won't throw you at the mercy of his Homeland Security goons once it suits him, you know."

Sally bristled at the suggestion. "I think it's you we should be worried about!" she growled. "You're an official suspect in Lady Lagrange's death! You could just as easily fabricate information about us to secure your acquittal."

"True," Zeus agreed pleasantly and went back to staring out the porthole.

Outside, the orbiter grew larger. It looked like a giant wheel with four spokes. It rotated around a long, narrow axis, almost like an elongated, white spine. Two ships – one a bulky, rusted transport about ten times the size of ours and the other a sleek, narrow luxury cruiser – were docked on one side of the spine.

Our ship accelerated. In short order, the orbiter grew so large it overwhelmed the view outside. Eventually, we slowed down and rotated along the axis of approach.

The ship shuddered as the landing gear made contact with the orbiter. We came to a full stop.

A dull clang came from the direction of the bulkhead.

Through the porthole opposite, a dull, red flash of light could briefly be seen on the Earth's surface. It disappeared almost as quickly as it had flickered into being.

Even though there was a lot going on, I took a stretch and paused. Maybe he was uncouth. Maybe he wasn't, in fact, someone you could take home to mom. Even so, I hoped Van Johnson had somehow managed to escape Hallowed Hills settlement. After all, he had risked his own life to save the rest of us. I had never seen or heard of anyone doing that before.

There was some scratching outside the bulkhead. Before anyone could react, it swung open.

A familiar figure stepped into the ship, panting. He had a thick beard and soiled overalls and when he spoke his voice was rasping and gravelly.

Lance Trevor looked around and caught sight of me. "He's

waiting," he announced and collapsed to the floor. "Says you're to come alone."

"Who in the dome are you?" George spat even as Zeus grabbed for his laser pistol.

But Sally recognized him. "Doesn't Terry want to see me?" she asked, standing up.

Lance Trevor shook his head. "He was very specific. First the clone." He jutted his hairy chin in my direction. "Everyone else stays put."

"Who is he?" Zeus demanded of Sally, refusing to lower his weapon.

"Lance Trevor," Scorpio said quietly, carefully looking the man over. "Isn't it obvious?"

"He's in the corridor outside. He wants to have a talk." As I stepped past him, Lance displayed a row of crooked, decaying teeth.

There would be no trap. He really was waiting in the corridor outside. Just like Lance said, he wanted to have a chat.

I wanted to have a little chat, too. After all, I was curious what I had been doing all this time.

Chapter 13

The one thing everyone agreed upon about clones is that one would eventually destroy the other. We would mindlessly seek each other out and then –

Well, that was just it. I couldn't connect the dots. There was someone else out there who looked and acted just like me, with all the same memories and habits and whatever else it is that makes one of us different from the rest. I knew that. It bothered me.

No, the feeling was deeper and harder to ignore. It *disturbed* me. There hadn't been a minutestretch since I first found out that the thought was far from my mind.

But maniacal, pathological, homicidal rage? I didn't feel any of it. I wasn't going to stick a knife in his neck or try and nail him with my laser gun. I'm a lot of things, but I'm not a cold-blooded murderer. I never will be.

The narrow, curving corridors of the orbiter were eerily silent. I could hear the electrical grid humming, punctuated by the occasional, hysterical crackle. Up ahead somewhere one of the glow panels kept going out and coming back to life again.

The orbiter was deserted. Of course, I thought to myself. I would have cleared it out of people, too. After all, this was a private affair.

Our ship had been outfitted with huge magnets to induce a sense of gravity, but the orbiter was far too large a place for a similar approach. According to guidelines made public by Developmental Engineering, the fields produced by the magnets are only safe up to a certain, officially approved strength, and the orbiter would clearly require too many.

Naturally, this threshold had been discovered using the most rigorous, scientific standards.

Whatever that means. There is no available data on the rate of cancer or spontaneous, fatal mutation among frequent space travelers. It would, in fact, be treason to search for it. Of course, most frequent space travelers don't live long enough to come down with cancer.

The sense of gravity there on the orbiter was provided by the centrifugal force of the outer rim spinning around its center. The floor where I placed my feet was pointed away, my head towards the hub.

I was upside down, walking on the ceiling.

"Hello," I said from somewhere behind me.

I turned. There I was, standing with hands on my hips. We stood, separated by a short but safe distance, looking myself over.

We were wearing the same overalls, the same shirt, and the same boots. It was all standard fare in the Bunker, but somehow out there on the orbiter, face to face, it seemed important.

How can I explain what I felt? No matter what I tell you, you will never know. The only people who could possibly understand have stood there staring themselves in the eyes just like me, and there aren't very many of them.

All I can say is that it was like looking at myself in a mirror. Except what I saw had a life of its own. It didn't move the way I moved and it wouldn't shrink or disappear if I walked off. George Walker, it didn't even have the same expression on its face.

It was wrong. I felt it in my bones. I was me. So who was this?

Funny thing was, it was just as wrong for the other one. I could see it in his eyes looking back at me. After all, there wasn't anyone else on Gaia who could read them better.

Which one was the reflection? And where was the mirror?

"It's about time," I replied and blew out a long sigh of relief. "I didn't think those cancerheads were ever going to agree to put in here."

I laughed nervously. "Suspicious?"

I nodded my head. "Paranoid is more like it."

"Is Sally in there?" I gestured back the way I had come.

"Sure. She can't wait to see you."

"I thought so. But we've got time. There are a few things I want to ask you."

"Let me guess," I said, smirking.

"You want to know what I've been up to."

We both smiled at each other, but neither of us moved a muscle.

"I have no idea what's supposed to happen next," one of us admitted.

"Me neither," I replied.

"I thought I'd just play it by ear."

"I knew you were going to say that."

"Why'd you send Lance after me?"

I shrugged. "Why not? It seemed the best way to get my life back. Not to mention –"

"– screwing up Scorpio's plans. Yeah, I know."

"I can't have another one of myself running around causing trouble and being a general nuisance."

"Exactly. It's just that he seems kind of incompetent."
"Lance has his uses."
"How'd you meet him?"
I sighed. "Wow. You know, it's a long story."
"It's okay. We've got time."
"Sure," I said, smirking. "Did you ever manage to get your hands on the Self-Destruct Mechanism?"
"Sure."
"Wow. Okay. Lance didn't tell me that."
"Was he on the surface?"
"Yeah."
"Keeping an eye on us. Sure. What'd he report?"
"Not here." I looked around. "Why don't we head over to the gravity chamber? It's a much better place than these hallways. They're cramped."
"Sure."
"Okay."
I gestured, and I followed.

We had only gone a few steps down the corridor when I threw the first punch. I was trying to take me by surprise. The target was the right kidney, a painful spot to land a sucker punch. I hoped it would take me down without much of a fuss, but almost the same instant I set in motion I swerved and deflected the attack with a quick, blocking thrust using both hands.

We stared at each other for a short but meaningful moment. The electrical grid hissed and cackled. Somewhere behind us, the light dimmed and resurged.

We knew exactly how we thought, where the punches were supposed to land and what the timing would be. It was useless to try and overpower each other.

"Come on."
"Yeah, let's go."

We walked side by side. I led me down the narrow, slightly curving corridor. Occasionally, we passed a door or a dark, narrow opening, but it wasn't until we reached a trapdoor in the ceiling that we veered off our path.

There were some rungs running up the side of the wall. I climbed them, braced myself, and pushed open the trapdoor. Gesturing for me to follow, I disappeared into whatever lay beyond.

What lay beyond was a long, well lit corridor – a tunnel is more like it – that stretched upward as far as I could see. It was narrow and cramped. The line of rungs continued unbroken past the trapdoor. On the opposite wall was a matching set. I clambered over to the empty ladder and quickly caught up with me.

We made our way slowly, neither one ever getting much ahead of the other.

"As soon as they told me they wanted a brainscan I knew something was up," I said as we plodded upward.

"I know," I replied. "Who under the dome needs a brainscan when you've come down with the flu? You reprogrammed the medibot to send me home. Then you took my place."

We both smiled. "None of those typhoids knows I can code."

"Not even Sally."

"You didn't tell her, did you?"

"No." I swallowed uncomfortably. "She's not interested in talking to me."

I laughed derisively.

The gravity was getting weaker. Which way was up was becoming less of a certainty and more a conviction.

"What did you do with all the people?" It was a question that had been bothering me since I arrived.

"Oh, I locked them up in the transport."

"Don't you think they'll try and escape?"

"I doubt it. The outer lock's seal is broken. The door doesn't even close all the way." Suddenly, an aggressive, injured look took hold of my face. "Why? What'd you think I did with them?"

"Oh, nothing," I responded smoothly and decisively. "I was just curious."

"Isn't it what you would have done?"

"Sure," I replied, nodding my head vigorously. "I just didn't know. About the transport, I mean. After all, this is my first visit. You've been here a while." I spoke quickly, hoping to talk past the fact we must have seen the ships docked to the orbiter coming in.

"So you managed to get your hands on the Self-Destruct Mechanism." I let out a low whistle. "Honestly, I didn't think you would."

"Yeah, you did everything you could to stop us. Are you going to try and stop Scorpio from using it?"

"Probably. Yeah. I mean, ever since I found out how he tried to use me, I've been doing my best to get him tagged. I don't see why I should stop now."

"At least you were out on your own. They had me with them the whole time. There wasn't anything I could do."

"So you're not in with them?"

"In with them?"

"On their side."

My nose crinkled up. "No, of course not. I don't like being tricked up that way, either."

I seemed to be getting excited. "Maybe we can work together."

"Work together?"

"Sure. Why not?"

Indeed, why not? My brain didn't see any reason. Just because everyone else said we had to be at each other's throats didn't mean they were right.

A light went on in my head. "That footage on the tube. Of you sweating it out on the asteroid. It was staged."

I smiled appreciatively. "Not staged, no. A laser cannon was targeting me and I really only did have a few secondstretches before I was blown to smithereens. But they didn't show what I was doing, did they? The image was a close up. Those smack addicts at Homeland Security cropped the video."

"They cut you out before the explosion."

"There never was an explosion."

"Obviously."

I was very proud of myself. "I managed to override the system."

I frowned. Sure, I liked to boast, but what was the point of exaggerating to myself? "You did what? How?"

I shook my head. "Most of the defenses are aimed at intruders. But I was already inside. Don't you get it?"

Yeah, I got it. "But there *was* an explosion," I pointed out. "You actually carried out the mission. You blew up the transceivers. Why would you go and do that?"

"Well, I tipped Raluca off first," I replied. "How else do you think she managed to take control of Hallowed Hills so quickly? Together, we made sure the communications equipment was repaired in short order."

I never knew I was such a high flier. "Raluca? How? She's an Alpha. You couldn't just call her up out of the blue."

"Lance Trevor."

"He's not in the Underground."

I shrugged. "Maybe he is, maybe he isn't. If he is, none of us knows about it, anyway. But he's a bodyguard with high ranking clients."

"Raluca!"

I nodded. "She was one of them. I told you he has his uses."

All the loose ends were starting to fit nicely together. "So, Scorpio arrives on Earth and walks into a carefully laid trap. He's tagged and bagged before even getting off the tarmac." I paused before I said, "Of course, they didn't bag us, did they? He actually recovered the Self-Destruct Mechanism."

I was growing more and more excited. There's nothing more pleasing than when a master plan comes together just like you thought. "I took precautions."

"Precautions?"

"Here's something you probably don't know. I sneaked onto that asteroid after they put it back in operation. Even if they *tried* to send anything through, it wouldn't do them any good."

"You installed a filter."

I nodded my head, clearly pleased to show off how smart I was. "All communications from Earth pass through that asteroid. But it won't process anything that comes from you or Scorpio or any of the others. Including myself."

Yes, it's exactly what I would have done. "Scorpio doesn't know. He hasn't tried to use it yet."

I noticed it was getting harder to put my foot down on the rung below. Up ahead, I could see that the corridor ended in another trapdoor.

"You don't know that. He could be trying now." I shrugged. "Either way, it won't do him any good. You can't disable it remotely. It's hardwired. So the only place he can go is back to the Bunker. Whichever one he picks, he'll be arrested."

"I'm a traitor, too."

"Yeah, we'll all traitors in the Bunker."

"No, really. It's official."

"No worries. I have contacts." I tried to lay my fears aside with a callous wave of the hand. "We'll get your situation sorted."

The gravity had almost run out. The end of the corridor was nearly at hand.

I didn't know why, but I felt like I was walking into a trap. Could I trust myself?

And if I couldn't trust myself, who in the Bunker could I trust?

The gravity chamber was aptly named, of course, for there was none.

We floated slowly through the still air separated by a meter or two.

I had already lost track of the floor.

I had never been on the inside of a icosahedron before.

Don't know what an icosahedron is? I didn't either until I stepped into one.

The room was like a sphere, but instead of a smooth surface there were twenty, identical, triangular shaped panels. They were padded with a soft, forgiving material. Forming a ring around the room, round portals had been set in some of them. It was through one of those that we had entered.

"Amazing place, isn't it?" I asked.

I must admit, I was fascinated.

I'm not sure where the light came from, but everything was bathed in a rich, vibrant blue. My teeth were a bluish white. So were the stripes on the sides of my overalls. So was the medibot tucked into one of the chamber's twelve corners.

Like the rest of the orbiter, this place was deserted.

I knew why I had brought us here. It wasn't just a fascinating place. It was a safe place. It was impossible to hide anything. The walls were padded.

"What do they use this room for?" I asked.

"Training, mostly. A lot of the people stationed here come to exercise. I like it because –"

"– it's fun to float around." I smiled. "Yeah, I know."

"Sure."

We floated around for a while.

"So here we are," I prodded after I thought enough time had passed.

"Okay, okay." I paused thoughtfully as I finished a somersault. "You really don't know about Delinda?"

The way he was looking at me, I thought maybe I should. Quickly, I scoured my memory, but there was no Delinda there. "She's a woman?" Something in my stomach tightened.

He nodded. "Yes, yes. She's a woman alright." Again, he eyed me uncertainly. "I guess the best place to start is after we switched places."

"Sounds about right." Already, I was settling in for a good story. This was the perfect place. I was relaxed. My hands were behind my head and I was tumbling in slow motion through the air. Every once in a while I'd bounce gently off one of the padded, triangular panels. "Last I know, you were headed for a meeting with Scorpio."

"That's right. And Sally. She was there, too."

"Yeah, I know."

"She told you?"

"I'm not sure. But I know she was there. And Alibaba and Starbuoy. They're dead now."

"Yeah, I know. Lance told me."

"Lance?"

"I told you he was down on the surface. But we're getting ahead of ourselves. Let's go back to the beginning. Just after you were born."

I took offense. "I was born thirty-five year-, five month-, and – let's see..."

"Ten daystretches ago."

"Yeah, that's right."

"Are we going to get on with this or what?"

"Go ahead."

"After the brainscan they took me to the morgue. It's Gamma clearance down there. That's where we had the meeting."

"That's where they tried to bring you on board."

"They told me about you. They said if I didn't agree they'd just kill me on the spot. At first I wasn't sure. After all, they thought I was the clone, expendable like you. Alibaba and Starbuoy were especially vicious. I didn't shed a tear when I heard those typhoids got snuffed out."

"The threats didn't work, though."

"Not at all. I called their bluff. That's when they changed their tune."

"Rewards this time."

I nodded. "Plenty. Security clearance, credits, an apartment of my own – private dining facilities! Scorpio stood there cool as stone and watched it all. I knew he was the boss. I also knew their promises meant nothing if he didn't intend to keep them."

"They didn't. They sent you off to die."

"I didn't know that at the time. Anyway, I realized all this endless discussion wasn't going to get me anywhere. So I agreed to what they wanted and they let me go."

"Just like that?"

"Well, I assumed I was being followed."

"Not by any of them. Someone else. From the Underground."

"That's right.

"It was Lance."

"Nope. I never did find out who it was."

"So how do you know you lost your tail?"

"How do you ever know that in a place like the Bunker?"

I was right. The constant surveillance is something we live with.

"Anyway, I slipped out through the tunnels that lead to the food pits in Q-13 sector."

"Food pits?"

"Yeah, they're connected to the morgue."

I swallowed uncomfortably.

"I know. It was already hard enough to get the slop down, wasn't it?"

"So you were heading for the asteroid."

"I took a detour first."

"I'll bet they weren't happy about it."

He shrugged. "What could they do? If we were seen together in public it might have tripped a surveillance program. Who knows. As long as they believed I was going – as long as I didn't try and disappear – I knew they wouldn't kill me."

"Sure."

"That's where I met Delinda."

"In the foot pits?"

"She was the director."

"Was?"

He flinched and looked away. "I'll get to that. Anyway, she was there on the floor with some technicians doing routine inspection when I climbed out one of the drainage pipes and – being a loyal citizen like the rest of us – demanded to see my security clearance."

"Scorpio forgot to give you a waiver."

"Right. But Delinda didn't turn me in."

"Why not?"

He shrugged. "My rugged charm, I guess."

"You led her on?"

"I did what I had to do."

"You told her about Scorpio."

"Not at first. I knew I was being watched and listened in on. I told her I was on a secret mission and here was her shot at quick advancement."

"She already had a Delta clearance."

"Who's happy with Delta when you can have Gamma?"

"You promised her Gamma?" The eyes were bugging out of my head.

"Sure. There was no way I could get it for her, but that didn't matter."

"Scorpio could."

"Exactly. Anyway, back at her apartment I met her bodyguard, Lance."

I frowned. "Her apartment?"

"It was the only place we could talk privately."

"Oh, okay. So Lance was her personal bodyguard."

"Yeah, her brother, too. Control assigned him to a security firm over at Defense. They hire out to all the big-wigs. She was one of his assignments."

"What help did you think you could get out of this Delinda anyway?"

"She got me a security clearance! I'm Delta now." He eyed me haughtily.

"Why would she do that?"

"Because!" he snapped and pumped his fist.

I started. "Okay, okay. George Walker. No need to get all riled up. It was just a question."

"Well stop asking and just listen."

There was a moment of uncomfortable silence before he said, "She'd been cloned, too."

"Cloned?"

"Yeah. A few yearstretches back. She signed up for a medical experiment run by some flaky private firm in Human Resources. That's how she got her Delta clearance."

"I see," I said darkly. Suddenly, it all started making sense.

"What?"

"Nothing. Go on. What was the experiment?"

"It was some kind of medical research. They were going to do tests on both the original and the clone and compare the results."

"But something went wrong."

"The clones got loose. She tracked hers down and killed it. In broad daylight, too. She didn't get arrested or anything. Pretty impressive, eh?"

I understood perfectly. After all, the two of them had shared the most intimate of experiences. They must have just melted in each other's arms.

Part of me was trying to deny it, but another part knew I didn't have the luxury of indulging my ego. Not if I wanted to survive. Events were going to unfold quickly, and I had to be ready. I had to be sharp.

"Don't judge me," he barked at me angrily.

"What about Sally?"

"Don't ask me about Sally, either!"

"What happened to Delinda?"

"I had to get rid of her."

"Why? She outlive her use?"

"She found out."

"About the mission."

"Yeah, and she didn't like it. Destroy Control? The whole Bunker would go to hell, she said. Wholesale murder and mass destruction. Who knows what would happen. She was afraid. Genuinely afraid. She was going to blow the whistle."

"But you wanted to get your hands on the Self-Destruct Mechanism."

So there you have it. Not only had I cheated on Sally, but I was a common murderer, too, inspired by simple greed. A credit-a-dozen criminal. The lowest of the low.

Wait. No, I wasn't. I hadn't done any of those things. It wasn't me floating around there. He looked like me. He had a lot of the same habits. But I wouldn't have turned a trick just to save my skin, not when there was some other way out of a boehner.

He had a gun. I always carry one whenever I can. I had to maneuver close enough so that when he reached for it I could stop him. I had to keep him distracted.

"So that's what Lance meant about revenge."

"Yeah." He snorted with contempt. "He went after me when he found out about Delinda. I thought I could make it to the asteroid first, but he's trained for this kind of thing. When he caught up with me, I managed to convince him I was you."

I felt a sudden and intense hatred for this pretender masquerading as myself.

"I told you not to judge me." He was growing angry, too.

"I'm not judging you."

"Yes, you are! I can see it in your eyes." His fists were clenched tightly at his side.

Mine must have been the worst kind of rejection. Who knows what excuses he had made up? It didn't matter. He might have been able to fool himself, but they would be no defense against me.

When he was a simple adulterer, the self-loathing might have been manageable. But calculated murder! Not committed in self-defense, but to further his own self-interest. I could only imagine. I don't want to imagine.

He was unable to escape from it. And now he saw this self-loathing framed in the same face he looked at every morning in the mirror. It was my face! My own, but untouched by the guilt and misery that comes from knowing you've done something unspeakably wrong and you can never put it right.

No wonder I provoked such a strong reaction.

But he wasn't the only one feeling explosive. I was consumed by a growing rage. You think you understand, but you don't. What lay behind it was more than the simple fact he had taken another woman and killed her.

I'm not a saint. I've never claimed to be. I know I have flaws. We all do.

There's a certain image I have of myself. Call it my ego if you want. I identify with it strongly. Maybe it's not who I am, but it's pretty damn close. Sure, it causes problems sometimes. It complains a lot and tempts me into making a lot of the same mistakes over and over again.

But they're my patterns, my mistakes. There's a certain comfort there. I can live with this image of myself. It's taken a while, but I've gotten used to it.

The monster in front of me, though, didn't jive with that image in my head, the one that I was comfortable with, the one that was me. Even worse, it was someone I hated.

How could I have ever become him? How could it have even been possible?

You want to know what I was feeling? I had to put an end to him, eradicate him, because only then could I be sure that he'd never existed at all!

"Do you know what Delinda told me?" he sneered as I closed in.

"What?"

"That the clone always wants to claim the identity of the original." He laughed, a stinging noise filled with malice. "As if it could change the fact it's just a copy. A thing with no mother, no father, no friends or thoughts of its own. A substitute, really. And there's no use for a second rate copy when the original is in perfectly good condition."

"You cancerhead," I spat between clenched teeth. "You killed Antinous, too. Didn't you?"

A curious combination of confusion and surprise took hold of his face. "What?" It looked like he thought I was playing some kind of trick.

But he was the one who played dirty tricks. He was playing one now. "You sent Lance to do your handiwork when no one was around!"

The rage boiled over. I left the realm of thinking and reason and went back to the primal part of being where terrible things can happen.

And they did.

When he reached for his gun, I was ready. I lunged and pulled the hand back. We struggled briefly for mastery, but like most everything produced in the Bunker, the pistol was flimsy and cheap. Within a matter of moments the battery had become hopelessly disengaged from the body, and it was useless.

There's no need for me to describe to you our titanic struggle. It's a memory I want to leave untouched.

Don't get me wrong. I'm not ashamed of what I did. It's just that talking about him also somehow brings him back to life.

I'll tell you this much: it was one of the strangest experiences I've ever had. Forget the fact we were fighting in zero gravity. I'm sure plenty of other people have done that. It was weird because we were almost the same person.

Almost. You see, in the last monthstretches we'd lived different lives. We'd had different experiences. So we weren't exactly the same after all.

It was only a matter of time before one of us landed a punch. After that, the advantage just got bigger and bigger. That blow opened the door to another, and another.

I was the lucky one. I got the first punch in.

Who knows what made the difference. The physical activity of trudging around in the wilderness down on Earth while he was floating up there in the gravity chamber? Maybe his guilt sapped his strength. I don't know. I don't care.

He's dead. You can trust me on that. I'm not proud of what I did. But it couldn't have ended any other way.

Even though I was sure he was dead, I kept on hitting him. His whole body was turned into a bloody pulp. It was only when I couldn't recognize myself in what was left of his face that I managed to break out of the haze.

Panting, I looked around the gravity chamber. Hundreds of round, red spheres of various sizes – some as large as my fist – floated eerily about the room. Mixed in among them were bits of cartilage and bone.

Thank the dome we're in a gravity chamber, I thought to myself. The blood won't cling to anything. If only I'm careful enough to get all the globules, there wouldn't be any traces.

And then I laughed. So this is why he had brought me here! He thought he'd be the one doing the cleaning up.

I think I laughed for a long time. If anyone had come in and seen me then, they'd have had every reason to believe I was a raving lunatic.

Eventually, though, I knew I'd have to get to work. Destroying him was only half the job.

I couldn't use any of the available cleanbots because there'd be a record of the activity. It's not that I couldn't have hacked into the data store, but it takes an awful long time to chase after the residuals. And time is exactly what I didn't have much of. All I had left had to be spent on the medibot.

I grabbed the messy corpse and pulled its head roughly to one side. Somewhere in that fleshy neck was his I-chip.

"Hey, doc!"

The box-like contraption with all the extensions slowly came to life. "Has someone been hurt?" The whining, mechanical voice was emitted through a set of dingy speakers lacking low tones.

"Get over here. I've got a job for you."

Chapter 14

When I pushed open the bulkhead and entered the ship, George and Sally were lounging listlessly in the center of the room, throwing dice. Lance was sitting up against the wall near the entrance almost exactly where I had left him. Zeus was seated, staring emptily out a rear porthole, twiddling his thumbs.

The dice slipped out of George's hand and rattled to the floor. The four of them stared at me dumbly as if I had stepped out of the forward viewing tube.

I looked them casually over. "Where's Scorpio?"

"Terry?" It was George. The fat bastard licked his lips nervously. "Is that you?"

I laughed. "Who else would it be?"

Sally climbed to her feet. "The real one?"

I held out my arms. "The one and only!"

She yelped and ran to me.

Zeus rose warily to his feet. "How do we know for sure?" He ran a thick hand through his wavy, blond hair and peered at me as if he had found some way to tell the difference.

"Scan him." The voice was Scorpio's. He had come to the doorway leading to the barracks. The eyes behind the squarish lenses were red and swollen. I suspect he had been crying.

George had the honors. "Yep," he affirmed at last, staring at the readout of the hand-held device. "It's Terry alright." He looked up at me, a smile spreading across his face. "I never thought I'd be happy to see you."

But I wasn't paying him any attention. I was holding my girl. The missing piece in my world had been fitted back into place. I was content just to feel whole again.

"Not a scratch on him," Zeus observed dryly.

I disengaged from Sally, although we still clung to each other around the waist.

"You caused us a lot of trouble," Scorpio began darkly and stepped into the room. I imagined he had a lot to get off his chest.

I shrugged. "I did what you wanted me to do, didn't I?"

Scorpio grabbed the stick from under his arm and began to chop at the air. "You switched with the clone. We should have been doing business with you all this time. Instead, we had an impostor. Then –"

swish! "– you put it on Ten Things I Hate About Treason. What were you thinking? The clone might have been eliminated before we could use it. Not to mention the danger to Van Johnson. And just now –" swish! "– you induced Control to destroy Hallowed Hills settlement on Earth." He took another step into the room. "We barely made it out alive. Finally, there are the suspicious deaths of Lady Lagrange and –" he swallowed thickly "– poor Antinous. You'll have to account for those."

"The clone was responsible for Antinous' death," I responded coolly. "If anything, you should thank me for knocking him off."

"The clone?" The words had been spoken so quietly I had to read Scorpio's lips.

I nodded. "He admitted as much before I killed him." Out of the corner of my eye, I studied Lance, but I couldn't get a good read on him. "He had some kind of poison and was sneaking it into Antinous' food. It probably overcame him while he was in the river. That's why it looked like he drowned."

A look of intense relief passed over George's face.

"Are you sure?" Scorpio eyed George the way a hunter watches a much sought after prize escape his grasp. "How'd you get it to open up?"

"What happened back there was between him and me. All you have to know is that we told each other everything. Trust me. The meeting was more intimate than you could ever know."

"It could have been lying." Scorpio's teeth were clenched.

I shook my head. "I'd know."

"Why?"

"Why what?"

"Why did the clone do it!" Scorpio screamed and slashed at the air with his stick.

I was treading on dangerous waters. I knew I had to play my hand perfectly or the game would be up.

"He knew how much Antinous meant to you, and he also knew you were the only one who could locate the Self-Destruct Mechanism."

"No. I would have sensed it. If anyone, *you* were acting against us. The way I figure it, Kuasimodo and you are linked up back at the Bunker. You're acting in concert."

I shook my head. "The clone turned against you, Scorpio. Think about it. I was on your side, so he wanted to trip you up. It's as simple as that. By killing Antinous, he thought you'd be so unnerved the mission was bound to fail."

There followed a heavy silence. Scorpio stared at me, eyes bugging from his head, trying to decide whether or not to believe me.

I thought it was best to keep talking. "It was the clone I was after. You know how it is between the original and the copy. I did my best to avoid collateral damage but –" I shrugged indifferently. "You shouldn't have kept him with you."

Scorpio's eyes narrowed suspiciously. "How do I know you're telling the truth?"

The smile on my face widened. "Scorpio, I'm Terry Renfield. I always have been."

Sally squeezed me around the waist.

"You killed it just like you promised?" Lance stood up. A few crooked teeth peeked out between his chapped lips.

"You'll never see him again. That's for sure."

"I want to go see for myself." He stomped eagerly out of the bulkhead.

Of course, there was nothing for him to find. I had incinerated the body and all the debris that belonged to it and deposited the ashes into the solar wind.

I swallowed and pressed on. Better to give them all the bad news at once. "There's something else you should know. Something you're not going to like." Quickly, I detailed what I had learned about the communications filter.

"Now why would you go and do a stupid thing like that?" Scorpio demanded. The toes of one of his black, animal skin boots began to tap at the ground.

"What kind of flapheads do you take us for, anyway?" George complained.

"Relax! He's on our side," Sally insisted and looked up at me. "Aren't you, honey?"

"Yes! And I still expect to be rewarded just like you promised."

"Tell me why you installed the filter," Scorpio suggested, "and I won't have you ejected into space."

"Insurance." It was a perfectly reasonable explanation. "To make sure I really will be rewarded like you promised. Otherwise I might *already* be floating around outside in space."

There was another moment of strained silence that was eventually broken by Zeus' chuckling. "He's clever, this Typhon."

"Is he now?" Scorpio whispered. "All he's done is make me mad. At a time when – in fact – I'm very inclined to indulge my anger. What happens after he goes and removes this filter? What's his insurance policy then?"

"There's no need to remove it," I pointed out. "It only filters out communications signed by you, me, Kuasimodo, and Complicity." I jutted my chin in Zeus' direction. "He could upload the Self-Destruct Mechanism."

All eyes turned on Zeus.

He wasn't keen on obliging, of course.

"I won't do it!" We could hear him shouting from the bridge. "Stop asking me!"

The rickety vessel we had arrived on was out of fuel, but the sleek luxury cruiser docked next to the transport was not. Before rejoining the others I snuck on board, hacked into the security system, and granted myself access. Later on, I told the others I had beat the key out of one of the prisoners.

We skipped out, leaving the orbiter deprived of all its communications capabilities. There was plenty of Vitamim and water, and the air-recycling system could keep them alive indefinitely. It was safe to assume that by the time they got in contact with anyone else from the Bunker, we would all be dead or entirely safe.

Or – more likely – they would all have killed each other in a frenzy of paranoid suspicion.

Either way, it wouldn't matter.

The vessel was very modern, very clean, and very fast. Scorpio estimated we'd arrive in the vicinity of the communications asteroid within a matter of weekstretches.

We spent some time wandering around the ship. There were several small but private suites. The beds were soft and comfortable, the floors carpeted. Each had a private toilet and shower.

A private toilet and shower! I was shocked and enraged by the waste. There was hardly enough water as it was. And these people were using it to wash away filth and dirt!

Near the aft of the ship, there was a small place outfitted with various tools for environmental control: a refrigerated box with a door and handle, and near it several round, metallic surfaces that would quickly grow scalding hot. Inside the box was the most curious thing of all: water cooled down so much it had become solid. I held some of the stuff in my hands. It melted quickly.

Lance told us the room was a kitchen and was used to prepare food, the kind that Betas and Alphas had access to.

I spent a lot of time in that room, trying to imagine how it would be used and what kind of meals could be prepared there. What did they look like? The slop was always the same.

I thought of that curious foodstuff Scorpio had been eating when I first met him. What had he called it? An apple.

What would you do with an apple in a place like this? Or had it already been done to it by the time I saw it?

Until that moment, I was just trying to survive. I hadn't been very keen on helping them. After all, they had pulled me in against my will. It's my nature to resist. But now – well, the world inside my head had changed. I wasn't fixated on the confrontation with the other anymore. I could actually take the time to look around, and now it was through eyes that were able to see more clearly.

I wanted this conspiracy to succeed.

It was wrong that the vast majority of us had been crammed into barracks eating slop three times a day, our lives planned out from the very beginning, with no real choices and no real risks, just to support the lifestyle of a few privileged smack addicts we never even knew existed.

I wanted my shot, too. A real shot, not just the illusion of one, a spoon-fed opportunity to prove to myself I was just an average flaphead married to his mediocrity.

If ever I was ready for anything, I was ready for this.

Funny thing was, it seemed like I was the only one.

The others were less than enthusiastic. Several of them had been killed. They had been at it for too long, and the final victory always seemed just out of reach.

For example, they had the Self-Destruct Mechanism, but they couldn't use it.

The argument Scorpio and Zeus were having was typical of their dilemma. It put everybody else on edge because they all had their doubts.

"Why should I hitch my wagon to yours?" Zeus shouted. "You're known criminals! All of you! As soon as we get anywhere, you'll be picked up and gassed!"

Scorpio's answer came soft and muddled through the doors to the bridge where we had gathered.

"It's your boehner, not mine," Zeus responded derisively. "I don't want anything to do with it."

"But we both want the same thing!" Scorpio's voice had picked up. "Why did you have your Olympians in the first place?"

When he answered, we could hear that Zeus had grown subdued.

"It took me a long time to build them up. Now they're gone. Scattered or dead in the bombardment."

"That's right! But here we are, and I've got the Self-Destruct Mechanism."

If Zeus replied, we couldn't hear him.

"Let's be straight with each other for once, Andreas. Every Alpha wants to take out Control. It's a fact. But none of us can get very far on his own. That's why no one's been able to do it. We're all too busy jockeying for favor. Whose favor? Control's! George Walker, it's absurd! All we have to do is cooperate!"

After that, Zeus stormed out of the bridge. We scattered before him like rats abandoning the Barry Goldwater Neighborhood Dining Experience in Q-15 sector when they switch on the heating units.

"You better hope I don't catch you cancerheads next time!" he roared after us.

Later on, as we lay next to each other in one of the luxurious beds, Sally said, "You were real busy after we split up. I'm so curious... Or can't you tell me about it?" She looked up and smiled playfully.

"There's not much to tell," I responded carefully. "I think you know everything already."

"But what about your security clearance?" She snuggled up closer.

"Oh, that." I paused uncertainly.

She cocked her head to the side and laughed. "What's wrong, Terry? You get involved with another woman?"

A pang of guilt washed over me. It must have shown on my face, because she drew her breath sharply in and pulled away. "George Walker," she breathed. "There *was* another woman."

Oh, no, I remember thinking to myself. I've just got her back. I'm not about to lose her a second time. Clarity and a sense of purpose filled my mind.

I grabbed her by the hand. "No, baby," I told her earnestly. "There wasn't anyone else. The whole time only you."

"I don't believe you."

"Look me in the eyes."

She did.

"I had help from a woman named Delinda. She was the director of one of the food pits in Q sector. She got me the Delta clearance. She was in love with me but I never betrayed you."

As I spoke the words, she stared deep inside me, probing.

"She's dead now."

"You killed her?"

I shook my head. "Someone else. For some reason that had nothing to do with me. But her death solved a nasty problem. If I'd tried to run away she'd have turned against me."

She held on to her anger and suspicion a few stretches longer before they finally broke. "Oh, Terry," she breathed, collapsing against me and burying her head in my chest. "I'm sorry. It's just that you're the only one I've got in this damned place, and if you ever betrayed me, I – well, I don't know what I'd do."

I knew exactly what she meant. Our mates were the only consolation Control allowed us. Everything else had been taken away.

I wanted to unplug this whole stinking world. I just hoped the others still did, too.

When we were in the vicinity of the asteroid, Scorpio and Zeus called us out to the bridge for a meeting.

"Okay, Terry," Zeus began, "now's your moment to shine."

"We wouldn't be here if he hadn't installed the damned filter in the first place!" Scorpio murmured softly. His stick was clasped tightly under one arm. A white knuckle grasped the handle firmly.

"Right," agreed Zeus. "Which is why he's going to go sneak past the security and remove it personally."

"He's done it before," Lance said and winked at me.

"And he knows exactly where it is and how to deactivate it. Don't you, babe?" Sally looked up at me expectantly.

"Sure."

"Once the filter's out of the way, Scorpio and I will beam the Self-Destruct Mechanism into the local server node."

George looked up hopefully. "And then – ?"

Scorpio's face was as cool as stone. "And then when Control goes offline we'll seize the initiative."

To be sure, I didn't understand why we were here.

"You can beam the Self-Destruct Mechanism into any server node," I pointed out. "Why does it have to be this one?"

"Stop making trouble," Scorpio replied icily and glared at me.

"You all are traitors," Zeus observed. "This is the only node we can hit."

"It's secured just like all the others. The chance of being arrested –"

"– is much smaller here, Typhon," Zeus interrupted. "As Lance and Complicity have already pointed out, this is tried and true territory for you."

I didn't like it. None of us knew what agreement Scorpio and Zeus had come to. All we knew is that the arguing had suddenly stopped.

But I was running short of arguments. From their point of view, there was no good reason I *shouldn't* have been able to find and disable the filter.

"The security system's probably been upgraded," I said. "To prevent an intrusion just like I managed last time."

I could see that Scorpio was getting fed up. "Terry," he told me, "if there's anything you've proven in the last monthstretches, it's that you are a miracle worker." He paused and fingered the handle to his stick. "Go out and work miracles."

I was about to say something, but he interjected before I could manage. "Don't come back if you don't."

To make matters worse, they were sending Lance and George with me.

"It was hard enough on my own!" I shouted. "How am I supposed to pull this off with baggage?"

My protests fell on deaf ears.

"You'll need help," Zeus pointed out. "Like you said, the security will be tighter. There might be goons this time, and Scorpio can't call them off."

Like hell he couldn't. Even if he was officially a traitor, there were most certainly people out there who owed him favors. Unless they all thought he had no chance of being rehabilitated, which – given the circumstances – was a fair possibility. Still, the alarm bells were going off in my head.

Were they keeping Sally as a hostage?

"We need her for logistical support," Scorpio told me.

Sally didn't seem to be thinking along the same lines as I was, and there wasn't a good opportunity to draw her aside. Maybe she was oblivious to the danger (I doubted it) or maybe she had some angle of her own she wasn't telling me (that must have been it).

George and Lance were just as happy about being sent along as I was.

"Wait a stretch," George protested, his eyebrows furrowing suspiciously. "Don't we get a say? When Control's offline there won't be Alphas or Betas anymore. Or do you expect to boss us around instead?"

Well, it was an interesting question. "I sure as the dome am not going to risk my neck just to replace Control with you two typhoids,"

I stated and planted both feet resolutely on the ground.

Zeus and Scorpio exchanged glances.

"And I don't see why I'm expected to go along!" Lance piped in. "I never was a part of your conspiracy and I'd prefer to leave it that way!"

Scorpio fixed Lance with a meaningful eye. "The moment you showed up at the spaceport looking for the clone, you got involved."

Lance glared back, trying to think of something clever to say.

I could see that Scorpio was close to losing his temper.

Suddenly, Zeus spoke up. "Citizens. Citizens!" Surprised, we all gave him our attention. "Don't you see what we're doing? We're so full of suspicion and paranoia that we're turning on each other, and for no reason at all. Don't you see that if we all do our part and simply *trust* one another – just this one time! – a whole new world will open up? Can you imagine what it would be like?"

He paused and looked us over. "Maybe Scorpio and I have gone about this the wrong way," he admitted. "Maybe we've given you the impression we've got our own agenda, that we mean to take over the Bunker or something sinister along those lines."

"Well," I said, daring to speak aloud what the rest of us were already thinking, "just a few daystretches ago you were dead set against beaming up the Self-Destruct Mechanism under your own credentials. Now you expect us to blindly follow your orders without telling us what changed your mind?"

Zeus nodded his head feverishly. "Fair enough. Like I said, we might have gone about this the wrong way. Old habits are hard to break. Even for us.

"I'll tell you why I'm helping out. It's the same reason why Lance will help us, too."

Lance grunted dismissively at the suggestion. "Let me guess," he sneered and glanced in my direction as if for support. "Freedom? Is that it?"

Zeus shook his head. "Nothing so ephemeral as that."

"Nothing so what?"

"Revenge." The word hung suspended before us like a cement block floating in the air.

"But I've already got my revenge," Lance objected meekly. "Terry here killed the clone. What do I need revenge for?"

"Why did the clone kill your sister in the first place?"

Lance shrugged. "You guys, I guess."

"Wrong. It was Control. It never gave the order directly, of course.

But Control acts to keep us harming each other. It has almost unlimited computing power and all the levers of decision making at its fingertips."

"I could use some revenge," George interrupted.

Our eyes turned to him.

"Yeah," he said, nodding his head dejectedly. "I fell in love when I was young. We had a child. Elisa was her name. Control decided she was too intelligent for her own good." He shrugged. "Anyway, after she was gone, my wife started behaving erratically. It wasn't long before they came for her, too."

"There you have it." Zeus looked at me as if waiting for my own, very touching, personal confession.

"Look, you don't have to convince me. I'll go."

"Really?" An eyebrow lifted curiously. "But just a moment ago –"

"My reasons are my own."

Again, Scorpio and Zeus exchanged glances.

"What's your reason?" Sally demanded of Zeus.

"My Olympians," he answered simply. "Lady Lagrange. All of them."

"Then why don't you just beam in the Self-Destruct Mechanism right now?" she pressed. "No one would have to leave the ship."

"I've tried," he responded smoothly. "But something's wrong. That asteroid isn't receiving *any* transmissions right now. The only way to access the equipment is directly."

We all took a moment to swallow that ominous development in silence.

"I want a gun," George insisted.

"You'll all have one," Zeus replied reassuringly.

"Okay, it's settled," Sally announced. She brought her hands together. "Let's cook up a plan."

The four of them drew closer and began a discussion in earnest.

I took the opportunity to have a little private conversation with Scorpio. "Look," I said, stepping close and whispering in his ear, "I know something's wrong. I also know it's out of my hands. Whatever happens –" I swallowed thickly. "If I do what you want, will you just make sure nothing bad happens to Complicity?"

A soft look spread across Scorpio's face. It looked strangely out of place there. He pulled me aside.

"You were able to lay my mind to rest about dear Antinous," he told me softly. "I am grateful." He cocked his head to one side and fixed me with one of his famously intense stares. "Insofar as I can prevent it, nothing untoward will happen to her."

I was relieved.

He said more. "Be alert," he told me. "The others are expendable."

I nodded, giving him my full attention.

"I wouldn't be too concerned about your personal safety, Terry Renfield, if that's who you really are. As you have shown time and again, you are a citizen of infinite resources."

I thought I detected a warning in his words.

"Hey, Terry!" It was George. He was standing, hands on his hips, a look of impatience on his face. "We need you over here!"

I wanted to ask Scorpio another question, but he had already turned his back on me.

Within an hourstretch, we had left the ship.

"You and Scorpio were getting pretty chummy before we left," Lance hissed as we crept along the rocky tunnel.

"Yeah," George agreed. "What was that all about?"

Asteroid 70927-Z is about a kilometer in diameter and very irregularly shaped. It's orbit lies for the most part between Earth and Mars and has a very singular peculiarity: there is always a direct line of sight from both planets when they are separated by the sun. Well, almost always. Long enough for it not to matter, anyway.

A great deal of communications equipment has been vested in the center of this tumbling space boulder. We were heading for it now.

Just as Zeus had predicted, there were goons this time. They radioed us as soon as we appeared on their radar.

I told them our ship (they could see it far in the distance) had been taken over by social deviants intent on blowing up the asteroid. Did they have any big guns we could turn on them?

They did, but they'd need our help manning them.

The quibble touched down near the center of the asteroid in a small but smooth patch near the only dome in sight. The dome wasn't high, but it was thick. Capping a conveniently large and deep crater, it had been designed to minimize the area necessary to create an enclosed space.

They let us in. As soon as we were out of our ecopacks, we drew our guns. Lance shot one of them outright, but George and I got the others to surrender. We gagged them, tied them up, and locked them in a storage locker.

The area under the dome was mostly open space. There were a few buildings, including a makeshift barracks and chemical toilets.

Everything had been constructed with a tight budget in mind.

Inside one of the structures was the entrance to the underground complex. I was glad to discover the tunnels were pressurized. It would have been uncomfortable traipsing around a rocky, uneven surface in that much bulk, not to mention hampering my reflexes.

"I wanted to make sure he and Zeus weren't going to let us dangle once we got here."

George and Lance, following closely behind, paused and exchanged nervous glances.

"And?" George pressed.

I stopped and turned around. "And what?"

George stuck his chin out. The radio Zeus had given him hung loosely from his belt next to his hip. "What did he say?"

I shrugged. "It doesn't matter what he said. I was interested in how he said it." I went back to leading them down the tunnel as if I had already explained a great deal.

Of course, I had no idea where I was going. My only hope was to find a terminal before they started to suspect something was flappy.

There was the occasional, lonely lightbulb hanging from wire every now and then, but so far no terminals.

"Are we there yet?" Lance demanded sourly.

"Stuff it," I growled. "I'm trying to remember the way."

To be sure, there was only one way to go. Occasionally we passed a door and I took a moment to peek inside. "Just to make sure there are no goons," I told Lance and George.

Most of the chambers held rusting, inoperable equipment. Once I thought I found what I was looking for, but there was no power.

"Are you sure you know what you're doing?"

Eventually, though, my luck turned. One of the chambers contained a bank of consoles that appeared to be working. I have no idea what that pile of dials, knobs, and touchscreens was supposed to do, but my eyes quickly zeroed in on what could only have been an outlet to the network.

"Guys, do you mind waiting outside?"

They minded.

There was nothing for it, so I sauntered on over to the outlet, activated the screen, and began tapping away.

George and Lance crept up behind me and watched what I was doing. George was too stupid to understand, but Lance was almost as sharp as he was smelly. "George Walker," he breathed once he saw me obtain an Alpha clearance and proceed onto screens he never even knew existed. "You're a hacker."

"How do you think I got out of here the first time?" I breathed absently as I searched around for any indication of where the filter might be. Normally, I would also be concerned about cleaning up after myself, too, but this time I didn't bother. After all, I was logged in as Zeus.

Lance giggled and patted his laser pistol. "Hackers are traitors," he pointed out and giggled again. "Maybe we should just shoot him now and throw ourselves at Control's mercy. It ought to count for something."

I paused for a stretch, ready to lunge for cover if I had to.

"Quit kidding around," George grumbled. "A bloke's got to concentrate."

A few stretches later, I stood up. "Okay, I got it."

"You removed the filter?" Lance asked suspiciously.

"Partly," I replied. "There's still some hardware to disable. Then you can radio back to Zeus."

I had found a schematic of the tunnels. Most of the operating transceivers were accessible via a shaft that led further into the heart of the asteroid. It wasn't far up the corridor.

"Come on," I said. "It's just down here."

What was I doing? It was hard to have a plan when I didn't know what awaited me. If there really was a filter – and I was hardly convinced – then I thought it most likely to be in the vicinity of the transmission gear. But what would it look like? And once I found it, what was I going to do with it?

They followed me in silence. Sure enough, a minutestretch or two later we came upon a trap door set in the floor.

"Down there?" George's nose crinkled up.

I pulled it open. A greasy, musty odor wafted up to us out of the blackness. Somewhere down there, pulleys and gears ground together angrily.

Lance took a step back. "Is this some kind of trick?"

"This where we have to go," I said.

"What's down there?" he wanted to know, staring warily into the shaft.

"The main battery. Don't worry about the noise. The shaft is safe."

Lance shook his head. "You're a flaphead if you think I'm climbing down that ladder."

I sighed, took out a flashlight, and aimed the beam into the shaft. "See? Nothing to be afraid of."

Indeed, after about five meters the rough hewn passage ended in another trap door.

"You go first," George suggested in such a way I knew it was useless to argue.

The air down there was hot, the ladder greasy. The rock walls were sweating. The horrible groaning of the unseen machinery came at me from all directions at once.

Above, framed by the entrance to the shaft, I could see George and Lance's nervous faces peering down. They looked as if they expected the walls to suddenly clamp together and crush me.

When I got to the bottom, I bent over to pull open the trap door. As soon as I yanked on the handle, an alarm went off. A small security camera emerged from the rock next to my face. The tiny, red eye was pointed squarely at me.

Oh shit! I thought to myself.

"Don't worry," I could hear George telling Lance. "This is where he tripped up before. Remember? It was all over the tube." He chuckled. "He'll have it disabled in no time."

There must be an access panel somewhere along the wall, I thought to myself. Desperately I began searching. My fingers glided over the rock, feeling for any regularly shaped depressions. Within moments, I had found it.

Inside was a bevy of wires, transistors, and – yes! This is what I was looking for. A tiny touchscreen.

It was flashing angrily.

Sweat started to pour down my face, stinging my eyes. I kept having to blink in order to see what was on the screen.

"SECURITY BREACH. REMAIN CALM. THANK YOU FOR YOUR COOPERATION."

I tried my cleverest, sneakiest tricks, but I still couldn't get a login prompt.

"What's taking so long?" Lance wanted to know.

I had managed to disable the alarm once before. Why couldn't I do it now?

I stood there, staring stupidly into the panel while the alarm continued to shriek. The wheels and the cogs of the machinery below kept thumping and grinding.

Whoever ran this place had obviously learned from their mistakes. I had never encountered security like this before. It was impenetrable.

I wonder, I thought to myself dreamily, if there isn't a second clone somewhere, just starting his daystretch over in Q sector. He'll be drilling away at rocks in Deeper Delvers, Inc, when suddenly he'll catch a glimpse of someone on the tube who looks just like him. The anchormen will be laughing at my implied destruction. Then a clone of George will call him up on his PA and fire his ass.

"He has no idea what he's doing," I heard George say. "Look at him. He's all frozen up."

"What?" Lance croaked.

"Don't you see? He's never been here before." The radio at George's side was heaved into the air.

"You mean, it's not Terry Renfield down there?"

That's when I saw it. The assassin bug was creeping along near my feet. Just the size of a closed fist, it was far more dangerous than it looked.

I held my breath.

"Zeus! Come in, Zeus! It's me, Kuasimodo!" Three meters above my head, he shook the radio violently. "Why doesn't this damned thing work?"

A lot of things manufactured in the Bunker don't work. Doubtless, it's what George was thinking at that very moment. But somehow, I knew that wasn't it.

I had to suppress the urge to laugh out loud.

I can take care of myself, he had told me. Of course!

Scorpio and Zeus were gone. They had left the moment we entered the dome.

Scorpio had told me something else, too. *The others are expendable.*

The assassin bug darted suddenly up the wall. It's amazing how quickly those things can move once they've spotted a victim.

The alarm continued to shriek.

"What's he doing?" Lance asked curiously. I couldn't see it, but I knew he'd drawn his gun. "He's just standing there!"

The assassin bug raced up the shaft out of sight.

Stay calm. Don't breathe.

Just by doing nothing, I could do a lot.

Chapter 15

As soon as I opened my eyes, I knew I was back in the confined spaces of the Bunker.

I was lying on a plank in the cramped cargo box of an armored battlepod. It shuddered ominously as it rocketed over the uneven transtube floor. A high-pitched, constant whine could be heard somewhere below. The windows were blacked out, but it was still possible to see the dim procession of the lightbulbs mounted on the transtube wall as we raced by.

My mouth still stung from the spray the Search and Extraction Team had put me down with. They must have pumped me up with meds, too, because I couldn't move a muscle. Even so, my hands were tightly bound with flextex wire. Apparently, they weren't taking any chances.

I wasn't alone. A low bench wrapped around the inside of the cargo box. On it, squirming to get comfortable, sat a few members of the Search and Extraction Team. When I came to, they were making bets on the likelihood of "termination on arrival", their expression for someone tagged and bagged within the hourstretch.

I found a reason for hope in their banter. After all, if *someone* among them was willing to risk a few credits on my living a little longer, there must have been *some* chance to salvage the situation, right?

Or so I told myself.

"Oh, look, he's awake," one of them said.

"How can you tell?" It must have been a newbie.

"Look at the eyes, stupid. It's the only part he can move."

Well, I could still breathe. I could still control my diaphragm. There were other muscles I still had use of, too.

One of the lads in back laughed maliciously. "You know, we picked up a target once who had no control of his sphincter. Control had it taken away for some minor infraction of the rules. The damned thing was always open."

"What's a sphincter?"

"It makes it so you don't shit when you don't want to."

They all pondered that revelation for a stretch.

"Did he carry some kind of bag with him?" one of the younger, more inexperienced goons wanted to know.

"Yeah. It was a lot of fun when we took it away, too."

We all took a stretch to ponder that, too.

I gathered from the rest of their conversation that they had kept me down the whole trip back to Mars, some three weekstretches. They must have had a more powerful ship than we did on the way out. Wistfully, I wished I had caught a glimpse of it.

Eventually, the battlepod got off the transtube, made a few sharp turns, and pulled to a sudden stop.

The double doors to the cargo box opened. More goons were standing outside in the bright, artificial light. Turns out I was on some kind of stretcher, because before I knew it I was being pushed out and hefted recklessly to the ground.

We were in some kind of commercial zone. The ceiling – made of rough sheets of corrugated steel plates fit poorly together – was just high enough so we didn't have to stoop over or crawl. Who knows how many floors the designers had crammed into the space allotted to this complex. The ground, too, was dotted with spots of rust and sharp, dangerous edges.

They were just like every ceiling and floor I had ever seen in the Bunker, except maybe at the spaceport which was carpeted. But that's where the familiarity ended. It was clearly an area that required a security clearance, and until recently I hadn't had one.

All around, I could see flashy storefronts where they sold products and provided services for a fee. Except the wares being pawned here weren't just PermaChunky and Blue Flavor, and a citizen could do more than just his laundry.

The entrance to Earnest Ernie's Exercise Bungalow – whatever that means – was just ahead. Its presence was advertised by bright, pink, neon letters. Most of them flashed and glittered, but a few refused to glow at all. A curious machine had been mounted in a little stand just off the sidewalk. It consisted of two wheels joined by a bar with a seat near the middle and pedals underneath. I imagined it could be used to extract confessions. My suspicions were only confirmed by the horrible grunting and the hopeless moaning drifting out the half open entrance.

Next to it, there was a busy joint advertising handbags, wigs, and makeup. Judging from what was on display in the racks outside, the only colors they came in were garish and glossy and clashed unpleasantly with the surroundings, wherever you happened to take them. I think I knew some of the brands, but the names escaped me. Hanging over the entrance was a strobe light. The heavy blows of a bass line rumbled just below the background noise in the corridor. Whenever anyone came out, the area was suddenly awash in the screeching that passed for music at Duo Dimensional Fashions.

On the other side, there was The Golden Dragon. It must have been some kind of dining facility, because a few patrons were cramped over near the entrance vomiting all over the large, plastex representation of what looked like a giant cat with wings. Some private security guards were beating them with sticks even as the poor sods retched.

I took a deep breath of the stale, recycled air. It was good to be back in a utopia.

A few citizens had gathered on the sidewalk to gawk at the battlepod. A pair of Homeland Security goons was already heading over to convince them it was better to leave than to bleed.

"Come on," one of the others ordered gruffly and nudged a colleague. "Get him inside."

Much to my horror, they started to wheel me towards Earnest Ernie's Exercise Bungalow.

Inside, it was a smelly, sweaty affair. There was a crew of janitors armed with mops whose responsibility it was to keep the building safe from any rogue hygiene inspectors who might be shopping in the area. They darted in between the smelly, sweaty patrons, most of whom were strapped into one of those terrible contraptions like the one in the corridor outside, trying to keep up with their personally tailored exercise programs. A few splashes of blood on the floor were a warning to those who could *not,* in fact, keep up that their personally tailored exercise programs would continue without them if necessary.

The security camera mounted on the wall awoke and swiveled towards us.

"Alright, everybody out!" The Homeland Security goons went to work clearing the area.

When the last of the unfortunate patrons of Earnest Ernie's Exercise Bungalow had been carried out and we were alone, one of them approached a small touchscreen mounted in the far wall and tapped out a code. Unsurprisingly, a section of the wall fell away, revealing a well-lit, sanitized looking space. All I could see beyond was a straight, metal chair bolted to the floor. It had been fitted with straps for the ankles and wrists.

One of the goons went to work untying the flextex wire that had cut off the circulation in my hands. "Okay," she said to someone standing behind me. The bonds fell away. "You can inject him now."

A needle slipped into my arm. A few stretches later, I noticed I could wiggle my toes and fingers. The next to be freed from paralysis were my forearms and lower legs, then the upper parts, and so forth.

"Get up."

I did as I was told.

"Don't just stand there. Get a move on!"

I was hit roughly in the small of the back with the end of a truncheon. Stumbling, I took a few steps in the direction of the opening.

The bright, white light streamed out towards me.

Well, there was nothing for it. Against my better judgement, I stepped into the light.

"GREETINGS CITIZEN TERRY. THIS IS CONTROL. I HAVE A FEW QUESTIONS FOR YOU. PLEASE ANSWER AS QUICKLY AND ACCURATELY AS POSSIBLE. THE SECURITY OF THE BUNKER DEPENDS ON IT. THANK YOU FOR YOUR COOPERATION."

I had been strapped into the metal chair, restrained with the straps, and gagged with a large, rubber ball.

This squarish room was rather small, unable to accommodate more than ten persons. The only furniture was the chair. A railing had been installed around three sides. Lounging against it to my left was a grey haired gentleman, eyeing me with scarcely concealed amusement. He was wearing a silver, reflective jacket over his overalls. A helmet had been pushed up onto his forehead so he could see. Most importantly, he was unarmed.

He may have been unarmed, but the room was not. Four laser cannons had been mounted into the ceiling. All of them were pointed at me and humming warmly.

The fourth wall where the railing was absent was taken up almost entirely by a large screen. Embedded in the screen was an immense, red eye. Like the laser cannons, it was staring right at me.

"YOU HAVE BEEN IDENTIFIED AS CITIZEN TERRY RENFIELD Q-16 SECTOR ASSIGNED TO DEEPER DELVERS INC PROCUREMENT. YOU ARE THIRTY-FIVE YEARSTRETCHES OLD AND YOUR CURRENT MATE IS SALLY XINHUA Q-15 SECTOR. YOU HAVE THE DELTA SECURITY CLEARANCE. PLEASE CONFIRM."

The rubber ball seemed to be getting in the way.

"PLEASE CONFIRM."

I thought I could hear the laser cannon revving up. Couldn't Control see that I was unable to answer? But even as I entertained the thought, I knew there was no way to know what Control was actually seeing. There were too many programmers – some legit and others rogue – between it and me.

It was at that moment that the grey haired gentleman approached and removed the rubber ball from my mouth.

"Yes!" I cried out anxiously.

"PLEASE ANSWER AS QUICKLY AND ACCURATELY AS POSSIBLE. THANK YOU FOR YOUR COOPERATION." There was a pause before Control said, "CONGRATULATIONS CITIZEN TERRY. YOU HAVE PERFORMED SEVERAL INVALUABLE SERVICES FOR THE BUNKER. SHALL I ENUMERATE?"

"Please," I responded carefully.

"TOGETHER WITH CITIZEN ANDREAS FOKKER YOU HELPED EXPOSE CITIZEN RALUCA IOANNOU AS A MEMBER OF THE UNDERGROUND. AS YOU KNOW THIS IS A MOVEMENT DEDICATED TO SUBVERTING LIFE IN THE BUNKER AS WE KNOW IT."

"I did?" The words slipped out unnoticed.

"YOUR MODESTY IS UNNECESSARY CITIZEN. I HAVE ALL THE RELEVANT DATA AT MY DISPOSAL."

The grey haired gentleman looked at me sternly.

I cleared my throat. "Glad to be of service."

"SIMILARLY YOU HELPED REVEAL CITIZEN LANCE TREVOR TO BE A MURDERER. WITHOUT YOUR HELP THE DEATH OF CITIZEN ANTINOUS LOPEZ WOULD HAVE REMAINED A MYSTERY."

"Yes, Control," I agreed. I felt like I was starting to get the hang of this. "It was a sad and sordid affair."

"OF COURSE AS IS SO OFTEN THE CASE CITIZEN LANCE WAS JUST A LINK IN A MUCH LONGER CHAIN OF WRONGDOING. FORTUNATELY BEFORE HE CEASED FUNCTIONING HE WAS ABLE TO IDENTIFY THE REAL MASTERMIND BEHIND THE CRIME."

This must have been Scorpio's doing. After all, Control had no hard evidence whatsoever about Antinous' death. It happened in the outside, far away from all the security cameras. Unless, of course, the satellite imagery picked it up. But somehow I doubted it. Nothing in the Bunker worked that well.

"IT IS UNFORTUNATE THE BODY WAS DESTROYED ALONG WITH THE REST OF HALLOWED HILLS SETTLEMENT. IT WILL THEREFORE BE IMPOSSIBLE TO VERIFY THAT THERE WAS INDEED ONLY A SINGLE ASSASSIN."

Now I knew it for sure. Control thought he had been shot to death.

"Yes," I agreed. "As far as I could tell, citizen Lance was acting alone."

"ONE MIGHT WONDER WHY IT IS THAT YOU CHOOSE THE COMPANY OF SO MANY SOCIAL DEVIANTS."

"Because," I answered smoothly, "it's the only sure way to expose them without risking the lives of innocent citizens. Especially Wards of the State. We wouldn't want anything to happen to them! Gathering hard evidence requires personal risks. But I make them gladly in service to the Bunker."

"NOTED. SHALL WE CONTINUE?"

"Yes."

"YOU EXPOSED A TERRORIST CELL OPERATING OUT OF HALLOWED HILLS SETTLEMENT WHICH PRETENDED TO BE WORKING ON A NEW DESIGN FOR ONE OF OUR ULTRA TOP SECRET STEALTH VENDING MACHINES. THEY WERE IN FACT SIPHONING OFF THE BUDGET FOR THEIR OWN EVIL PURPOSES. THIS TERRORIST CELL USED ADVANCED MEANS TO HIDE THEIR ACTIVITIES INCLUDING THE FAKING OF LIVE VIDEO FEEDS TO MAKE IT SEEM TO ME THAT THE STEALTH VENDING MACHINE WAS ACTUALLY THERE. DOES THIS NOT SEEM INSIDIOUS TO YOU?"

"Yes, of course it is, Control! That's why I exposed them."

"IF I CANNOT TRUST THE DATA WHICH I RECEIVE HOW CAN I REALLY KNOW WHAT IS GOING ON OUT THERE?"

It seemed like a familiar problem. "I am sure this is only an exception."

"YOU ARE OVERLY OPTIMISTIC. I HAVE ALL THE RELEVANT DATA AVAILABLE TO ME AND THEREFORE MY ANALYSIS IS SUPERIOR TO YOUR OWN. PERHAPS NOW YOU UNDERSTAND WHY I MUST BE ON CONSTANT ALERT FOR SIGNS OF TREASON."

"You can always trust your most loyal servants, Control."

"BUT WHO ARE THEY?"

"Well, there's myself."

"HOW DO I KNOW FOR SURE? YOU MIGHT NOT EVEN BE

SITTING THERE."

The interview was starting to take a dangerous turn. "Allow me to assure you that I am, Control."

"PERHAPS I SHOULD HAVE THE LASER CANNON SHOOT AT YOU. IF YOU ARE INDEED PRESENT YOU WILL CEASE FUNCTIONING AND THE CLEANUP CREW SHOULD ARRIVE WITHIN THREE MINUTE- FORTY-SIX SECONDSTRETCHES."

My mind raced. How was I going to stop Control from testing the limits of its own paranoia by killing me? "Your proposition would prove nothing. If I could be falsified, so could the cleanup crew. And any other reaction you expect to observe."

There was a short pause. "NOTED. SHALL WE CONTINUE?"

"Yes, Control."

"UNFORTUNATELY THE TERRORISTS ALL CEASED FUNCTIONING DURING THE SUBSEQUENT DESTRUCTION OF HALLOWED HILLS SETTLEMENT. DOUBTLESS THEIR INTERROGATORS WERE INVOLVED IN THIS CONSPIRACY WHICH IS WHY I WAS DEPRIVED OF THE MEANS OF DISCOVERING HOW THEY MEANT TO DISPOSE OF THE FUNDS THEY HAD STOLEN."

"Can't you arrest their interrogators?"

"THEY CEASED FUNCTIONING AT HALLOWED HILLS SETTLEMENT AS WELL."

"I see." I paused before I added, "I will do my best, Control, to keep my eyes and ears open for any further information concerning this terrorist ring."

"NOTED. SHALL WE CONTINUE?"

"Yes."

"LASTLY YOU WERE INSTRUMENTAL IN UNCOVERING THE PLOT HATCHED BY CITIZEN LANCE TREVOR AND GEORGE VARUKAS TO DESTROY THE TRANSCEIVERS ON COMMUNICATIONS ASTEROID 70927-Z."

"It was dangerous work, Control. I was only able to stop them at the last moment. And at great personal risk to myself!"

"YOU PERFORMED WELL UNDER THE LEADERSHIP OF CITIZEN FELIX TUBMAN MY TRUSTWORTHY HEAD OF HOMELAND SECURITY. HE HAS RECOMMENDED THAT YOU NOT BE TERMINATED."

I wasn't quite sure if I should be pleased. "Thank you, Control."

"YOU ARE WELCOME." There was another pause before Control said, "CITIZEN TERRY RENFIELD YOU HAVE PROVEN

YOURSELF WORTHY OF REWARD. YOUR POSSESSION OF THE DELTA SECURITY CLEARANCE IS HEREBY CONFIRMED. IN ADDITION TWO THOUSAND CREDITS WILL BE DEPOSITED ONTO YOUR CARD AT THE END OF THIS INTERVIEW."

"I was only doing my duty, Control."

"MARKS OF EXCELLENCE HAVE BEEN ENTERED ONTO YOUR PERMANENT RECORD."

"Thank you, Control."

"YOUR PATRIOTISM SHALL NOT GO UNNOTICED. YOU HAVE BEEN EARMARKED FOR FIFTEEN MINUTES OF FAME."

I swallowed thickly. "Great."

"IS SOMETHING WRONG CITIZEN?"

Being rewarded had never felt so good. "No, of course not."

"YOU ARE LYING. MY BIOSENSORS REPORT THAT YOUR HEARTBEAT IS ELEVATED AND YOUR PUPILS ARE DILATED."

"I'm not feeling well, Control. It must be all the excitement."

A slot opened up in the wall near the grey haired gentleman.

"HERE CITIZEN TERRY. TAKE THIS. IT WILL HELP YOU."

A tiny, yellow pill was dispensed into the slot. It bore no markings whatsoever.

The grey haired gentleman took it, walked over, and placed it in my mouth.

I held on the tip of my tongue for a few stretches, hesitating.

"IS SOMETHING WRONG CITIZEN?"

"What is it?"

"SWALLOW IT. IT WILL HELP YOU."

I had no idea what I was taking or how it would affect my biochemistry. But did I have a choice?

I braced myself and swallowed.

"VERY GOOD."

"Is that it, Control?"

"YES CITIZEN TERRY RENFIELD. THIS CONCLUDES THE INTERVIEW. YOU MAY GO NOW."

Good, I thought to myself. If I get out of here quickly enough, I can have my stomach pumped.

The grey haired gentleman approached.

"JUST ONE MOMENT PLEASE."

The grey haired gentleman settled back against the railing.

"I HAVE A FEW MORE QUESTIONS ABOUT SOME INFRACTIONS OF THE RULES. THEY WILL ONLY TAKE A STRETCH."

My heart sank.

"THANK YOU FOR YOUR COOPERATION."

Control's tone changed ever so slightly.

"DUE TO THE QUANTITY AND SERIOUSNESS OF THE ACCUSATIONS AGAINST YOU I FEEL IT IS BEST TO GROUP THEM BY SUBJECT. DO YOU CONCUR?"

Before I could get a word in, Control continued. "THE SYSTEM OF LETTERED SECURITY CLEARANCES WAS DESIGNED TO ENSURE THAT ONLY THOSE TRUSTWORTHY ENOUGH BE PRESENT IN THE APPROPRIATE LOCATIONS OR HAVE ACCESS TO THE APPROPRIATE MATERIALS."

My mind began to race for a strategy. "Yes, Control. I can't agree more!" Only a clear but simple strategy offered any hope of getting out of here with all my parts in their proper place.

"I MUST WONDER THEN WHY YOU CONTINUE TO FLOUT IT WITH SUCH ENTHUSIASM."

There was, of course, only one strategy I could rely on. "I don't know what you are referring to, Control. I am one of your most loyal citizens. I do not flout any of your regulations."

"UNTRUE. FOR EXAMPLE YOU WERE RECORDED SEVERAL MONTHSTRETCHES AGO IN THE MORGUE UNDER THE ADAM SMITH SERENITY CLINIC WHERE YOU WENT FOR TREATMENT. THIS IS A GAMMA RESTRICTED AREA."

What was the best way to argue with an all-seeing, all-knowing computer? "I was onto the conspiracy to blow up the transceivers on the communications asteroid, Control."

"YOU SHOULD HAVE REQUESTED A WAIVER FROM MYSELF."

"At the time, I didn't know you existed."

"A HIGHER CLEARANCE CITIZEN THEN."

There was, of course, only one defense that would serve me. I had to play on Control's weakest point: it's own, self-admitted paranoia! "I didn't know who was involved and who wasn't. I suspected, though, that the sinister plot reached into the highest levels." I shrugged nonchalantly. "Of course, if you feel that my methods were inappropriate and disloyal, I'll gladly accept the punishment. After all, to act in defense of the Bunker is the meaning of my life."

There was a slight pause as Control busily computed, or received a new feed of data, or some lurid combination of both, such as the case may be. "NOTED. SHALL WE CONTINUE?"

Inwardly, I breathed a sigh of relief. "Yes, Control."

"THERE IS NUMEROUS EVIDENCE THAT YOU WERE PRESENT ON PLANET EARTH IN BOTH HALLOWED HILLS SETTLEMENT AS WELL AS THE OUTSIDE. THESE AREAS ARE BETA RESTRICTED."

"How else could I have gathered information about the stealth vending machine?"

"KNOWLEDGE OF THE ULTRA TOP SECRET STEALTH VENDING MACHINE IS GAMMA RESTRICTED."

I swallowed thickly.

"ANALYSIS SUBSEQUENT TO ITS DESTRUCTION HAS REVEALED THAT HALLOWED HILLS SETTLEMENT WAS A VORTEX OF TERRORIST ACTIVITY. VIRTUALLY EVERY CITIZEN PRESENT WAS INVOLVED IN MULTIPLE CONSPIRACIES AT ONCE. BE AWARE THAT YOUR CONFESSION NOW WILL BE WEIGHED HEAVILY IN YOUR FAVOR. IF IT SHOULD LEAD TO THE APPREHENSION OF DANGEROUS CRIMINALS YOUR COOPERATION MAY RESULT IN THE COMMUTING OF ABROGRATION OF YOUR SENTENCE. ON THE OTHER HAND IF YOU DO NOT CONFESS YOU WILL BE PUNISHED TO THE FULLEST EXTENT OF THE GUIDELINES. DO YOU HAVE ANYTHING YOU WISH TO TELL ME?"

Now that it had been destroyed and it was impossible to carry out interrogations, citizens everywhere who were able were transferring blame and guilt to the unfortunate deceased. For yearstretches to come, Control would probably continue to uncover a series of threats to the peace and security of life in the Bunker, threats that would – unfortunately – trace their roots back to this veritable black hole of accountability.

"But, Control, I was the one who tipped you off! I called in the alarm, remember?"

"SEVERAL TIMES DURING THEIR INTERVIEWS CITIZENS VAN JOHNSON AND ANDREAS FOKKER IMPLICATED YOU IN ACTS OF TREASON. ARE YOU SURE YOU WOULD NOT LIKE TO SPEAK IN YOUR OWN DEFENSE?"

"Those liars? They're trying to set me up! In fact, there's a few things you might like to know about them, too, Control! You might start to think differently once I've told you."

"CITIZENS VAN JOHNSON AND ANDREAS FOKKER HAVE A HIGHER SECURITY CLEARANCE THAN YOU. ARE YOU SUGGESTING THEY HAVE TOLD ME DELIBERATE LIES?"

Tricky. It was hard to dispute accusations if I didn't know what they were. "Citizen Van Johnson has an illegal supply of meds. I saw them myself."

"ACCORDING TO MY DATABANKS CITIZEN VAN JOHNSON IS NOT CURRENTLY ON A REGIMENT OF MEDICATION."

"Exactly! He has a box he carries around. In it are hundreds of pills."

"YOU HAVE SEEN THIS BOX?"

"Yes, Control. He offered me some."

"HE TAKES THEM FOR RECREATIONAL PURPOSES?"

"Yes, Control."

"WHERE DOES HE GET THEM?"

"I don't know."

"WHAT KINDS OF MEDICATIONS ARE INSIDE?"

I shrugged.

"YOUR COMPLAINT IS INCOMPLETE."

"But –"

"ACCUSATIONS AGAINST CITIZENS SHOULD BE APPROACHED WITH THE UTMOST CAUTION AND DETAIL. YOU HAVE FAILED TO LIVE UP TO THESE HIGH STANDARDS. FALSE ALLEGATIONS AGAINST A FELLOW CITIZEN CAN HAVE SERIOUS IMPLICATIONS FOR YOUR CONTINUED WELLBEING. ARE YOU SURE YOU WOULD LIKE TO PROCEED?"

Whatever the meds I had taken, they were starting to take effect. My thoughts still came, but it felt like I had to force them through the nozzle of a tube of toothpaste before I could get at them. I sat there uselessly trying to sort them out.

"NOTED. SHALL WE CONTINUE?"

What followed was a list of more security infractions, more unheeded regulations, and a few violations of the General Guidelines on Sanitation and Hygiene.

"More than once, I tried to get citizen Lance Trevor to take a chemical bath, but he refused."

"YOU COULD HAVE BEEN MORE PERSUASIVE."

"Not without resorting to violence, and use of violence without a waiver is strictly forbidden."

"YOUR KNOWLEDGE OF THE WHITE PAPER ON PATRIOTIC CONDUCT IS REFRESHINGLY THOROUGH."

"Thank you, Control."

I found that I was falling in and out of passivity. The spells were like those wispy clouds I had seen back on Earth. They broke up the sharp clarity of the blue sky and blocked the terrible light of the sun beyond.

It was after another such period of listlessness that I remember Control saying, "ONE OF THE TERRORISTS' MOST EFFECTIVE WEAPONS IS THE DISRUPTION OF OUR ECONOMY. AS YOU KNOW THE PRODUCTION OF GOODS AND SERVICES IS REQUIRED BY THE WELL BALANCED AND ZERO SUM SUPPLY CHAIN FOR WHICH I AM PRIMARILY RESPONSIBLE. ACCORDINGLY THE WANTON DESTRUCTION OF PRIVATE AS WELL AS PUBLICLY OWNED PROPERTY IS STRICTLY FORBIDDEN."

Oh, shit! I thought to myself.

"YOUR MATE SALLY XINHUA HAS BEEN RECORDED RECKLESSLY ENDANGERING THE LIVES AND PROPERTY OF MOTORISTS IN THE TRANSTUBE."

One of Control's more humane white papers suggests that mates officially entered into the Communal Registry will never be required to give testimony implicating each other. In practice, however, few people ever actually invoke this rule, as it tends to draw even more suspicion and the inevitable terminations.

"We were being chased."

"BY LOYAL SERVANTS IN HOMELAND SECURITY. WHY WOULD YOU BE RUNNING AWAY FROM THEM?"

There were any number of reasons I could have given, but none of them was beneficial to my health. "They never identified themselves to us properly."

"AGREED AND NOTED. SHALL WE CONTINUE?"

"Yes, Control."

"USE OF A MODEL 7X AUTOPOD IS RESTICTED TO THOSE OF DELTA CLEARANCE AND HIGHER."

Yes! I thought to myself. When I get out of here, I'm going to get my hands on one of those, even if it's the last thing I do. "I thought we had already closed the book on the violations of security clearance."

Control paused a moment. "PERHAPS THIS IS A SIGN OF

TREASONOUS ACTIVITY."
"I would agree, Control. Someone may be interfering with your memory banks even as we speak."
I faded out again. When I came back to myself, Control was saying, "– EMBEZZLEMENT OF SIX THOUSAND CREDITS TO AN ANONYMOUS CARD IN YOUR POSSESSION."
What? There are anonymous Cards?
"No, Control! It's not true at all!"
"I SEE. SO YOU WERE IN FACT SOLELY RESPONSIBLE AND CITIZEN YURI HAD NOTHING TO DO WITH THIS TREASON. YOUR CANDOR IN THIS MATTER IS APPRECIATED. HOWEVER EMBEZZLEMENT IS A SERIOUS CRIME AND YOU WILL NOT ESCAPE PUNISHMENT."
Who was citizen Yuri? "Control," I began, "citizen Yuri is a model of proper behavior. Perhaps she deserves fifteen minutes of fame?"
"NEGATIVE. FIFTEEN MINUTES OF FAME ARE AWARDED UNDER THE STRICTEST OF CIRCUMSTANCES LEST THEIR IMPORTANCE BE DIMINISHED BY COMMON FAMILIARITY."
Obviously, someone was trying to dump his treason off onto me, someone I didn't even know. But if I was going to be in a position to return the favor, I needed a second name. "Perhaps then you will permit me to thank citizen Yuri in person."
"THANK HIM?"
"Yes. Imagine what would have happened if he hadn't gotten involved at all?"
"AGREED. HIS ADDRESS WILL BE PROVIDED TO YOU AT THE END OF THIS INTERVIEW SHOULD YOU SURVIVE IT."
"Thank you, Control."
I considered asking what my current chance of survival was. If anyone would have known, it was Control. But I quickly decided against it. After all, there is nothing so demoralizing as the truth.

"YOU DO REALIZE THAT MY WARDS OF THE STATE EMBODY THE PRECIOUS FUTURE OF THE BUNKER AND ALL THAT IS GOOD AND WHOLESOME?"
I thought Sally's friends in the Underground had taken care of that surveillance.
"Naturally."
"THEY CAN DO NO WRONG."
Of course, someone might have kept a reserve copy. Someone

might have arranged for it to be reinserted if something unpleasant happened to her. "I cherish them as my own."

"WHY THEN DID YOU VICIOUSLY MURDER TWO OF THEM?"

It was impossible to tell. There wasn't enough information to go on. I started to respond, but Control interrupted me. "IT HARDLY MATTERS HOW YOU ANSWER NOW DOES IT?"

This was one of those rare truths spoken by anyone in the Bunker. "I'm sorry."

"YOU ARE SORRY?"

"There is no excuse, and there is no punishment to match the crime."

"WE CAN CERTAINLY TRY TO COME UP WITH ONE."

I swallowed thickly.

"IMMEDIATELY FOLLOWING YOUR REPREHENSIBLE ACTIONS IN THE TRANSTUBE YOU WERE INVOLVED IN THE ERADICATION OF THE SEARCH AND EXTRACTION TEAM THAT WAS FOLLOWING YOU."

I frowned. "I had nothing to do with that steam bath."

"SO YOU ADMIT YOU WERE PRESENT WHEN THEY CEASED FUNCTIONING."

"Yes, but –"

"I SEE." There was a brief pause. "YOU WERE ALSO ULTIMATELY RESPONSIBLE FOR THE DEATH OF THE CITIZEN ANTINOUS PREVIOUSLY MENTIONED."

"Responsible? But I'm the one who turned in the real killer!"

"YOU COMMISSIONED CITIZEN LANCE TREVOR WITH THE TASK."

I rolled my eyes. "Next you'll be telling me I've been accused of murdering Lady Lagrange!"

"CITIZEN LADY LAGRANGE'S DEATH HAS NOTHING TO DO WITH YOU. ACCORDING TO CONFESSIONS PREVIOUSLY OBTAINED SHE WAS MURDERED FOR REASONS THAT ARE ABOVE YOUR SECURITY CLEARANCE."

"Murdered?"

"YES."

"But her death was an accident! How could anyone know which ecopack she'd wear?"

"WOULD YOU LIKE TO MAKE A CONFESSION IN THIS REGARD?"

I swallowed thickly. "No."

"VERY WELL. NOW THAT WE HAVE WORKED THROUGH THE VIOLATIONS OF SECURITY CLEARANCE AND CHARGES OF MURDER WE CAN ADDRESS THE LAST REMAINING COMPLAINT AGAINST YOU."

"Great."

"IT IS ALSO THE MOST SERIOUS."

Not so great. "More even than the unfortunate deaths of the Wards of the State?"

"INDEED IT IS MORE SERIOUS THAN THAT."

Ouch. What could it possibly be?

"YOU POSSESS KNOWLEDGE OF THE FORBIDDEN ARTS OF PROGRAMMING AND THE SUBVERSION OF COMPUTERIZED SECURITY SYSTEMS OTHERWISE KNOWN IN COMMON PARLANCE AS HACKING."

My mouth hung open. "I don't know what you're referring to."

"THE PUNISHMENT FOR THIS INFRACTION IS IMMEDIATE TERMINATION."

A low whine came from the laser cannon mounted on the ceiling as they charged up.

This is it, I thought and closed my eyes.

Except it wasn't.

I sat there with my eyes closed for a few, long stretches, and when nothing much happened I tried opening them again.

The great, big, unblinking eye was still there on the screen in front of me. The laser cannon were fully charged and hadn't yet found anything better to point at.

The grey haired gentleman, however, was holed up in the corner tapping away on a tablet dangling from a few wires out of a small hole in the wall. When he noticed me looking, he winked.

Eventually, he pushed the tablet back into the open compartment and slammed the wall panel shut.

When Control did not speak, he frowned and banged the back of the panel a few times with his fist.

"CITIZEN TERRY RENFIELD DUE TO THE GRAVITY OF THE CRIMES OF WHICH YOU HAVE BEEN FOUND GUILTY I WOULD NORMALLY ORDER YOU TO UNDERGO MEMORY WASH AND CORRECTIVE SURGERY. HOWEVER AFTER THE INTERVENTION OF CERTAIN HIGHLY TRUSTED CITIZENS I HAVE DECIDED INSTEAD TO PUT YOU ON PROBATION

UNTIL SUCH TIME AS YOU HAVE PROVEN YOURSELF
WORTHY OF RELEASE. IN ADDITION YOU WILL BE FINED
THREE THOUSAND CREDITS AND DEMOTED TO THE
EPSILON SECURITY CLEARANCE."

"I appreciate your leniency, Control."

"YOU ARE NO LONGER EARMARKED FOR FIFTEEN
MINUTES OF FAME."

I was desperately relieved. "Thank you, Control."

"MARKS OF SHAME HAVE BEEN ENTERED ONTO YOUR
PERMANENT RECORD."

"Of course, Control."

"YOU MAY GO NOW."

"Really?"

"YES CITIZEN. REALLY."

The grey haired gentleman approached and began to undo the
straps.

A last warning came from Control before the eye blinked out and
the screen went dark.

"STAY   VIGILANT   CITIZEN   TERRY   RENFIELD!
TERRORISTS AND TREASON ARE EVERYWHERE."

Chapter 16

So that's how I got my Epsilon security clearance.
Every morning now when I go to work at Deeper Delvers, Inc, I take a slightly different route. I don't operate a mining drill any more. My office is George's old office, and my desk is George's old desk. I've hung my own snaps up on the wall and cleared out most of the junk he left behind. Other than that the place pretty much looks the same.

It's the same old crew, too, minus the team leader, of course. Now Clyde is team leader. He's not so bad at it, either, once you get used to the smell.

During my probation I couldn't talk about our unauthorized adventure, not even with Sally. I wore that collar for a monthstretch, you know. Clyde and the boys used to make jokes behind my back. I could hear them, but I never interfered. They're not a bad crew, really, although now that I'm not out there with them in the dusty pits they have a hard time making the quota.

Still, I do what I can. Even if they don't know for sure what's out there lurking behind the Anthem of the Patriot, I think they have some idea. Everyone does in the Bunker, even if you don't have a security clearance. You see, the boys treat me with some measure of respect – even though they still have trouble calling me "sir" – which is more than I can say for George, the fat bastard. They show up to work on time even when they've been drinking and at the end of the monthstretch they put in a few extended shifts. If necessary I'll dust off my boots and go out and join them. Somehow, we always manage to scrape by.

I never told them why I disappeared so suddenly, and they never asked me what happened to George. There are some questions it's just not safe to ask in the Bunker. But I like to think everyone's happier with these new arrangements. I know I certainly am.

Not long after I got back, I was transferred out of Barracks One at the bottom of Q-16 sector. I've been assigned a space in a communal living facility in Q-15, an exclusive, Epsilon clearance area. There are only fifty of us quartering there, and the beds are separated by flimsy, grey panels. They don't go all the way to the the ceiling, but even so, there's only one bed per cubicle. It's certainly more privacy than I've ever enjoyed before.

I still eat at Endurance Community Dining Hall, of course. They scan our Cards at the end of the line just like they always did, but now they serve me from a different cauldron of slop. It's still slop, mind you, and if I don't eat it fast enough it hardens into an indigestible grime, just like it always did. But floating around in it are small lumps of something substantial. I'm not sure what they are, but they have taste. Not only do they have taste, but it even changes once in a while. In the Bunker, a matter as small as taste is an enviable luxury.

I've even had my first apple. One evening at the end of my daystretch they took me aside into an little-noticed alcove and dropped one on my tray. I recognized it instantly. It was dotted with brown spots and someone had already taken a bite out of it, but the memory of berries and nuts was still very fresh in my mind.

Scorpio was right. I had no idea what I was missing when I refused his offer, back when I first met him in detention on the outskirts of a Homeland Security gulag. It seems like centurystretches ago.

Some things never change, though, no matter how much Control pretends to trust us. The hygiene inspectors still show up, and my friend who hands out napkins can't help me anymore. At first I thought I'd bully them, but it turns out H&C is thoughtful enough to send out inspectors with the same security clearance as those they are meant to bully.

Of course, now I have another way to avoid most of the fines and other unpleasantness they are capable of slinging my way.

I crept up the wide, mostly empty corridor in L-7 sector. There were a few cracked, dusty tubes hanging from the ceiling. They were all showing a fresh, new and eagerly anticipated episode of Ten Things I Hate About Treason hosted by Van Johnson.

I don't feel as harshly towards Ten Things I Hate About Treason hosted by Van Johnson as I used to. After all, even though I can hardly brag to anyone about it, I am one of the few citizens who ever survived the show. How about that?

Whenever I see Van Johnson up there on the tube, I can't help but smile. I'm glad he made it out of Hallowed Hills, even if he did try to implicate me to Control. After all, it's a matter of survival when you're dealing with Control. I understand.

Audition For Freedom, on the other hand, didn't fare so well. They tried to pass off some other woman to host the show, but she didn't cut it, and after she put in a memorable appearance on Ten Things I Hate About Treason, it was cancelled.

A few weary citizens passed. They were oblivious to me, their attention held riveted by the glowing tubes. Most were stumbling the other way. Up ahead there was another intersection. According to the map I had been given, it would be the last.

The place was crawling with guardians. A barricade had been thrown up in the very center. I had been warned about this, too.

The line to get through was short and moved quickly enough. A surly woman with a shaved head stood at the end, flanked by heavily armored colleagues. They brandished their high-intensity blasters while she scanned my I-chip and took my Card.

"Charles Lebron," was the name on the readout.

"Epsilon, eh?" she said, lightly fingering my Card, and gestured impatiently for my papers.

I handed her the thin packet.

She leafed through them, taking her time. I patiently studied the burn marks on the walls.

"Okay," she finally grunted and threw the documents back at me. "Get the hell out of here."

Only too happy to oblige, I moved on.

Up ahead was the ball bearings factory. Few people if any were expected to be about now that the current shift had already started. The lights were dim or not burning at all.

A friendly, female voice came over the loudspeaker. "This area is restricted to authorized personnel only. Thank you for your cooperation."

It's funny. Now that I'm in on the secret, I see and hear signs of Control's twisted personality everywhere.

Control is very careful about who is allowed into its factories, especially the ones dedicated to necessities such as stainless steel ball bearings. It is concerned that someone or someones might sneak inside and try to blow them up. Rightly so. Nowadays, I happen to know a few people who enjoy doing just that.

Up ahead was one of the workers' entrances. A turnstile blocked the way. Standing nearby was a lone citizen, looking bored. Projecting from the wall above him was a security camera. The red light underneath wasn't showing.

He spotted me approaching and stood up straighter.

He got a bit nervous when I hesitated and reached for what I assume was a gun, but then I got over feeling stupid and made the damned sign.

I pushed the palm of my right hand against my forehead and

wiggled the fingers.

Who thought this stuff up? I wondered to myself crossly.

A look of relief passed over the man's face as he returned the secret sign. "You're Complicity's boy?" he whispered and quickly scoured the area for witnesses.

"Yeah. What about the camera?" I wanted to know.

The man shrugged. "It's broken."

I smiled. "I wonder how it got that way."

"I wouldn't wonder too much. It might be bad for your health." He took a moment to size me up.

"You must be Rulda," I said.

"And you're Typhon. I've heard a lot about you. You killed John the Baptist." He nodded with grudging respect. It was difficult for any citizen to do. "Thanks."

I hate that name. Sally told me when they get inducted into the Underground most people get to choose their handles, but not me. Mine was handed down from above. It's how I know Zeus is alive and well and thinking of me fondly, even if chances are slim I'll ever see him again, that unhygienic typhoid.

Sally and the grey haired gentleman who had been present at the interview championed my membership in the Underground. He said he was impressed with the way I handled Control.

You need at least two sponsors to be accepted. Not that I really wanted in, but Sally thought it was a good idea. Otherwise they might have come after me.

"You know where the leaflets are hidden?" Rulda asked as he jabbed the turnstile with a screwdriver.

"Yeah. They're – "

"Don't tell me! I don't know and I don't want to!"

Fair enough.

Rulda glanced around one last time for good measure. "Don't worry about the camera inside," he said as I passed, snickering. "It's having some technical difficulties."

I had memorized the schematic of this part of the factory. The chemical showers were just this way, along this dark corridor and through these doors...

The lights were on in the locker room. It was a bad sign, because nobody was supposed to be there.

I could hear voices on the other side of the nearest bank of lockers.

"Thanks, but I can't tonight. My girl's working overtime all this weekstretch."

"Too bad. Me and the boys will be over at Brady's watching Bloodbrawl."

"Maybe next time."

Thankfully, the voices were receding.

"Why's she working late?"

"I don't know. She's over at Sights and Sounds. Ever heard of it? Part of H&C. She sorts and files the reports that come in about the state of the various sectors."

"So?"

"So apparently there was some kind of disaster over in F sector because whole departments are being closed down. She's got to work off the paperwork."

I could hear a little chuckle. "F sector you say? Those boys over at Control. I don't know what they have up their sleeve, but your girl and everyone else at Sights and Sounds is being taken for a ride."

"How do you mean?"

"Just take my word for it. There's nothing unusual going down in F sector."

"Well, it's what the reports say. Why would someone at Control fake a meltdown in F sector?"

"Who knows? But I wouldn't get involved if I were you. There's probably an Alpha behind it."

"They all are over at Control."

There was the sound of a door being yanked open. The lights went out and the voices were cut off.

I drew out a flashlight from my utility belt and headed straight for locker number 609. Inside, as expected, there were neat stacks of familiar, glossy leaflets.

There wasn't much time. The next shift started in a few hourstretches. If I had to skip out before I had managed to slip a leaflet into the pocket of every worker's trusty overalls, MentalistX would be mad. After all, this job was my idea. I talked it up at our last meeting over his strong and surprisingly personal objections.

MentalistX is my handler in the Underground. I don't like him, and I don't think he likes me, either. Still, there's nothing he or I can do about it. One daystretch if he doesn't get me first I'll make sure he regrets it, but until then I'll just have to swallow my pride and do what he says.

As for Scorpio, I never did see him again. I doubt I ever will. Sally was furious he abandoned the project when there was nothing to stop

213

us from finally disabling Control. I've heard her say some really nasty things about him, things that make me cringe and hope they don't make it into the surveillance.

It's true, I kept telling her. There was nothing else to stop us. Nothing else, that is, except ourselves. The way I see, we are our own biggest problem.

But Sally doesn't agree. We just don't see eye to eye on this.

I knew Zeus had won their argument the moment I found out they were sending us down to the surface. After all, the Self-Destruct Mechanism was in our hands. It could have been beamed into the network at any server node, and as Alphas they certainly had access to those.

At first, I spent a lot of time wondering what Scorpio's motivations could have been. Was he ever really serious in the first place?

It's impossible to say for sure. For all I know, he had a whole different angle than he let on. He could have been involved in schemes and been moving against enemies totally invisible to us. There simply isn't enough information to go on.

My gut, though, tells me his heart was in it.

I think citizen Delinda, a woman I've never met before, has come the closest to explaining Scorpio's sudden change of heart. We all hate Control, you see, but we hate the absence of Control even more. I'm sure it didn't take long for Zeus to convince Scorpio of that.

I would have gone through with it. But I also know I'll probably never get another chance. Sally's more optimistic. That's part of the reason I love her so much.

I don't harbor Scorpio any resentment. After all, I saved his life and he let me live. It's a fair deal, wouldn't you say?

Which brings me back to those leaflets. I wrote them myself. I'm doing my part, you see. It's the reason I agreed to join the Underground in the first place. I love Sally, and I'll do what I can to spare her any grief (which is more than I can say for her!) but my decision had nothing to do with fear.

Those leaflets tell people about Earth. Not the radioactive wasteland Control wants them to think it is, but the real thing. It tells them about trees and the sky and what it's like to eat real food.

It tells them the story of a citizen with a Beta security clearance who leaves the safety and comfort of our underground utopia to brave the uncertainty of an unscripted life.

This is a story without a predetermined ending. A lot of citizens have a hard time with it.

When information is hoarded and kept locked away from those it could benefit the most, it becomes subversive to carry around the key. That's what I do nowadays. In the dark corners of the Bunker when no one is looking, I pass on subversive information. If I can reach just a precious few, then maybe they'll pass the torch on to someone else.

If enough of us are carrying torches, the light will shine brighter and brighter, and more people will notice of their own accord.

Like I said, I'm doing my part.

One day, Control will go offline. Not in my lifetime, I know, but one day.

January – November 2011, Amsterdam